CALDERWOOD

Leila A. M. Martin

Orange Spectacles Press

Author's note

Calderwood combines hallmarks of a classic Gothic novel with elements of the darker brand of fairy tale, which means it's got all kinds of suspenseful and spooky stuff. Hopefully you're here because that's your vibe. But in case any of these specific things are a problem for you, be aware that the book includes snakes (they talk), dark cellars, disembodied voices, characters questioning their own reality, enclosed spaces, predatory behavior/manipulation, seduction, borderline SA, implications of cannibalism, a runaway/lost child (off page, in the past), and a scene by a grave.

1

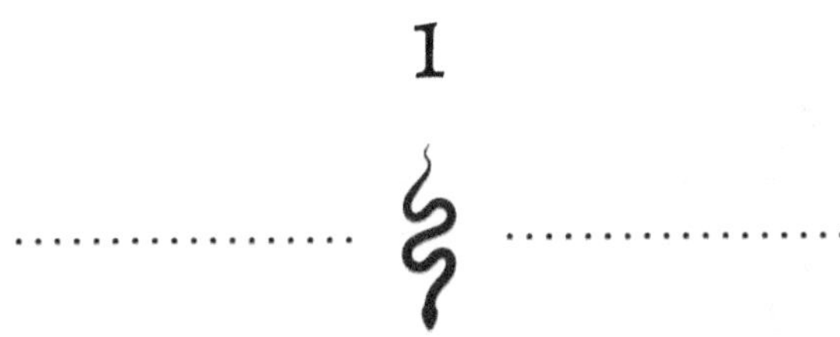

ARLO READE ARRIVED FOR her first day of work at Calderwood ready to make apologies for being late. But when she knocked on the servants' entrance of the grand house, no one answered.

She scrunched her brows and peered through the nearest window. From the little Arlo knew, or had heard from others who'd worked in them, country houses were supposed to be bustling in summer. There should be the sounds and smells of cooking and fires, at the very least. But there was no one in there, not that she could see. No footmen hurried by, no brooms swished, no butler gazed down his nose at the comings and goings of what should have been a sizable staff.

If Arlo didn't know better, she'd think the place was empty.

"Hello?" she called. She knocked again.

The door flew open, making her start and drop her worn carpet bag. The penny dreadful she'd shoved into the bag's hinged opening at the end of the carriage ride slipped out, slapping the paving stones with an accusatory thwack.

Arlo stooped to reclaim it, only to freeze in an awkward half-crouch when she heard the gentle but imperious sound of a throat being cleared. She looked up.

A harried-looking woman in a dark dress stood in the doorway, graying red hair pulled into tightly woven plaits that marched from above her ears to meet in a neat coil at the back of her head. The faint lines around her eyes creased a little more as she looked from Arlo to the much-thumbed booklet on the courtyard paving stones and back.

"May I help you, miss...?"

Arlo fought an embarrassed blush as she snatched up the penny dreadful and tucked it under her arm with the cover against her body. Of all the first impressions to make. But she couldn't leave now. She'd come too far, and there was nothing behind her worth keeping. She pulled an envelope from her bag, straightened, and held it out.

"Arlo Reade, ma'am. I'm here about the placement." When the woman's expression didn't change, she added, "Maid of all work?"

"Ah." The woman took Arlo's papers, then pulled in a deep breath and squared her shoulders. "Well," she said, suddenly all business, "I'm Mrs. Hollister, the housekeeper. Have you worked as a maidservant before?"

Arlo blew a stray curl out of her face and half-scowled when the golden strands caught on the straw of her hat brim. "No, ma'am," she said. "But my mother was in service in the city before she had me, and I helped her with taking in laundry before she died. She told me what to expect."

"Hm," Mrs. Hollister said. "Come in." Her sensible skirt flared as she spun and walked back into the house. Arlo followed, stealing one last glance at the courtyard before the dark doorway swallowed her.

Mrs. Hollister brought them into an office tucked just to one side of the courtyard door. Arlo skirted past a small table and chairs to reach a large, tidy desk near the back wall. The housekeeper sat behind the desk, facing Arlo and the room beyond.

"Please, have a seat." She gestured to the empty chair opposite the desk, slid the papers from the envelope Arlo had given her and scanned them, her face a perfect vault.

Arlo's skin prickled with the stillness as she waited, the house's silence an oppressive weight all around her. She strained her ears to hear what should have been there, only half-listening as Mrs. Hollister told her the rules of the house and asked whether she had a sweetheart, whether she might be pregnant, and whether she understood that her family could not visit her in her place of work.

"Yes, ma'am," Arlo said. "That is, no. I don't have a sweetheart, and my family..."

Tears started to prick at the corners of her eyes. She looked down at her hands folded in her lap, willing herself to take deep but silent breaths until the urge to cry had passed. As she did, her glance caught a smudge on her shirtwaist that might be coal dust or the residue of printers' ink. Damn, and she'd tried to be so careful. But at least the spot had distracted her. She cleared her throat a little and looked up again, meeting the older woman's eyes.

"There's just me."

Mrs. Hollister pursed her lips. "I see." She turned toward a tall pigeonhole bookcase against the wall, running one finger over the mostly-empty openings until she pulled out a hand-sized book bound in black fabric. It had *Rules* debossed in silver foil on the front cover. "Well, you have us, such as we are." She held the book out for Arlo to take. "Welcome to Calderwood."

Arlo took the book, its cover rasping gently against her fingertips.

"I'll show you to your room." The housekeeper led Arlo across the house, past a larder and pantry and up a narrow set of stairs to the second floor. They stopped at a closet for a folded pile of white linens before going all the way down the hall to a room at the northeast corner of the house.

"This is you," she said, opening the last door on the right. "There's a bathing closet two doors down on this side. You are to take one bath per week, on Saturdays." She eyed Arlo's blouse, and Arlo just knew she was looking at the smudges. "I advise you not to skip. Cleanliness is next to Godliness, after all."

Arlo stepped into a room much finer than she'd expected. It was designed to share, a fact that softened some of the nervous tightness in her chest. Of *course* there were other servants at Calderwood, or would be. Perhaps the house was just getting a late start this year, and Arlo had been the first to arrive.

Satisfied, she breathed a little easier as she took in the details.

Each side of the space was a perfect copy of the other, as though an invisible mirror line had been drawn down the middle. But where most maids' rooms were plain, all straight lines and bare bones, this one had two decorative alcoves carved with elaborate tangles of tumbling vines, each one with a narrow bed snugged underneath. The owners of this place must have loved it very much, to have installed something so ornate in a place where the family would never get to see it.

The curving walls swept toward the far end of the room, where two open east-facing windows let in the last of the morning's light. A light breeze ruffled against Arlo's cheek, carrying with it the green scent of the hills in summer.

Between each bed and its window stood a narrow wardrobe and short dresser, there to hold whatever clothing the occupants might have. Not that Arlo had very much. She shifted a little as a frayed bit of cording tickled her inside her corset. She'd need to patch that soon.

Arlo stepped further in, then hesitated. "Which side is mine?"

Mrs. Hollister shrugged. "Take your pick."

Arlo chose the bed to her right. She put her bag down next to the small washstand by 'her' window, then peered out at the property behind the house. There was a small copse of trees just outside the servants' wing, singing a hushed lullaby in the gentle wind. Arlo wondered whether that was how Calderwood had gotten its name, though it seemed a bit of a stretch, as it wasn't *much* of a wood. Beyond it, lush green hills rolled to the horizon.

"It's lovely," she said, sliding the long pin out of her hat and putting both down on the dresser. Then she eyed the bed opposite her, which was bare, the wardrobe and closet empty of any trinkets. "When will the others arrive?"

Mrs. Hollister dropped the folded bedding on Arlo's bed before joining her by the window.

"That's my son, Jonathan," she said, as if Arlo hadn't spoken.

In the slanting afternoon light, Arlo followed the housekeeper's gaze to find a man of indeterminate age leading a horse around a paddock near a stable.

"Also the Calderwood coachman and groom, though you won't see much of him. He doesn't come to the house except to take Master Tristan into the village or city as needed."

Arlo waited to see if the woman would say more, but that seemed to be it.

Silence rushed back in, falling between them like dust motes until Arlo thought she could damn near feel it dancing across her skin. The quiet stillness of this place made her want to run through the hallways and shout at the top of her lungs. She bit her tongue instead, drawing long breaths through her nose as she fought down the building tension at the back of her neck.

"Well." Mrs. Hollister turned from the window. "I'll leave you to unpack. Your duties begin tomorrow."

Arlo bobbed a curtsy. "What time do I wake you?"

"You don't."

"Sorry?" Arlo was certain the lower servants were supposed to wake the upper ones. Mrs. Hollister had never answered her question about the others, but as the maid of all work, surely Arlo ranked lowest in the house. Her confusion must have shown, because the housekeeper folded her fingers against her palms to make gentle fists, then released them with a sigh.

"Miss Reade," she said. "I feel I must tell you that you may find this house...unusual. Master Tristan is a good man, but a bit of a recluse. He lives alone here, and never entertains. Much of the house is closed off, so you and I are responsible for only a handful of rooms."

"You and I?" Arlo echoed the housekeeper's words with widening eyes. "Are we...is there no other staff?"

Mrs. Hollister sniffed. "We don't *need* any other staff. I carried on quite well by myself until recently. Our employer doesn't require much, which is good news for you, as you're the only servant in residence. I live in the village, but I come during the day to oversee the cleaning and deliveries, and to take stock of items the house needs to run. Of course, I'm not here on Sunday mornings. Perhaps

I'll see you at church?" She asked in the pointed way that expected an answer.

Arlo's stomach dropped a little. "Does Mister Calder attend?"

Many wealthy, upstanding families went to church every Sunday. It was unthinkable for staff not to be there as well, never mind the chores they'd need to make up when they got back on the so-called day of rest. But Arlo had grown skeptical about God after he'd taken her mother. Once her father had died, too, Arlo had resolved that if God cared so little for her, she'd return the sentiment in kind.

"No," Mrs. Hollister said. The word sounded like a burr in her mouth. "He doesn't."

"Nor I," Arlo said quietly.

The housekeeper sniffed again. "You two will get on like a house on fire." She made a subtle but sharp sign of the cross over her face and shoulders.

Arlo shook her head, questions churning through her mind like a shifting mass of starlings. Eventually, one fought its way free.

"I hope it's not too rude a question, but why does he have no staff, apart from us?"

Mrs. Hollister took a deep breath and pursed her lips as if deciding how best to deliver the answer in a way that laid no judgment on the man who paid her wages.

"From what I understand, Calderwood had a brief flurry of activity when it was first built. But within a handful of years, the family apparently decided to withdraw and keep to themselves.

"Master Tristan maintains the tradition of his parents and grandparents before him, keeping most of the rooms shut and unused, which means he doesn't need much in the way of help. We're responsible for managing only his meals, laundry, and cleaning in the few rooms he *does* use.

"I've handled it up to now, but the work involves a great deal of bending and lifting, and my back isn't as strong as it used to be."

"Ah." Arlo began to nod when a sharp crack exploded into the quiet. She flinched at the sudden noise and spun, heart in her throat, eyes wide. But it was only a broom lying in the corner, still vibrating the slightest bit with the impact of its fall. She swallowed, a sudden sense of trepidation buzzing like an anxious hornet somewhere below her collarbone. When she turned back to Mrs. Hollister, the woman had an expectant look on her face.

Arlo wiped her hands on her skirt, then retrieved the broom. It was perfectly ordinary, the wood handle warm from where it had stood in a shaft of sunlight, but a chill pricked along her spine as she propped the stave back in its corner. There had been no strong wind in the room just now, no cat or other critters that Arlo could see. Nothing to knock the broom over.

A chill rattled her shoulders, shaking a question loose before Arlo quite knew she was asking.

"Will I be safe here?" She swallowed. "Alone?"

"Safe?" Mrs. Hollister's voice was brittle around the edges. She cleared her throat. "Of course you'll be safe. Though going to church does help, if you'd like to strengthen your relationship with the Divine." She fixed Arlo with a meaningful glance before flicking her attention to the open door. "And do lock your door at night. Just in case."

"In case of what?" Arlo asked, though she already knew the answer. Most grand houses required servants to leave their doors unlocked at all times. It wasn't uncommon for lascivious employers to take advantage of the policy, and maids who fell pregnant were dismissed immediately.

With just the two of them here, it would be easy for Mister Calder to have his way with Arlo, if the fancy took him. Being asked to lock her door meant that she had permission, however tacit, to deny him that chance.

"Come downstairs in half an hour," Mrs. Hollister said. "I'll take you around the house and to meet our employer before I go home for the night."

Arlo blinked. Servants at her level almost never met their employers. The butler and housekeeper did the hiring, gave orders and managed any friction among the household staff. They filtered grievances into finer words to present for consideration *only* if they couldn't handle things themselves, and the lower staff were *never* allowed to speak directly to the family.

At least, so Arlo had always thought.

"Meet...?"

"I don't want him to see you and not know who you are."

"Ah." That made sense; as awkward as it would be to have to interact directly with her employer, she'd hate to be taken for some kind of thief sneaking around looking for riches. "Half an hour, then."

The housekeeper nodded and bustled off.

Arlo reached for the catch on her bag, then stopped as the enormity of her situation rolled over her. Until her father's death, she'd never been on her own before. Now she was alone in a new place, with nothing and no one familiar. She heaved a huge breath in and out, feeling the bulk of the house's presence settle like a heavy blanket over her shoulders. A fat, black fly buzzed at the window, hitting the glass with a series of soft thumps.

It was depressingly easy to fill the wardrobe: she had only one other shirtwaist, a wrapper to go over her nightgown, and the black dress and white apron she'd spent the last of her meager savings to buy, knowing she'd need to supply her own uniform. Her nightgown, spare shift and drawers went into the dresser. Then she shook out the bed linens, releasing the gentle scent of lavender and sage into the room. After dressing the bed, she sat down on its edge with the black book of rules in her hands.

"The maid of all work at Calderwood," she murmured, trailing one finger down the page as she read aloud, "must maintain the fireplaces in the common rooms of the house; sweep all floors and stairs; dust all surfaces; clean all carpets; polish all furniture and stair rails; wash sheets and other linens no less than once per week; plate meals and do the washing up. Responsible for emptying and cleaning all chamber pots and commodes. Must also answer the door during the day if the housekeeper is indisposed."

She flipped to the next page, which had nothing else about her duties, instead advising her to keep herself apart from any male servants in the house. She snorted. No worries there.

She lay back on her bed and stared at the arch over the bed opposite hers, taking a longer look at the sinuous curves carved into the wood, a jungle of vines in bas-relief. She tried to trace a single line with her gaze as it undulated through the others. Time stretched, slowing as she lost herself in the complex pattern. The fly's buzz seemed to grow until it surrounded her, a low humming like a distant storm.

"Miss Reade?"

The housekeeper's call snapped Arlo back to the present. Had it been half an hour already?

She stood up, smoothed her skirt, tugged at her shirtwaist and headed downstairs, clutching her rulebook like a talisman against the strangeness of this place.

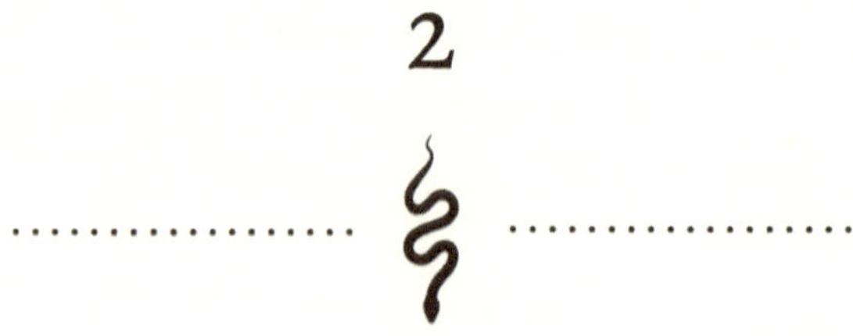

2

CALDERWOOD WAS ALL STRIPED light and shadow as Arlo followed Mrs. Hollister through the halls. The kitchen and scullery had felt somewhat familiar, though larger than any she'd seen before, and her room was snug and lovely. But the main house was another thing entirely.

The scale was so much larger than Arlo was used to, it seemed impossible to take in. Four narrow two-story windows made of palm-sized diamond panes stood like a row of soldiers along the great hall, two on either side of the front door, watching Arlo as she fought the urge to scurry past. The thick glass transmuted the last of the afternoon light into something thin and watery, barely enough to see by.

Arlo shuddered at the thought of these halls in true dark. Part of her wanted to run back to the city, to the familiar people and places she knew. But that was ridiculous. The people were a large part of why she'd left.

After her father's death had left Arlo alone, his friends had been ever so solicitous in their offers of support—but those offers only ever involved marriage to them or their sons.

"A pretty girl like you, already twenty-six?" they'd said, with knowing nods and meaningful glances. "High time you had a husband."

The men at the textile factory where she'd worked had been just as bad. She'd even heard them talking when they didn't think she was around, laying bets on why she wasn't married already, and who'd be the first to "turn her gown green" and other such disgusting euphemisms.

Arlo wasn't against finding a husband, but she didn't want any of *them*. She wanted a man who saw in her more value than just a pair of hands to clean up after him and a pair of legs to thrust between. It was clear she wouldn't find a man like that in the places she normally occupied.

That alone might not have been enough to make her leave. But then the landlord had come to collect the rent for the tiny, cramped flat she'd shared with her parents and deliver a not-so-subtle offer that if Arlo found herself coming up short without her father's income, there were...other ways to pay.

She'd wriggled away from where he'd tried to pin her against the wall and bolted, thinking of nothing but escape. A few streets away she'd come to her senses and panicked at the sound of approaching footsteps until she realized it was only the lamplighters about their work. It had been seven years since the Ripper had roamed the streets, but that didn't mean they were safe.

She'd hurried home only to find that the haven it had been when her parents were alive was gone, replaced by four flimsy walls and a thick air of grief, now redolent with the fug of the landlord's lingering breath and body odor.

There was no way she could stay here alone. She could find lodgings elsewhere in the city, keep her factory job...but did she want that? Or was this a chance to start fresh somewhere else?

The next morning, she'd gone to the nearest registry office looking for a placement outside the city. The registrar had said that most of the country houses had already engaged their seasonal staff, but...yes, here was a possibility. What about Calderwood? They were three hours' ride outside the city and wanted a maid-of-all-work to start immediately.

It was perfect. Arlo took it.

But this place was nothing like what she'd expected.

Mrs. Hollister stopped before a grand set of double doors, wrenching Arlo's mind back to the present. One of the doors stood ajar, just open enough for a sliver of warm light to escape. In the silence, Arlo could hear the scratching of a pen on paper, the mutters and grumblings of someone at work.

The housekeeper knocked, then swung the door open wide.

"Master Tristan," she said.

Arlo peered in over Mrs. Hollister's shoulder, and barely managed to suppress a gasp of surprise. When the woman had told her their employer was a bit of a recluse, she'd thought he'd be...old. Eccentric. Maybe he'd have a family in the city, waiting for him to die so they could fight over his wealth.

But Master Tristan, as the housekeeper called him, couldn't be more than thirty. His skin was clear and shaved smooth, which gave him an unusually boyish look that wasn't helped by the mess of dark curls that crowned his head. They were longer than was fashionable, though not quite long enough to tie back neatly.

He ran a hand through them now, leaving a smudge of ink on his forehead.

"Hollister," he said. When he looked up, Arlo saw that dark half-circles lay like rugs under his eyes, belying the youthful look of his grooming. His voice was pleasant, though he sounded ragged, further cementing her impression that he'd heard of sleep in passing but had never managed to get any. In the lamplight, his eyes could be any shade from dark blue to dark brown, but they were large and open, with lashes that stabbed Arlo's heart with envy.

"Master Tristan," the housekeeper said, nodding her head once in an informal bow, "your new maid, Miss Arlo Reade."

Arlo stepped forward and bobbed, ducking her head. "Good day, sir."

He didn't answer, but Arlo heard the soft scrape of his chair as he pushed it away from the desk and stood. The carpet ate his footsteps as he came around the desk and rested his weight on the front edge.

"And do you?" he asked.

Arlo looked up and cocked her head to one side, questioning. "Do I what, sir?"

"Read."

Her sharp inhale cracked on the air as she realized what he meant. "Oh! Yes, sir. I do."

"Really?" Surprise took some of the weariness from his voice, but then his mouth twitched into a patronizing smirk. "Ladies' magazines, things like that?"

Arlo bristled, thinking of the story she'd read on the coach getting here, about a bloodthirsty killer roaming the night for victims and the detective hunting him down. Part of her wanted to scandalize him with every gory detail of the story she'd devoured on the coach this morning just to wipe that condescending little smile off his beautiful lips. But maybe that wasn't the best idea.

"Not...exactly, sir."

"No?" Tristan asked, his voice warming with the beginning of true curiosity. "What, then?"

Arlo heard Mrs. Hollister snort gently and pressed her lips together, fighting an embarrassed flush as she remembered that the housekeeper had seen *exactly* what she'd been reading.

"Detective stories, sir."

"Oh?" he asked, sounding quite perked up now. "Rue Morgue? A Study in Scarlet? I adore Poe."

Arlo nearly gasped with delight. "Yes!" she said. Then, remembering herself, "sir."

Years dropped from his face as he smiled. For just a moment, his boyish curls and smooth chin suited him. Then, he glanced out the nearby window.

"Ah, Hollister," he said, his face going once again haggard. "Isn't it a bit late?"

"Yes, sir. Now that introductions are done, I'll be going, if you don't mind."

Mister Calder nodded his assent. "Of course. Good night."

"And to you, Master Tristan." She bowed again to him, then nodded at Arlo. "See you tomorrow."

"Yes, ma'am."

Arlo watched her go, then turned back to find her employer sitting behind his desk as if he'd never left it.

"Master Tristan?" she asked. The space between them seemed infinite, yet something about the house felt cloying now that she was alone with him, like a hand hovering just over the back of her neck.

"Please," he said, looking uncomfortable. "Calling me 'master' seems ridiculous when it's just the two of us. You're my employee, not my slave."

"Sir?" Arlo asked.

"Yes," he said. "That's better. Sir, if you must, or you may call me Mister Calder." He picked up his pen to start scratching again at the pile of papers in front of him.

"Yes, Mister Calder," Arlo said, trying out the name as if she could feel it in her mouth.

"Is there anything you need?" he asked, without looking up or lifting his pen.

"No, sir."

"Best turn in then." He signed the bottom of something with a jagged flourish that caught on the paper, splattering tiny drops of darkness across the blotter. "Ah," he said, snatching at a handker-chief to dab at it.

"I can—" Arlo started forward.

Mister Calder held up one hand. "Go."

Arlo bobbed a last curtsy, then turned with her skirt flaring and nearly flew up the stairs to her room.

Arlo's three brass hairpins ticked faintly against each other as she laid them one by one on her small dressing table. She ran her fingers through her long hair, then pulled it over one shoulder to weave into a loose plait. The sun was already gone from this side of the house, but the last fingers of afternoon tickled the leaves in the stand of trees outside her window. The dancing light dimmed as she watched, the last of the sun sinking until tomorrow.

She had never in her life heard of a servant in bed before sunset, not unless they were ill. And even then, employers could dismiss their staff at any time, for any reason. It was unwise to stop working unless you were physically unable to carry on.

Still. It was her first night away from a place she wasn't sure she'd ever call home again. Maybe her weariness showed on her face, since Mister Calder himself had sent her to bed.

But she'd get an early start tomorrow—the sun coming through her east-facing window would see to that. And despite the unusual situation at Calderwood, she did want to make a good impression. There was something sort of sad about the young master, all alone in this big house.

Well, alone except for her.

Arlo reached for a bit of string to tie off her braid and stopped. Her brows drew down in concentration as she cocked her head, listening to the clock tick in the hall. She caught another sound couched inside its steady beat; an echo trailing just after every tick, not quite synchronized but too regular to be the creak of settling floorboards. It could have been a branch in the wind, only there were no trees close enough to tap the window, not to mention the fact that it was clearly coming from the other side of her door.

Then there was a whisper, the barest sound of someone talking only to themselves, and the last reasonable explanation clicked into Arlo's awareness with a frisson of alarm, lifting the hairs at the back of her neck.

Someone was in the hall.

But who? She was the only servant in residence, Mrs. Hollister had said so, and Mister Calder's rooms wouldn't be anywhere near the servants' quarters.

Had the housekeeper forgotten something and come back for it?

Or was her employer more lecherous than he'd seemed, and eager to try out his new housemaid?

Lock your door, Mrs. Hollister had said. *Just in case.* And Arlo had fully planned to, but it was barely even dark. She'd thought the instruction had been meant for bedtime, when she'd be asleep and at her most vulnerable. Now she wasn't so sure.

The tread continued, even and unbothered and terribly slow, until it stopped.

Just outside her door.

Arlo's heart tripped, her body poised like a fox on the edge of fleeing. Her gaze fixed on the door handle, waiting, while her back and shoulders and stomach all thrilled with dueling urges: one, to rush out of her chair, to throw the bolt and gain her safety; the other, to stay perfectly still.

Would the floorboards creak again? Would the doorknob turn?

Silence crept from her like tendrils of fog through city streets, until the whole room seemed muffled, the walls huddled closer, and time stretched longer between the beats of her heart. A breeze sighed through the trees beyond the window.

Arlo's bedroom door opened toward her with a slow creak.

She gasped and flung herself at it, fingers scrabbling for purchase even as her frantic gaze searched for any sign of her would-be assailant. She had every intention of slamming the door shut when she got a clear view of the hallway and stopped short, overbalancing and grabbing the edge for support.

No one was there.

Arlo's breath left her in a gust, both relieved and incredulous. She stepped back into her room, shut the door, and shot the bolt with trembling fingers. The hall clock chimed the hour, its solemn peals giving way to a ticking as pure and clean as spring water, as regular as a heart at rest.

At that, Arlo laughed. It was a weedy, strained thing, hardly a laugh at all, but it still managed to break the spell her own silly fear had cast over this place. She wiped tears from her cheeks and shook her head in gentle self-reproach. It was natural to be nervous in a new place, away from everything she'd ever known, but the change was clearly getting to her in ways she hadn't expected.

Of course Mrs. Hollister would tell her to lock her door, if it was prone to falling open like that at the slightest breeze. What a nuisance it would be to have the thing swinging on its hinges all night, when maids had little enough sleep to begin with.

Arlo bound her braid where it had started to unravel and slipped into bed, staring up at the ceiling of her little alcove. Her body was slow to accept the evidence of safety, vibrating with every beat of her pounding, frantic heart while a fine prickling of sweat made the sheets sticky against her neck. She shifted, turning onto her side in the unconscious, protective curl of an animal or a small child.

Things would be better in the morning. She had to believe that. She snuggled in deeper, pulling a blanket over her shoulders despite the warmth of the room, and hummed a lullaby her mother used to sing to her.

As slow and tentative as a new fern, the notes unclenched the grasping fist of unease, lengthening her breath and weighing down her eyelids until Arlo finally drifted off to sleep.

3

IN THE MORNING, ARLO consulted her rulebook. The first order of business was to stoke the kitchen fires. But Mrs. Hollister had said that Mister Calder had all his meals delivered from the village. She couldn't imagine food came for the servants, too—or, servant, singular, since the housekeeper didn't live here and probably ate at home.

She'd need to empty chamber pots and open curtains at some point, but Arlo decided a quick trip to the kitchen wouldn't go amiss. If nothing else, she might want to have a fire going for tea if Mister Calder wanted any. And, to be frank, a little tea for herself would be lovely.

When she arrived downstairs, Mrs. Hollister was already there, slicing a loaf of bread on the long central table. The village was half an hour's walk away, and the woman had still beaten Arlo here. She flinched, expecting a reprimand, but Mrs. Hollister only twitched her tight mouth in what Arlo had to assume was her version of a smile.

"Good morning, Miss Reade."

"Good morning, Mrs. Hollister." Arlo looked around the kitchen, then knelt by the stove to rake yesterday's ashes out into a metal pail and lay fresh kindling.

The housekeeper gave an approving nod as Arlo coaxed the fire to life. "Toast and eggs in the morning," she said, "for us and Master Tristan."

Tristan. It was a nice name. Arlo wished she could say it out loud, feel the shape of it in her mouth as easily as Mrs. Hollister did. But the woman was older than their employer, and had obviously been here for ages. She'd probably burst into indignant flame if anyone else called the man by his given name. Besides, he hadn't invited Arlo to do so. Sir, he'd said, or Mister Calder.

His eyes flashed in her mind as she remembered his delighted smile at her taste in stories. She blinked, dragging her attention back to the here and now.

"Eggs?" she asked.

Mrs. Hollister pulled back the cloth covering a basket on the counter. "Chickens are in a coop on the grounds," she said. "I usually stop on my way to the house."

Arlo nursed the new fire until it crackled and spat, then shut the stove door and pressed the back of one hand to her forehead. It was already warm, the freshness of dawn melting into the heat of a summer day.

"And the bread?"

"From the bakery in the village. Get that pan heating." Arlo took down the pan Mrs. Hollister pointed to and laid it on the stove top. They worked in companionable silence, making toast and eggs and tea enough for three. Mrs. Hollister showed Arlo where they kept the plates and cutlery.

Arlo opened the wood-paneled door of a small icebox in the larder to put the butter away and frowned. Apart from the butter and a small jug of cream, the box was otherwise empty. She went back to the table, brow creased.

"Why is there so little food here?" Yesterday's tour had revealed little more than a few sacks of assorted grains in the pantry, and nothing in the way of meats or cheeses or other things that should be staples in a wealthy kitchen.

Mrs. Hollister pointed toward the courtyard door. "A cart from the village comes round daily with Mister Calder's afternoon and evening meals, as well as a few other staples from the inn. We make do for ourselves, and he prefers it to keeping a cook."

A bell rang just as they finished arranging their employer's meal on a tray. Arlo looked up at the label under the tinkling bell.

Main Bedroom.

"Right on time," Mrs. Hollister said with a satisfied nod. She picked up the tray and thrust it into Arlo's hands. "Bring this up. Take the main staircase."

"But I've never been—"

"Take a right at the top and go all the way down. He's on the opposite end of the house from you, last door in that hallway. There's a small table just outside. You can't miss it."

Arlo took a deep breath and nodded. The tray hardly clattered as she carried it up. How strange this was, for her employer to take breakfast in his room. Still, it wasn't as though he had a family to eat with. Maybe it was too much, eating all alone in the large dining room. At least it meant one less room to clean.

She turned right at the top of the stairs and followed the hallway down to a door with a small table to one side. Arlo put the tray on the table, knocked, and picked it back up again to wait.

"What is it?" Mister Calder's voice came through the closed door.

"Breakfast, sir," Arlo called.

She waited, listening as he moved around the room. The door opened a few minutes later to reveal Mister Calder in his nightshirt and dressing gown.

His dark hair was even wilder than last night, if that was possible, loose curls falling over his forehead in charming disarray. Arlo could still see a shadow of the ink smudge from the night before, lurking just near his hairline. He started to step out of the room, then reeled backward when he saw Arlo standing in the doorway.

"Good God!" he exclaimed, shooting his arms out to either side of him to grip the door frame, as if guarding the room from intruders. "Miss Reade?" he asked. "What are you still doing there?"

"I—" Arlo clenched her teeth a little. Necessaries were necessaries, but did she have to say it out loud? Still, he truly looked as if he'd expected her to leave the tray and vanish into thin air. "Can I empty your commode, sir?"

Mister Calder paused, then stepped into the hallway and pulled the door shut behind him.

"Miss Reade." As he looked down at her Arlo could see that his eyes, like hers, were blue. But where hers were so light they were almost a pale gray, his were the deepest twilight hue she'd ever seen. "Let me make one thing clear to you. Excepting your own quarters, you are to keep to the downstairs areas of this house."

He ticked them off on his fingers. "The kitchen. The library. The hall. Anywhere that needs cleaning or tending. That is what I hired you to do." His words were clipped, his manner imperious and cold. He was, in this moment, worlds away from the gentle young man he'd seemed to be last night.

"The upstairs rooms are shut, except for mine, and your responsibilities do *not* extend to my rooms in *any* capacity," he went on, holding her so fast with his gaze that she felt like a moth on a pin. "You will leave the breakfast tray on the table. Correspondence on my desk in the library. And you will never, *never* set foot in these rooms," he said, jerking a thumb over his shoulder. "Is that clear?"

Arlo tore her wide-eyed gaze away from his before he could see the tears pooling in her eyes.

"Yes, sir," she whispered, before turning on one heel and fleeing back to the safety of the kitchen. She slowed her steps just before entering and tried to hold her breath to keep from crying, though she knew as soon as she saw the look on the housekeeper's face that she wasn't fooling anyone.

"Good Lord, child," Mrs. Hollister said, her gaze almost soft with concern. "What happened?" She pushed a cup of tea toward Arlo, who sat down and sipped at it until she felt better.

"I brought up Mister Calder's breakfast," she said. "I tried to get in to empty his commode, but he...he sent me away."

Mrs. Hollister looked horrified, which made Arlo want to climb into a hole and pull it in after her.

"Didn't you see the table?" the older woman asked, aghast.

"I did," Arlo said. "But I couldn't empty—"

The housekeeper huffed a tight little sigh, laying one hand flat on the tabletop between them.

"Miss Reade, we are not to enter Master Tristan's room for any reason. Meals, linens, anything he might need goes on that table outside the door. You may knock to alert him to the presence of a delivery, but he's very strict about his privacy. Do you understand?"

Arlo's mind flashed like a flip book through several ghastly scenarios. He'd been so excited on discovering their shared love of Poe's writing. Had he perhaps taken real-life inspiration from the work? Did he have someone's heart beating under the floorboards? A tin full of teeth? A woman or perhaps a cat cruelly murdered and bricked behind the wall?

But there was no way. Tristan Calder might be stuffy and a little distant, but his eyes were kind. And perhaps it was time for Arlo to lay off the penny dreadfuls for a while. She wiggled her jaw, loosening the muscles she'd begun to clench.

"Yes, ma'am."

"Well," Mrs. Hollister said, moving her hand so that her fingers brushed Arlo's once before she picked up her cup again. "Chin up. Now you know."

Arlo nodded and took another sip of her tea.

The housekeeper pushed away from the table and brought her cup and saucer to the sink. She gestured for Arlo to follow.

"You can clean these up later. For today, I'll take you around with me and show you what to do."

Arlo followed the housekeeper to the closet where they kept brooms and brushes for cleaning the carpets, then out to the courtyard storage space where mops and buckets waited to clean the bare floors.

There'd be no need for any servants at all if Mister Calder was willing to stoke the kitchen fire and sweep his own floors, maybe do a little laundry on occasion. But Arlo wasn't about to complain. No matter how odd this house might seem, it had been her ticket out of the city. She would just do her job, and keep out of Mister Calder's way. It couldn't be that hard in a place this big.

Before he came downstairs, Arlo brushed the library rug while Mrs. Hollister swept out the fireplace and laid new kindling. As the housekeeper emptied the commode chair in the little alcove off the main room, she explained that their employer was often up late working or reading. She reassured Arlo again that there really was no need for either of them to tend to his rooms. He took care of them himself, to preserve his privacy. Besides, he did very little in there but sleep. Their Master Tristan spent almost all of his waking hours working here, in the library.

Arlo thought of his face again: the piercing intensity of his deep blue eyes, the wild hair falling over the sharp lines of his cheekbones and brow. Was it possible that he was mad? But no; surely, Mrs. Hollister would have said something.

Wouldn't she?

Arlo shivered. Yes, the best course of action was probably to avoid her employer. Leave linens and meals on the table outside his door and try to stay as invisible as possible while going about her chores. *Like a ghost.* She smiled, then frowned.

Mrs. Hollister had said that this house had seen its share of tragedy. What if there *was* a ghost in these halls? What if...

No, she told herself, with a jerky shake of her head. Her door had opened last night because old houses couldn't always be trusted to keep their doors shut. That was all. Anything else was just Arlo riling herself up, the product of too many sleepless nights devouring the latest penny stories of monsters and adventure and murder most foul.

She helped Mrs. Hollister rearrange the grate in front of the fireplace, then followed the housekeeper out of the room just as Mister Calder's boots clattered down the stairs.

"Ah," he said, though Arlo couldn't see him with her eyes downcast, her face averted. "Good morning, Hollister. Miss Reade."

She chanced a look up and flinched at the brief accident of meeting his eyes. It wasn't enough time to read the expression there; only to know it was complex. The tips of her ears burned with embarrassment and she scurried out of the room.

"Will you be in the library again today?" Mrs. Hollister asked as Arlo flung herself around a corner with her back against the wall, breathing hard.

"I have business in the city," he said. "Have Jonathan bring around the coach, will you?"

"Very good, sir," the housekeeper said. "Will you be back tonight?"

"Before nightfall," Mister Calder answered. "Or soon after. But you don't need to stay. The girl will be here."

"Of course," Mrs. Hollister said. Arlo squeezed the tip of her tongue between her sharp, flat front teeth. *The girl.* Last night he'd seemed almost friendly, dispensing with the customary formalities between them. But this morning he wouldn't even say Arlo's name when he wasn't speaking directly to her.

She couldn't let it matter. She'd let her guard down yesterday, but she wasn't here to be friendly with her employer. She was here to clean his carpets, plate his meals, and stay out of his room.

Arlo took a deep breath and pushed off the wall, her determined steps carrying her back to the kitchen and her half-finished cup of tea.

Mrs. Hollister showed Arlo around the rest of the house after their employer's departure, listing the things she would be responsible for and showing her how Mister Calder liked them done. Arlo suspected it was more a matter of how Mrs. Hollister liked things done; Mister Calder seemed hardly to notice the house around him. She'd been in all of the rooms he used, and the only one with runners over the base carpet was the library, a testament to how much time he spent there.

She thought about it while she and Mrs. Hollister rolled up the runners and took them out into the courtyard, hanging them over the high-strung lines and beating them with wide, scrolled-metal paddles. Dust bloomed into the air, dancing in the sunlight.

What would make Mister Calder want to keep himself cloistered away in a place like this? Arlo was sure there were neighbors for miles around who would bite their handkerchiefs in two for the chance to shove their marriageable daughters in the direction of someone so wealthy, and handsome to boot.

Perhaps the tragedy had been a wife, lost to childbirth or illness. It was impossible to tell—Mister Calder kept no portraits around the house. There were still-life scenes and landscapes aplenty, but no faces on the walls, nor in small frames on side tables.

It was almost as if it had always been just him, alone and eternal, roaming these halls. A ghost in his own right.

Arlo shook her head. She needed to stop that kind of thinking. She took the runners inside and laid them out again, covering the paths her employer seemed to tread the most.

Mrs. Hollister shepherded Arlo through the rest of her chores, and was ready to leave by mid-afternoon.

"And that's it?" Arlo asked. "There's nothing left to do?"

"That's everything. If Master Tristan were here, you'd also need to warm and deliver his evening meal. But as he's out for the day, you'll start that duty tomorrow." Mrs. Hollister wiped her hands on the long cloth hanging on the wall. "Be sure to polish the flatware before putting it away," she said, with a glance at the leavings from their morning's tea still sitting by the kitchen sink.

Arlo nodded as Mrs. Hollister removed her cap, pinned on her hat, and went out into the afternoon sunshine. She washed up the tea things and slotted each bone-handled spoon into a velvet-lined hollow in the cutlery box.

And then...there was nothing to do. The housekeeper was gone, Mister Calder had said he'd be away until nightfall, and Jonathan was with him.

Arlo pressed her lips together, then wiped her hands on her apron and headed for the library. Surely Mister Calder wouldn't mind if she perused his collection, especially since he'd made it clear they shared a fondness for detective stories.

And even if he *would* mind, he wasn't here.

Arlo searched the spines for something of interest, finally pulling down a volume of poetry—not her usual fare, but the title intrigued her. She sat in the south-facing window seat to catch the afternoon light, tucking her legs underneath her skirts and settling her back against the wall. "Morning and evening," she read, "Maids heard the goblins cry:

"Come buy our orchard fruits,
Come buy, come buy:

Apples and quinces,
Lemons and oranges,
Plump unpeck'd cherries,
Melons and raspberries,
Bloom-down-cheek'd peaches,
Swart-headed mulberries,"

Arlo whispered the words aloud as she read them, imagining the rich flavor of each fruit as she named it.

"Wild free-born cranberries,
Crab-apples, dewberries,
Pine-apples, blackberries,
Apricots, strawberries;—"

As the afternoon dimmed toward evening, the sounds of her reading seemed to linger, the sibilance of every *s* hovering in the air for the barest moment before it dissipated. Arlo looked up, neck prickling with the sense that someone was there, though she knew she was alone in the house.

"All ripe together," she went on, after an uneasy glance into a shadowed corner,

"In summer weather,—
Morns that pass by,
Fair eves that fly;
Come buy, come buy:"

The subtle hissing seemed to increase as she read: *ssssummer; passssss; evesssss.* Then the staccato clop of hoofbeats cut through the lulling roll of sibilants, and Arlo stood so fast she swooned a bit, light-headed. She took a few steps to catch herself on the back of Mister Calder's chair. It was there that he found her, bent over his desk, waiting for the swimming in her head to pass.

"Miss Reade," he said from the library door. She gasped and curtsied.

"I'm so sorry, sir," she said, snatching her hand away from the chair. She straightened from her dip but kept her head bowed, her neck and shoulders tensing as she braced for his displeasure.

He was silent for a long moment, unmoving. Then his steps took him toward her, past her, to the book she'd left lying in the window seat.

"For what?" he asked. He lifted the book, turned it over. "For reading?"

"For not asking permission, sir."

Mister Calder sighed, then turned toward her, gently tapping the slim volume against his open palm. "Miss Reade," he said. "I'm afraid I was a bit rude to you this morning, wasn't I?"

Arlo nearly fell again. This time, not from dizziness but from shock. Men in Mister Calder's position did not apologize to servants.

"Sir?" she asked, unsure whether he was setting some kind of trap for her. She heard the carriage continue down the drive toward the coach house and stables, and realized how very, very alone she was with her enigmatic employer.

"You startled me, is all," Mister Calder continued. "I thought Hollister would have told you about my...particulars."

Arlo bobbed again. "She did, sir. That is, she told me there was a table. I just didn't realize I was supposed to leave things there and not enter."

"Well," her employer said, "now you know. Here." Arlo looked at his hands to see the book of poetry pointed toward her.

"Sir?"

"You may borrow this, if you like."

Arlo reached for the book and took it with another bob. "Thank you, sir."

"Of course," he said. "Now, it's getting late."

Arlo glanced out the window. It *wasn't* late, not really; it was barely past sunset.

"Has your lordship eaten?" she asked. She didn't know if he was actually titled—the world of wealth and titles was a mystery to her, and the placement agency hadn't said—but he was certainly the lord of this house.

And while his excitement over books had caused Arlo to let her guard down, his sharp words from earlier had shattered that tentative camaraderie. He had all the power here, whether or not he was comfortable with it. She was just a servant. Best she didn't forget it.

But Mister Calder tsked, quirking one side of his mouth in an almost-smile. "Miss Reade. What did I say?"

Arlo's nostrils flared as she took in a silent, frustrated breath. After the scolding she'd received mere hours ago, she was to dispense with the formalities again? Why couldn't this man make up his mind?

"Did *you* eat then, sir?" she asked, her voice a little sharp as she emphasized the informality of the address.

It didn't seem to touch a nerve. "I did," he said. "Good night."

Arlo deflated, indignation draining all at once.

"Good night, sir." She left the library, pulling the door shut as Mister Calder sat down at the desk. Whatever the rules were about servants staying in their rooms with locked doors at night, they didn't seem to apply to her employer.

Well, it was his house.

If he had eaten, that made one of them. Arlo went down to the kitchen for toast and tea. She listened to the house settle around her and read as she ate. In the poem, bold Laura spied a market parade of dancing goblin men crying their enchanting wares into the night. When the curious but penniless character caught up with the goblins and bought their fruit with a lock of her golden hair, Arlo touched her own curls in sympathy.

Meal done, she rinsed her cup and left it out to dry, then banked the kitchen fire. The coals hissed as she moved them into a tight heap to smolder until morning. Then she picked up the book and left the kitchen. Her footsteps rang in the quiet, whispering back at her from the slick, tiled walls in this wing of the house.

She made it past the pantry to the bottom of the servants' stair before she turned back with her head cocked, listening. There was a faint sound coming from somewhere nearby, an indecipherable susurrus similar to what she'd heard before.

It was possible Mister Calder was talking to himself, though she shouldn't have been able to hear him so far away.

Assuming he was still in the library.

"Hello?" she called, barely more than a whisper. The sound fell into Calderwood's quiet like the delicate rustle of a handkerchief hitting the floor. Arlo cleared her throat. "Hello?" she called again, stronger this time.

There was no answer. Was it an animal, maybe? Or local children breaking in for a laugh or to filch valuables from where they might be lying around? It wasn't as though this house was full of servants who might stop them.

But maybe they didn't know about Calderwood's new hire. Arlo crept through the darkening kitchen into the empty hall by the servants' stair and pulled a broom from where it hung on the wall, grabbing it in both hands, just in case. She followed the sound into the small hallway between the servants' stair and the pantry.

It was empty except for a door, painted the subdued but alluring green of a primeval forest shrouded in mist.

Something about it arrested Arlo's attention. She gentled her hold on the broom as a gust of stale air mumbled its way through the gap between the door and the wall. It smelled of earth and coal and some kind of rot, like green vegetables left to sit too long, and sounded embarrassingly familiar. Arlo let her breath go so fast her chest ached.

It was a *cellar*.

There was probably cold storage down there, hence the old-vegetable smell, and maybe larger reserves of coal than the small bin she'd seen in the scullery. She shook her head with a breathy laugh. All this country quiet was getting to her, and being mostly alone in this huge, old, darkening house didn't help. She hung the broom back on the wall and took the stairs up to her room two at a time.

4

A FEW DAYS LATER, Mrs. Hollister proved at least one of Arlo's suspicions correct when she declared it was time to refill the coal bin in the scullery. She handed Arlo the empty scuttle and led her to the narrow hall under the servants' stair.

"The dumbwaiter will be straight ahead of you." She opened the cellar door. "It's only the support structure down there, no walls, so keep your hands well away when the car is moving, unless you want to lose fingers. The coal box will be further on from there, at the back of the house under the serving lobby."

She filled Arlo's other hand with a lantern that swung from the end of a short pole to protect its holder from the heat of the three-wicked candle inside.

"Fill the bucket, and we'll use the lift to bring it up. Is that clear?"

Arlo nodded and stepped past the green door onto the landing at the top of the cellar stairs. The steps hugged the interior wall, which Arlo was amused to note continued to separate the servants' area from the main house even into the foundation.

Below the first few steps, the cellar was a void; a formless darkness that could have been a room or a galaxy without stars, for all she could see.

She started down, leaving behind the meager light coming in from the hall behind her. Her eyes should have adjusted, but the gloom never seemed to get any lighter.

The three-wicked candle in her lantern didn't help much, though the dark eased a bit as the dumbwaiter car came rumbling down.

It was on the smaller side, its top nearly level with her waist, its width half the reach of her outstretched arms. It was obviously designed for domestic use only, rather than heavier jobs like changing out furniture, or whatever it was wealthy people did.

Light from the kitchen leaked into the cellar as the gap widened between the upper floor and the top of the lift, highlighting the mechanism of rails, ropes and pulleys that enabled the car to glide up and down through the house's three levels.

The bones, Arlo thought.

Wooden planks like ladder rungs supported the vertical rails at narrow intervals, forming a kind of cage between the cellar and the floor above. Arlo eyed it for a moment, then skirted around to move toward the wall Mrs. Hollister had indicated.

On the east side of the cellar, she could just make out a tall wooden structure with a chute towards the bottom. That had to be the coal bin.

She put her lantern down and placed the empty scuttle under the opening, then tugged up on the handle of the small sliding panel that held the coal in. A cascade of craggy black chunks fell with a dusty clatter against the tin of the bucket. When it was full, she shoved the door back down and hauled the load toward the light, heaving it with a grunt into the dumbwaiter car.

She called up through the hole in the floor. "Ready!"

The small car started moving up, leaving Arlo in the diminished light of her single lantern. It pooled at her feet, shrinking her visible space while the darkness around her seemed to grow and deepen.

She shifted her weight from one foot to the other, then froze as she heard something move behind her. Panic danced on needled feet across every inch of her scalp as she squeezed her eyes shut and whispered to reassure herself.

"It's only a cellar. There's no one else here."

Every *s* she pronounced seemed to echo back at her from the surrounding stone walls, and she had that sense once again that something was watching her. She slapped one cheek and inhaled fast as Mrs. Hollister's footsteps thudded above her.

"Coming down!" The dumbwaiter rattled, scattering whatever echo Arlo thought she heard. She filled the bucket again, paying extra attention to the clack and hiss of the coal as it tumbled and settled inside the box.

That had to be the sound she'd heard before.

She was almost sure of it.

"Ready!"

The car retreated, leaving Arlo alone again in the dark.

She *was* alone. Wasn't she?

Apprehension crept up her legs to send tremors through her knees. She'd have a few minutes while the housekeeper lugged the full pail over to the coal bin in the far corner of the scullery. Perhaps she could have a look around while she waited.

Just to be sure.

It would be better than standing still, anyway. Standing still felt like waiting for something to pounce.

She picked up her lantern and walked along the interior wall. The first door, marked *Meats,* had nothing but empty shelves and hooks behind it. Then came the dumbwaiter cage.

On its other side was another door that, when opened, revealed racks of dusty bottles extending past where her light could reach. A wine cellar, then, stretching for who knew how long.

She passed the stairs to survey the wall running along the front of the house. It was as solid as the other had been full of doors, all the way to the northeast corner of the foundation.

Arlo turned again to follow the short wall on the north end of the house, trailing her fingers quickly along the bump and grit of the foundation stones. Then she felt something that wasn't stone at all: writhing vines? No, they were stiff in the light of her lantern, unmoving; not living plants, nor the desiccated husks of dead ones.

The carvings looped and twisted over each other, a tumble of movement caught in time. She brushed tentative fingers over the frozen undulations. They climbed from the base of the wall to higher than she could reach, and stretched nearly as wide as her full arm span.

Was it some kind of artistic study, left down here to rot? Or perhaps a practice piece for the person who'd carved the alcoves in her own quarters? The pattern was the same, or near enough. Arlo hadn't seen anything like them anywhere else in the house, but Calderwood was mostly a series of closed doors to her. Who knew what might lie behind any one of them?

She paused when her hand found a piece that, unlike the others, curved only slightly. Dissonance pricked like a pin at the base of her skull as soon as her fingers curled behind it. A handle? She moved her lantern closer, peering for a better look.

Yes, it *was* a handle.

And what Arlo had thought were vines and scrolls were nothing of the sort.

They were snakes.

They crept and curled, and Arlo flinched until she realized their movement was only shadows, the flicker of her candle that made them seem to dance.

What was a door doing here? The house didn't extend past this wall. An ice house might, dug deep into the hill to take advantage of the cool underground. The door didn't feel cold, like she thought it should if there was ice behind it. On the other hand, Mister Calder had all his meals delivered. Apart from the small icebox in the kitchen, he probably didn't *need* to keep anything cool.

But regardless of whether her employer made use of this door, Arlo had only ever seen decorations so elaborate in church, before she'd stopped going. Its beauty and size hardly seemed appropriate for something as simple and utilitarian as an ice house, especially down here in the dark with no one to see it. The incongruousness burrowed under her skin, drawing her curiosity like a magnet draws iron filings.

If it wasn't an ice house, what else might it be? The silence seemed to thicken, taking on texture around her as she stared with curious, hungry eyes, breath caught, wondering.

When the dumbwaiter rumbled down again, Arlo jumped so high it was a wonder she didn't hit her head on the floor above.

"Arlo?" Mrs. Hollister called when she didn't take the empty scuttle right away. "Are you there?"

"Yes!" Arlo rushed back in a whirl of skirts. "I'm here!"

They worked without speaking. Arlo filled the scuttle again and again to the strange, glassy music of coal against coal as it fell from the box.

"All right!" the housekeeper finally called, after what felt like an eternity. "That's the last one!" The dumbwaiter car began its long upward trundle, swallowing the light from above as it locked into place.

Apart from Arlo's lantern, the only light now came from the open door at the top of the stairs. It was enough to show her the way up, but not enough to reveal the door at the far end of the cellar.

Mrs. Hollister's footsteps thumped on the floor above, crossing through the lobby and kitchen to dump the last of the coal into the scullery reserve. Arlo knew she should go up. She started toward the stairs, but paused halfway into her second step. The urge to go back pounded through her, inexplicable but nonetheless impossible to deny. Just one more time, and then she would go.

She turned and took one step into the darkness, then another, to see how close she needed to get before the dancing shadows of the door were visible again.

It took longer than it should have. The dark down here was nearly thick enough to spread on bread, so oppressive it made her lantern seem feeble, as if it was sucking away the light. Another step. Then Mrs. Hollister called again.

Arlo cursed quietly and turned for the steps again, following the beacon of the cellar door back up to where the housekeeper sighed at her. She looked down. Her hands were blackened, her apron streaked with coal dust and fingerprints.

"Wash up," Mrs. Hollister said, waving Arlo toward the kitchen. "And clean your apron. No point getting coal dust all over the floors you're about to clean."

Arlo washed her hands and face, wincing at the sharp, oddly sweet scent of the orange sliver of carbolic soap. In the courtyard, she used a hard-bristle brush to slap and scrape the dust from her apron before washing her hands again. It was barely past breakfast time. She had a whole day of chores ahead of her: fireplaces, commodes, carpets and floors, plating meals and cleaning up after.

But all she could think of was that strange black door, waiting in the dark. And though Calderwood had been built long before she was born, she couldn't shake the feeling that, somehow, it was waiting for *her*.

When Arlo got to her room that evening, her single candle threw wild, capering shadows on the wall. She unpinned her braid from its crown around her head, letting the serpentine plait fall over one shoulder. In the dim, tricky light, it almost seemed to move.

She gazed at it for a moment, then took a sharp inhale and shook her head to dismiss the illusion.

It was that *door*. Every thought she'd had all day seemed to slither back to it. Her feet twitched, wanting to return to the cellar; her fingers itched with the longing to touch those strange, flowing carvings again.

But more than that, perhaps more time with the door would give some clue to its purpose.

Why was it there; why decorated like that? And what on earth would the Calders keep behind such a display? Did Mister Calder even know about the door, shrouded as it was in all that darkness? Or did he keep the cellar that dark *because* of the door, to hide it from all but the most prying of eyes?

Arlo wished she could ask. But how would she approach a conversation like that?

Oh, Mister Calder, pardon me for asking, but what do you keep behind the snake-covered door in your pitch-black cellar?

No, that wouldn't do.

But maybe she didn't have to ask him.

It was possible the housekeeper knew. But the more Arlo considered it, the less likely it seemed. After all, that door had followed Arlo out of the cellar and into every waking thought for the rest of the day. It had taken all her will not to run back down and drink in its details in some vague hope of slaking her curiosity. If Mrs. Hollister had ever seen it, wouldn't she feel the same? Wouldn't she want to go down and fetch coal or wine herself, just to have the opportunity to see those carvings one more time?

Actually, given Mrs. Hollister's clear dedication to the church, the first thing she was likely to want upon seeing a big, black door covered in snakes would be an exorcism. Arlo nearly chuckled at the mental image of the housekeeper sprinting up the stairs in a demented gallop, refusing to set foot in the house again until Mister Calder did something about that abomination in the cellar.

Besides, the woman was nothing if not brisk and efficient. Why waste time venturing further in, when everything she needed to do her job was already right at the bottom of the stairs?

No, there was no way the housekeeper had ever seen the door. And if Mrs. Hollister didn't know about it, Arlo wouldn't be the one to tell her.

She'd have to do this on her own.

Her chance didn't come the next day, or the following. But three days later, Mrs. Hollister asked Arlo to go down for a bottle of wine to accompany Master Tristan's evening meal.

"It's the first door on the right," the housekeeper told her, "at the bottom of the stairs."

Arlo nodded as though she hadn't inspected the cellar on her last trip down. She took her hand lantern and descended, lifting her shoulders a little to try and warm her neck as the temperature plummeted, the warmth of summer above giving way to the chill of the dark underground.

Arlo opened the wine cellar, selected the first red she saw, and placed the bottle gently on the bottom step. Then she turned around to face the north wall and walked until the meager glow of her lantern licked the curved, intricate carvings she'd so longed to see.

The door made her feel like she was falling, even as she stood on solid ground. But this time, it wasn't the design that took her breath away.

It was the voices.

The door seemed to whisper and hiss, sounds just on the other side of words, an endless stream of sibilant secrets reaching for her through the dark. Arlo had no idea what they said, only the certainty that if she could stay here and listen for long enough, they would start to make sense.

A prickling shiver brushed down the back of her head and landed on her shoulders. Her breaths came shallow and silent, as if the spaces between contained some magic that might translate the unintelligible noises into something she could understand. Her vision went vague, soft, as though the door was somehow sliding away from her, yet it was the only place to focus, the only thing in the room she could see.

And she *could* see. The whole door was here, as crisp and detailed as if this room was full of candles, and the seething noise around her built and wove into a strange almost-music.

And then it moved. She was sure of it this time: a flicker of forked black tongue at the corner of her vision. She held up the lantern to expose it and saw—nothing.

The carvings were perfectly still.

Arlo reached out with a trembling hand. She was a breath away from touching a small, wedge-shaped head when her employer's voice wrenched her from her reverie.

"Hollister!" he called, his imperious tone slashing through Arlo's trance, slamming her back to the present moment, to reality, to the dark. "Where is that wine?"

Arlo nearly choked on a gulped gasp, then bolted back to the stairway-side of the cellar, snatching up the bottle just as Mister Calder came clattering down the stairs so fast he nearly collided with her.

"Miss Reade!" he said, bracing his hands on her shoulders. For a moment, he searched her eyes with a wild, terrified gaze, his grip a tight spasm against her shoulder blades. Then he withdrew his hands and straightened. His eyes shifted, looking away from her and into the dark beyond.

She took the opportunity to gaze up at him, noting the disheveled curl of dark hair over his forehead and the planes of his face, severe in the low light.

"Sir?" she asked, already missing the warmth where his touch had been with a pang of guilty pleasure. Though she wasn't above noticing a handsome face or a fine figure right in front of her, she knew perfectly well that she shouldn't think of her employer in that way.

Still, there was something about this moment—just the two of them alone in the dark, with the mystery of that door hovering just beyond sight. It felt powerful, almost transcendent, a moment where anything could happen. It was as if she was balanced on the head of a pin or the peak of some great precipice, heady with altitude even as she knew it was possible to fall in any direction.

With a start, Arlo realized that he was looking at her again. But his gaze was shuttered now, his initial frenzy tucked safely behind an impenetrable wall of privilege and disdain.

Arlo held up the wine, pointedly ignoring the tiny tingles in the skin at the back of her neck. "Is this one all right?" she squeaked, keeping her gaze on the label to stop herself from staring as he pushed a hand through his dark hair, making it more rumpled instead of less.

Mister Calder took the bottle from her, holding it low to catch the light from her lantern.

"Fine," he said. "Come on." He gestured for her to go up the stairs ahead of him. She did, and felt his glare on her neck the whole way up.

"Oh, Master Tristan," Mrs. Hollister said when they emerged into the light. She reached toward the bottle. "Would you like—"

"No need," he said, curtness clipping his words as he picked up the wine glass from the half-laid supper tray. "I'll open this myself, and await the rest."

"Very good, sir," Mrs. Hollister said.

Mister Calder looked at Arlo for a long, unreadable moment before he turned on his heel and stalked away.

"Here," the housekeeper said, hoisting the tray and handing it to Arlo. "Take this to the library."

"Why doesn't he eat in the dining room?" Arlo asked, gesturing with her chin at the swinging door that separated the food staging area from the main house. "It's right there."

"It's not for us to judge our betters," the housekeeper said primly.

Arlo suppressed a snort. *Better* he may be, but Mister Calder's reaction had answered at least one of Arlo's questions. She hadn't missed the focus in his eyes when he'd looked past her.

He knew the door was there.

And he didn't want her to know it, too.

Her macabre imagination jumped once again to a scene the penny dreadfuls would be proud of: bodies piled in a cold room, victims of this mysterious man whose distant facade masked the heart of a killer.

But that was absurd. On the one hand, Mrs. Hollister had been here for years, and she was still alive. No one else came here, and although Mister Calder did occasionally leave the house, he never came back with bodies strapped to his carriage.

Arlo huffed a laugh through her nose, shaking her head and rolling her eyes at her own penchant for sensationalism. The explanation was likely a good deal simpler than that. The door could have been a gift, or a commission. Perhaps someone in Mister Calder's family had carved it. Maybe even Mister Calder himself. Given the church's dislike of snakes, it made sense that they'd keep it hidden.

Arlo's mouth curled up at the idea of her employer making his furtive way downstairs in the middle of the night to whittle away bit by bit at a secret project that would probably never see the light of day. But whatever his reason for keeping it hidden, Arlo wasn't going to ask. Not after the way he'd reacted. Not if there was a chance he'd forbid her from going downstairs again.

She turned with the tray in her hands and followed where her employer had gone. By the time she reached the library, he was already several sighs deep into some paperwork, the glass in his hand nearly brimming with deep ruby wine.

"Sir?" Arlo asked, hefting the tray. "Where would you—"

"Here," he said, shoving papers aside to make space. Arlo placed the tray in front of him and backed away, all without looking at him. She bobbed at the door, then turned to leave.

"Miss Reade?" His voice was gentle, tentative, with none of the thunder he'd wielded just minutes before.

"Sir?" she asked.

He was silent for a long time. Then, just as she started to turn, he said, "thank you."

Arlo felt her cheeks grow warm, remembering the strength of his hands on her shoulders, the raw vulnerability in his eyes, all so brief she could almost convince herself she'd imagined it.

"Sir," she said, and retreated, her steps scurrying in time with her frantic heart.

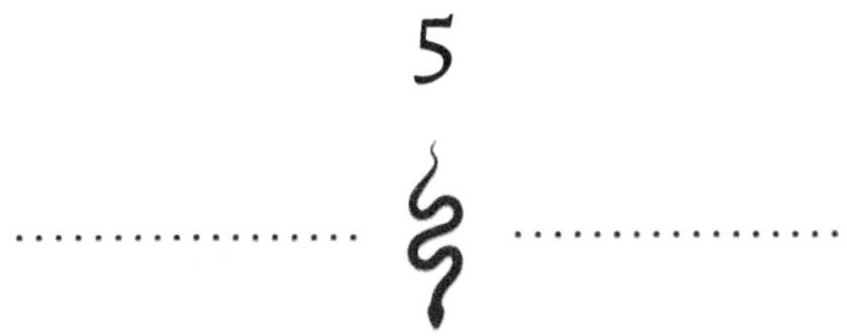

THAT NIGHT, ARLO SMILED as she felt something cool against her ankle where it stuck out from under the sheets. A refreshing breeze at this time of year was a precious thing, and she was glad she'd left the window open. It tipped her mind into dreams that were almost memories: the cool of the cellar; the warmth of her employer's hands on her shoulders.

The look in his eyes when she'd dared to meet them, full of concern. For her.

Warmth bloomed in her belly at the thought that they might have forged a connection in that moment. That there was something between them. She would never give voice to this longing in the light. Wouldn't even let herself think it.

But what harm was there in dreaming?

The dream-touch became hands, Mister Calder's hands—*Tristan's* hands, her mind prompted her, and her mouth curled up at the corners as she reveled in the stolen intimacy. His touch was gentle, feather-light, but strong, too; his softness a choice, not a weakness.

The caress slithered up over her knee, her thigh, tickling the edge of her shift as it crept ever-closer to parts of her body she'd never shared with another person. Arlo squirmed a little, mewling with pleasure, then stopped dead.

She *hadn't* left the window open.

Her eyes flew wide, as panicked as Tristan's had been on the stairs. She flinched hard, pulling both legs up to curl under her as she ripped the sheet aside and yelped at what lay there.

It was a snake, white as ash, undulating toward her. She skittered off the bed, flattened herself against the wall, and groped for matches to light a candle, never taking her eyes off the creature in the dark.

Her bare toes gripped the floor, preparing to run. Mister Calder's room was on the other side of the house, above the library in the southwest corner. Dreaming aside, Arlo's cheeks burned with mortified shame at the idea of running to him in nothing but her shift. But what choice did she have? Apart from her employer, she was alone in this house, and she'd never seen such a giant serpent in all her life.

Except...it wasn't.

Arlo's match flared and she lit her candle, then held it up one more time to get a better look, only to find that there was no snake at all. There was nothing but a bunched-up length of sheet.

At a quick glance in the dark it could *look* like a snake's supple curves, but in the light Arlo could see that her dreams seemed to have slithered away with her.

She tiptoed toward the bed, candle outstretched in a trembling hand, reaching her free fingers to grasp, to snatch, to whip the sheet away.

Nothing.

Arlo's chest went heavy, concave, until she sucked in a huge breath and let it out on a tentative laugh, wheezy with relief, her sheet still clutched in a white-knuckled hand. She didn't so much sit as collapse on the edge of the bed, cocooned in the noise of her own rushing blood.

As her heart slowed, she heard something else.

Words, just on the other side of meaning.

The door.

Arlo sat so still she could feel the hair on her arms rise and stand on end as she listened. There was something on the other side of that door, she was sure of it, and it was calling to her. But she was two floors up from the cellar. How was she hearing it all the way up here?

Part of her wanted to run back, to tear down the cellar stairs in nothing but her shift and bare feet, to look again on the strange carvings and listen to the music in the words she couldn't make out.

But she couldn't do it tonight. Not after that dream.

She cast a glance behind her, as if the snake that hadn't been there might have returned when she wasn't looking. Nothing lurked; nothing moved. Even the murmuring of the door subsided until it was as if it had never been.

Maybe she'd imagined it, a sound to go with her imaginary visitor. Her breaths sounded near to shouts in the silence. It took ages for her breathing to slow, her hands to still their shaking, her heart's rhythm to return to normal, and even longer for sleep to come.

Arlo slept fitfully and woke well before dawn, her mind a jumble of hands and snakes and the memory of whispers. She rinsed her face in the basin and attempted to rub the itch from her gritty eyes, but it barely helped. Her hairpins seemed extra sharp this morning, stabbing at her scalp as she jammed them into a braided bun that kept wanting to fall out.

On her third failure to get the thing to stay up, Arlo let the braid uncoil and sighed. As it fell, she heard a knock on the pocket door that separated the main house from the servants' quarters. She froze, then stood and went out to it. It was too early for Mrs. Hollister to be here, which meant...

"Mister Calder?" she asked, sliding the wall open just enough to see his face.

"Miss Reade," he said. His mouth sounded stuffed with exhaustion. The bags under his eyes were nearly the same deep blue as his irises. There was a shadow of scruff on his chin that made a scratchy sound when he rubbed at it, yawning. She wondered if he'd slept even less than she had. If he'd slept at all. "Are you having breakfast?"

"Not yet, sir," she said, with a self-conscious tug at her un-pinned hair. "I'm going down now."

"Eggs?" he asked.

"Yes, sir."

"Make me some too, please," he said.

"But—," she started, knowing that Mrs. Hollister would arrive in about two hours with fresh bread and bacon and cheese.

"I'll be in the library."

She bobbed, resigned to her fate. "Sir."

Early-morning mist still wreathed the hills behind Calderwood like a gentle sea. When the sun came up, the haze would glitter with golden seams before disappearing like a stain of breath upon a mirror. But for now it was gray, with dark eddies that spun from Arlo's skirt as she walked down the path toward the chicken coop.

She filled her basket with eggs from grumbling hens, then turned back toward the house. Every room on this side was unused except for hers; every window an empty, watching eye.

At least, they were supposed to be empty. As Arlo walked, she caught movement from one of the windows, the sense of someone watching her. A moment later, the sun crested the hills behind her, painting the bleak panes with pastel stripes of blue and pink that chased away the darkness and made Arlo squint and turn away.

When she looked again, the curtains were still; unmoving, untouched except for what must have been a trick of the light.

She returned to the kitchen and was halfway through cooking the eggs when Mrs. Hollister arrived, earlier than expected.

"You eat those," the housekeeper said, unpacking her basket. Arlo dished up the eggs and ate while she watched Mrs. Hollister set bacon to sizzle and bread to toast. When she saw there was no tea, she made a face before setting water on to boil as well.

Arlo, shamefaced, shoveled eggs into her mouth as politely as possible, then put her dish in the sink and took over preparations for Mister Calder's breakfast.

When she brought it to him, he was already hunched over the desk. It was still dark here, except for the light that filtered slantwise through the door that opened to the conservatory. Its walls, made entirely of glass panels with a faint green tint set in a metal framework, must have cost a fortune, though it stood empty now. Whoever loved to garden apparently didn't live here anymore.

Mister Calder's skin looked even worse than before in the greenish haze, like he'd only just risen from the dead, or spent the night fighting off a ghost.

Arlo nearly asked him whether he'd slept well, if he'd had bad dreams. But she thought of *her* dream—of what she'd been dreaming about before it turned into the snake—and then of how she thought she'd need to run to him in nothing but a shift, her hair all in disarray.

In the night, it had seemed wild and romantic, but now it was terribly embarrassing. Arlo cleared her throat quietly and set the tray down when Mister Calder sat up.

"Breakfast, sir," she said.

His gaze was cool and appraising when he looked up at her. Arlo felt she was being sized up for something, or judged. She bit her tongue, feeling her skin go hot and cold as he stared at her.

Could he know that she'd found the door? Was there some mark on her, some invisible, indelible stain that shouted her transgression? Or was he thinking about their exchange at the door to the servants' quarters this morning: Arlo alone, tousled and helpless?

After an eternity, he looked away. "Thank you."

Arlo nodded, then turned and forced herself to walk to the door when all her heart wanted was to run. But she couldn't run. Where would she go?

In fact, despite the size of the house, Arlo found over the next few days that she could barely stay away from her employer. She made no special effort to be near him—in fact, after the dreams she'd been having, it was easier if she stayed away. But Mister Calder seemed to have other ideas, because it became more and more obvious that *he* was making an effort to be near *her*.

He was everywhere, all the time, watching her polish the brass or sweep the carpets or mop the entry hall floor. She caught him over her shoulder, from the corner of her eye: watching, never saying a word. He often surprised her, treading silently into a room and spying, with her all unaware until she looked up. She'd do her best to keep from visibly startling, and he'd nod or clear his throat and walk away.

It was, without a doubt, the most bizarre thing she'd ever been subjected to.

Was he perhaps rethinking his decision to take pity on Mrs. Hollister's aging back?

But his expression was never suspicious nor angry; just a watchful, neutral blank. He never said a word, neither to praise nor criticize. And though Arlo had no prior experience working as a housemaid, his peeking around corners and refusal to make eye contact hardly seemed like the behavior one might expect from a rich man displeased with his servant.

If anything, they were more like the furtive efforts of a boy trying to get close to a wild animal without startling it away.

Arlo had grown up in the city, with people around her all the time. But apart from his occasional trips into town, Mister Calder had spent who knew how many years with only his aging housekeeper for company. It was entirely possible that his clumsy sneaking had nothing at all to do with the quality of her work, good or bad, and everything to do with the fact that he was lonely.

The next time he made an appearance, Arlo had to bow her head to tuck her smile away until his footsteps pattered their customary retreat.

It would have been sweet, if he'd been a shop boy blushing as he handed her something over a counter, trying his best not to let his attention show. And despite how tired he always seemed, he was still pleasant to look at.

But he wasn't the only thing trailing after her.

Everywhere she went, the scratchy, fine whispering of the door followed. It called to her, its constant pull like ants crawling under her skin. Indeed, the whole place seemed to conspire to lure her. The early-summer air became unseasonably oppressive, heavy with heat and the threat of thunderstorms that never came, making Arlo long for the cool retreat of the underground space.

Sometimes she'd catch the hint of words in the movement of her brush across the carpet, a counterpoint to the song that leaked up through the floorboards. The irresistible urge to dance seized her more than once, and she could only be grateful that it had never happened while her employer was lurking nearby.

She *needed* to open that door, to free her mind from the question of what lay behind it. Once she could be sure that it really *was* a disused cold cellar or ice house or something equally reasonable, she could shed this strange obsession and go back to her duties with a focused will.

It was only the memory of Mister Calder's reaction that stopped her. He hadn't actually forbidden her from going back down, but the panicked look in his eyes haunted her, sending an uneasy flutter down her spine every time she caught a peek of that green cellar door or heard the whispers calling, calling.

She endured it for four days. Then the tension snapped.

On her way back from sweeping the great hall, Arlo opened the door that separated the main house from the service suite and pulled up short when she found the housekeeper standing by the dumb-waiter.

"Mrs. Hollister?" she asked, eyes narrowing, brow heavy with confusion.

"Oh, good," the woman said, then hollered down the shaft. "Last one?" she called.

"I'll bring it up!" came a voice from below. Mister Calder's voice.

Arlo swallowed, her mouth suddenly dry. What was he doing down there? His errand came clear when he emerged a moment later from the doorway, his hands covered in coal dust, his shirtsleeves rolled to the elbow.

"Miss Reade," he said, favoring her with a nod. Arlo could do nothing but stand back as he passed her, carrying the coal scuttle down the hall and into the scullery where he dumped it in the holding bin.

"What is he doing?" Arlo asked in a furious whisper while the coal clattered into its new home.

Mrs. Hollister shrugged. "Sometimes he helps."

She said it so factually, as though it was normal for the master of a great house like this one, however empty, to pitch in now and again. Yet Arlo couldn't help the thoughts that started to nibble at her mind.

It was *her* job to fetch the coal. Was he trying to keep her away?

Was she going to lose her place?

She heard the courtyard door open and stepped around the corner to look out the big window, where she could see her employer working the pump, waiting for the gush and then running his arms and hands under the water, and his wet hands through his hair.

"Ah!" he said, striding in again. "That's refreshing." The smile he flashed at Mrs. Hollister didn't survive its trip to Arlo. He brushed past her, striding through the kitchen without so much as a glance in her direction. After all his obvious interest over the past few days, this sudden, blatant disregard for her existence lanced her heart like a pin left out overnight in freezing weather.

"Luncheon will be here soon, Master Tristan," the housekeeper called after their employer, apparently oblivious to the tension between them.

He paused, looking back at Mrs. Hollister with mild confusion on his face, as though he couldn't imagine why she felt the need to remind him of such an established routine.

"I'll be in the library, as usual."

The housekeeper raised an eyebrow. "Maybe you'd like a clean shirt before you eat?"

Mister Calder looked down. "Ah. Yes." He brushed at the streaks on his shirt, though the motion did nothing but make Arlo more aware of the dark hair curling along the line of his exposed neck. She thought she saw something near his collarbone, like the puckered pink line of a healing scar, but the shirt moved again to cover it up before she could make it out.

"Very good, sir."

He disappeared through the door into the main house, muttering under his breath. True to the housekeeper's word, Mister Calder's meals arrived within the hour on a small horse-cart from the village.

"Ah," she said, when the cart pulled up. "Good. Arlo, you'll need to handle the plating today. My daughter and her children are visiting for the next few days, so I'll take the cart back to the village now and help them get settled."

"Oh," Arlo said, having completely forgotten about the upcoming family visit the housekeeper had mentioned. "Of course. Will you be taking a few days off?"

Mrs. Hollister looked at Arlo as though she'd grown another head, eyes narrowing. "Of course not. I'll just be leaving a little early while they're here."

Arlo opened and closed her mouth, nodding, but said nothing while the housekeeper checked the food that came in for Mister Calder's meals. Once she was satisfied, she bade Arlo farewell and took her seat on the cart.

Arlo watched it rumble away. She plated the meal mechanically, her hands gliding and jerking and gliding again with the juddering pace of a faulty automaton while her thoughts compounded, as fast and forceful as a runaway train.

Mister Calder had been doing her job. How many *other* jobs might he do, if the mood took him? Did he even need the additional help? What would she do if she lost her position? She had nowhere she wanted to go back to.

Would the door stop tugging at her if she was forced to leave it behind? Why did it have that kind of power to begin with? It was only a *door*, for Heaven's sake.

Perhaps Mister Calder wasn't the only one who found all this country solitude strenuous on his mind. He'd apparently had so little to do that he'd taken to following her around the house, watching while she worked. What habits might Arlo pick up in time?

Maybe it would be a good thing to leave this place and all its enigmas behind. To find a tiny room to let, and perhaps a job in another part of the city. Selling her body was absolutely out of the question, and she was too old to apprentice in a trade, but maybe she could find work as a shop girl, or use her love of reading to find a position as a governess or a teacher.

But even as the mundane world unfolded its possibilities, the thought of leaving this place now twisted like a knife in her gut. She already knew that if she walked away, she'd regret it forever. This house held a bona-fide mystery, something she could sink her teeth into, like Sexton Blake from the Halfpenny Marvel stories, or even Poe's Dupin. Walking away now meant losing the chance to solve the mystery that defined her every waking moment in this house, and half her sleeping ones.

She shook her head, as though her thoughts were a sack of grain she could settle. Leaving was not an option. She'd been lucky to get this position, in a house where so little was required of her and her master was kind, even if he was a bit odd. Door or no door, she didn't want to lose that.

But it was obvious that Mister Calder didn't want her going downstairs. And if he was willing to do the parts of her job that required it, might he eventually decide he didn't want her here at all?

Arlo couldn't let that happen. She'd have to say something.

With a deep inhale and a squaring of shoulders, Arlo picked up the luncheon tray and carried it down the long central corridor, past the empty rooms to the library at the other end of the house. The sun had crested an hour ago. Steady summer sunshine slanted in through the tall windows, leaving bright-gold rectangles on the floor.

The door swung open on silent hinges at a nudge from her foot, and Arlo stopped at the sight beyond.

Her employer's desk sat in a pool of light that made every paper on it seem to glow. It turned his dark curls to gold around the edges and kissed the contours of his cheeks and his strong, straight nose so gently that it made Arlo want to kiss him, too.

She watched him at his writing for a moment. His hands were lovely and fine, despite the traces of coal dust that still blackened a line under his fingernails. Arlo's attention drifted for a moment. Her fingers tightened around the handles on either side of the tray she carried when she realized where her thoughts about those hands were leading.

She had to *stop*. She'd never thought about *any* man like this, and now, of all people, it had to be *him?* Beyond it being entirely improper—a sentiment the housekeeper would surely approve—he wasn't *interested*. He'd barely even looked at her earlier. And he still hadn't noticed her presence. She cleared her throat.

He nearly jumped from his chair. "Miss Reade!"

"I'm sorry, sir," she said. "I didn't realize you hadn't heard me come in."

He fixed his attention back on the desk, moving papers and pen aside to create a space for the tray, just like always. And, like always, Arlo set it down without a word. Her body twitched with the habit, already ingrained, of leaving as soon as the tray was down. But she planted her feet instead, sending a subtle tremor from her legs all the way up to her shoulders. With no tray to hold, she squeezed her hands into fists by her legs.

It took Mister Calder a few moments to realize she wasn't leaving. Then he asked, "Yes?"

"Mister Calder." An awkward lump collected in Arlo's throat as she worked out what to say.

Don't turn me out; don't send me back; I have nowhere without this strange old house.

"I just wanted to say thank you," she finally said, after squashing down the begging that threatened to take her tongue.

He held his expression like a secret, letting nothing through. Arlo bit the inside of her lower lip, then tilted her head. His mouth might be trained to give nothing away, but his eyes betrayed him.

He was curious. That was good.

"For what?"

"For...giving me a home, sir," she said. His brow started to twitch. Before it could knit or quirk or do anything else that might unnerve her, Arlo pressed on, nearly babbling to get it all out. "I lost both my parents and had to leave the city. All the other houses were staffed, but this position came up like a blessing, sir, a blessing. And I can't tell you how glad I am to have a place here."

She waited a beat, then another, with no response. Her heart battered itself against her ribs in the long stretch of his silence while she stared at the carpet, unable to meet his gaze. Finally, she couldn't stand it any more. She looked up.

Mister Calder was looking at her, his gaze steady, the sunshine pouring blue galaxies into his eyes. Then a cloud scudded by, obscuring the light and returning his eyes to their usual, unreadable twilight hue. He blinked slowly, as though processing her words.

"I see," he finally said, looking away.

Arlo's heart lurched. She was losing him.

"Please don't feel like you have to do the maids' work," she said. "That's what I'm here for."

He nodded. "Thank you, Miss Reade," he said. The words could have been gratitude or a dismissal, or both.

Say something else, she willed, silently begging him to ease her fears. But he lifted his fork and leveled an expectant look at her. She bobbed a curtsy and left. Every step she took through the house was a formless plea, a silent desperation to cling to this place.

Her feelings about Calderwood were as tangled as a kitten's ball of yarn. She didn't want to be forced back to the city to scramble for work. She had a lovely room all to herself here and stopped working well before dark, neither of which she'd find back in town.

She could marry...but she'd left her home specifically to avoid that. Perhaps she wouldn't have, if any of the men back home had been even a little like—no. She couldn't entertain that, couldn't even think it. Wealthy men didn't marry servant girls, no matter how otherwise odd they might be.

And beneath it all, the door, the door, the door. Its subtle voice caressed the edge of every moment, a relentless beckoning that coiled around Arlo's thoughts and curled like cool mist through her dreams.

The list of reasons she couldn't leave ticked over and over through her head as she worked at her tasks, her own particular clockwork, until it was time to set the supper things to warm. Mister Calder hadn't turned up to watch her all afternoon, and she found him still at his desk when she brought his meal. Whatever he was working on must be terribly important, to keep him at his post all day.

Then again, perhaps it was his own fault. Maybe he'd have gotten more done if he hadn't been following her around these past few days. She wished she could ask what he was so focused on, but it was hardly appropriate for her to question him, and the last thing she needed was to reinforce any idea he had that she was inclined to poke into places she shouldn't.

"Supper, sir," she said at the door, more to alert him to her presence than because she had anything to say. She didn't know what else she *could* say, if he had no response to her earlier outpouring.

"Ah," he said, looking up from his book. "Good evening, Miss Reade." His voice was level and pleasant. He set the volume aside so Arlo could put the tray down, then pointed to a side table where his earlier tray lay waiting.

"Thank you, sir," she said, retrieving it.

"That will be all, Miss Reade," he said. "Good night."

Good night, not good-bye. That had to count for something.

"Good night, sir," she said, and left him to his meal.

In the otherwise silent house, the whispers from the door followed Arlo upstairs, twining around her ankles like a thousand hungry cats. Tonight, she did her best to ignore it. She hummed an old song of her mother's to drown out the door, and when she slept, she managed not to dream.

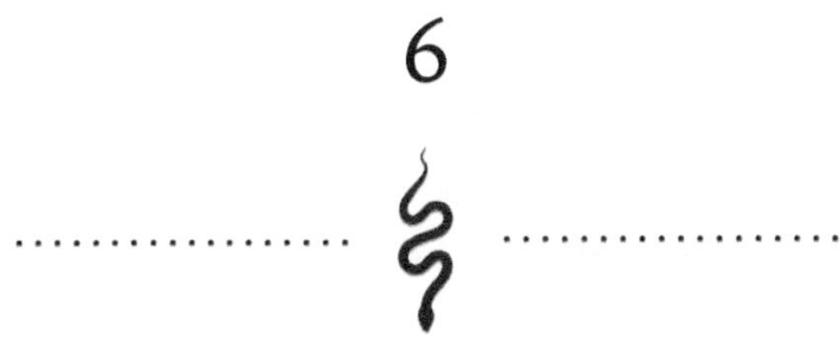

THE NEXT MORNING, MISTER Calder appeared at the door to the kitchen while Arlo and Mrs. Hollister prepared his breakfast.

"Master Tristan," the housekeeper said, tapping a spoonful of tea leaves into the bone china pot with a resonant chime. "To what do we owe the pleasure?"

"Good morning, Hollister," he said to the housekeeper. "Good morning, Miss Reade."

Miss Reade. Would he call her just *Reade* one day, like he did with *Hollister*? The thought of that kind of familiarity sent a pleasant flutter through her stomach, and she wondered what her given name would sound like in his mouth. The smell of eggs close to burning dragged her mind back to focus on the present moment.

"Sir." She turned back to the pan, flipping his egg and hiding the blush that heated her cheeks.

"It's actually Miss Reade I'd like to speak to," he said, though he made no move to dismiss the housekeeper, and she made no move to go.

Arlo's eyebrows creased with puzzlement, but she shuffled aside to let Mrs. Hollister take over the cooking.

"Yes, sir?"

"Miss Reade," he said. "When you're done here, please gather your things to stay at the village inn tonight."

Arlo's heart tripped, her lungs seized, too surprised to breathe. This was it. She'd gone too far; her gratitude had fallen on indifferent ears and now he was thinking better of taking her into his home.

She gaped at him, opening and shutting her mouth while her mind groped for something, *anything* she could do or say to change his decision. Should she burst into tears? Fall to her knees? Would any of it do a single lick of good?

She dragged in a wheezing breath, then doubled over coughing when it caught in her throat.

"Are you alright?" Mister Calder asked, while the housekeeper rushed over and thumped Arlo on the back.

"Yes," she said, straightening up. "But—"

"You'll recall," her employer said, cutting her off, "that my business sometimes takes me away from Calderwood for a time." He didn't phrase it as a question, but Arlo nodded anyway while she got her coughing under control. "This evening, I'll depart for the city and won't return until tomorrow evening. I'd like you to stay at the inn while I'm gone. I'll drop you there with Mrs. Hollister on my way to the city."

Arlo scrambled for an answer, then paused as his words sank in. *While I'm gone.*

Relief melted through her shoulders, almost making her sag. *While I'm gone* meant he was coming back. And, more than that, so was she.

She'd never stayed in an inn before. It had been all her working-class family could do to scrape together rent for the tiny flat they'd shared with no one but each other. They'd certainly never had the means to travel, except for one notable day at the seaside arranged by the shipbuilding company that employed her father. They'd boarded a four a.m. train, spent a few magical hours in a world of gritty sand and roaring surf, then piled back onto the returning train that evening. Arlo had slept on both train rides, and that was the closest she'd ever had to "lodgings away."

The inn was probably very nice, if the meals they delivered were anything to go by, and it wasn't as though Mister Calder didn't have the money to put her up there if he wanted to. But he'd hired her to work and live *here*, at Calderwood, and he wasn't dismissing her. Arlo jerked into a curtsy.

"Sir, begging your pardon, but I already have a perfectly good room here." She looked up in time to see his eyebrows jump. He could sack her here and now for daring to question his instructions, but he just looked surprised.

"Yes, but..." He glanced around the room. "This house can be frightening at night. Creaks and the like, you know. I don't want to cause you any distress, being here all alone in the dark."

Arlo fought to suppress a derisive snort. As though she hadn't been alone in the dark every night since she'd arrived here. Couldn't he see how silly this was?

"There's really no need—"

"Need or not," he said, interrupting her. "I'd prefer it this way."

Arlo tilted her head to one side. He'd been following her around, taking over any part of her job that required a trip to the cellar, and now he preferred for her to be out of the house when he wasn't here. This wasn't about money at all. It was about trust.

He'd been watching her ever since that day in the cellar, and it was obvious that this went back to the door. He couldn't be sure whether she knew about it, and he didn't want her finding out.

Its pull welled up as if Arlo's thought had summoned it, slow and sweet as molasses, licking at her awareness like the scent of something delicious on the wind. Mister Calder being out of the house overnight was too perfect an opportunity to miss. She couldn't let it slip away.

"Sir." Arlo clasped her hands in front of her, gaze tracing the dip and rise of her intertwined fingers. "I don't *know* anyone in the village. I appreciate your concern, truly. But I'm perfectly comfortable here, if you don't mind my saying so."

She chanced a look up at her employer to find him staring at her with his mouth slightly open. His gaze met hers for the briefest of moments before he looked down at the table beside him, pressing his finger against an imperfection in the wood grain, a dark almost-circle that glared up like a baleful eye.

From this angle, Arlo could just see an indent where one corner of his lower lip pulled slightly into his mouth, as if he were chewing it. When he turned back and spoke again, it wasn't to her but to the housekeeper.

"Hollister," he said, appealing to the older woman. "Perhaps you could take in our Miss Reade for the night?"

Mrs. Hollister shook her head. "I would, sir, but my daughter and her children are visiting for a fortnight. We're full up."

Mister Calder looked aside and twitched one hand into a fist in a movement that said *damn* without any words at all. Then he looked at Arlo again.

"You wouldn't have to socialize, you know," he said. "I can have them bring meals up to your room."

Arlo cursed inwardly. He'd offered a perfectly sound solution to a problem that didn't exist. It wasn't that she didn't want to be around people she didn't know. The city was full of people she didn't know, and she'd lived there all her life. The issue was that she wanted to be *here*.

She'd have to try one last tack: appealing to her employer's affection for the house. He must love it dearly; otherwise, why would he spend so much time here alone but for the servants?

"It would be a shame to let a fine old place like this stand empty," she said. "And, if I may say so, sir, in the two weeks I've been here, you've had no callers. I can't imagine anyone might try to visit while you're gone. I'll be perfectly safe." And then, just to make sure, she added, "Won't I?"

His shoulders twitched as if he'd been stung, but he said nothing. Then he drew in a deep breath, let it out, and looked at Arlo.

"Very well," he finally said. "If you'd truly be more comfortable here, far be it from me to turn you out."

Arlo sank into a deeper curtsy than her usual, using the opportunity to keep her face bowed until she could school the expression of absolute relief into something more professional.

"Thank you, sir," she said, when she rose. "I appreciate your concern for me. And just in case anyone *does* come knocking, I promise I'll keep the place locked up tight and never answer the door until you come back. You have my word."

Mister Calder gave her a short, sharp nod, then turned his attention to the housekeeper again.

"Please tell Jonathan to have my carriage ready before three."

"Of course, sir," the housekeeper said. She shot a look at the eggs she'd plated with the rest of his breakfast. "Where will you take breakfast this morning?"

Mister Calder followed her gaze. His mouth flattened, just for a moment, but then he relented and sat at the long table that ran down the middle of the kitchen.

"Here," he said.

Arlo gaped at him. Here? He only ever ate in the library, wouldn't even take meals in his own dining room, and now he wanted to eat *here?*

He shifted in his chair and looked up, his gaze flashing with challenge.

"Why not? I'm here already."

"If...you say so, sir," Mrs. Hollister said, missing less than half a beat as she transferred the plates from the tray to the table.

"Can I get you anything, sir?" Arlo asked.

"No," he told her, picking up his fork. "Not at the moment."

Arlo bobbed, and it was all she could do not to scurry out of the room. There was something so...*human* about him sitting in the kitchen of his great house, eating in the servants' space as if it was something he did all the time. She wouldn't put it past him, except for the scandalized look Mrs. Hollister was *almost* able to hide, which confirmed that this wasn't a common occurrence.

Still, it was his house. Who were they to tell him what he could and couldn't do here?

She grabbed the dustpan and carpet brush from the hall next to the pantry, pointedly ignoring the whispers from beyond the cellar door that seemed to stick to her skin. She'd go back soon enough.

A few hours later, the housekeeper called for her to see Mister Calder off. Arlo put down her tools and stood up, tucking a stray curl back under her cap. She went through the house toward the front door, where the carriage waited outside.

Mrs. Hollister was already there, standing at attention just outside the door while Mister Calder seemed to be having a word with her son.

"With Master Tristan away until tomorrow evening, we'll have very little to do. Can you do without me for tomorrow?"

"I believe so." Arlo's voice was level, though her heart sang. She'd planned to visit the door in the evening after Mrs. Hollister had left, but it was an extra comfort to know she'd be utterly alone in the house until at least tomorrow evening and wouldn't need to listen over her shoulder for anyone who might catch her where she wasn't supposed to be.

After a moment, their employer strode over to them.

"Go get settled, Hollister," he said. "I want a word with Miss Reade."

"Of course," the housekeeper said, turning toward where the carriage waited.

"Mister Cal—" Arlo started to say, but he grabbed her by the elbow when the housekeeper turned away and pulled her into the shadow of one of the columns that fronted the house, where they'd be mostly out of sight.

He hadn't laid a hand on her since that day in the cellar, and that had been brief and, she suspected, mostly accidental. This time, he touched her with purpose, and her whole body surged with the thrill. His eyes were serious; his wide, full lips pressed hard together with something he needed to say.

"You meant what you said, didn't you?" he asked, his fierce gaze searching hers. "You'll keep the house locked tight."

"Of course, sir." Arlo met his eyes and made a tentative move to pull her arm away, but his fingers gripped tighter, squeezing against her bones.

"You won't answer the door." It wasn't a question.

Arlo's skin went bumpy with a sudden apprehensive chill. Was there some double meaning in that? But her alarm subsided as quickly as it had come. He *couldn't* be talking about the door in the cellar. If he was that afraid of it and honestly believed she'd found it, there was no way he'd leave her alone in the house. Besides, it was in the cellar, underground. It wasn't a door she could answer.

She was going to have such a laugh when the buildup of this mystery turned out to be nothing more than an abandoned cold storage room. She really had been reading too many tales of ghastly terror, to let a door get to her the way she had.

But tonight, it would be over. Tonight she would finally know.

Mister Calder squeezed again. Arlo winced. She hadn't answered him.

"I promise." Her words were a gasp as his grip tightened. "Sir," she added, nearly whimpering, "you're hurting me."

At the same time, they heard Mrs. Hollister's raised voice carry from where she sat on the carriage bench.

"Master Tristan! Are you ready?"

He let go of Arlo's elbow all at once, jerking his hand back as fast as if he'd been caught picking a pocket. She couldn't tell whether it was her mewl that had stopped him, or the housekeeper's tone of voice. The woman clearly disapproved of anything that might be construed as lingering with the help.

Mister Calder held the offending hand up in apologetic defense, his grim expression gone, a concerned, guilty look in its place.

"I'm sorry. Are you injured?"

Arlo shook her head.

"No," she said, though she rubbed at her elbow, massaging away some of the hurt he'd left behind.

His hand twitched toward her, then stopped. He balled it into a fist at his side and cleared his throat.

"I'll be back tomorrow," he said. "Before sunset."

"Very good, sir." Arlo curtsied. When she rose, he was still looking at her. Then, after a long moment, he turned on one heel and stalked off toward the carriage.

Arlo took her place in the drive, the lone maid to see off her strange employer. The cloth of his jacket strained a little across his back as he reached up for the rail to guide his climb into the carriage. Although he didn't look up before closing the door, the curtain twitched aside to reveal one eye, dark in the shadows of the enclosed space, watching her as Jonathan clucked to the horses to get them moving.

The weight of his gaze lingered on her skin for much longer than he could have seen her.

Arlo waited for several minutes after the carriage was out of sight, just in case. Then she walked back into the house, locked the front door, hung her apron on a kitchen peg, lit a hand lantern, and went to the cellar.

7

IN THE HOUSE'S SILENCE, Arlo's steps echoed on the stone stairs. She inhaled the scents of earth and coal, dust and old damp as the cool air caressed her skin. There was the rustle of something moving in the dark beyond her lamp, the hushed clack as a piece of coal shifted and settled.

Then nothing.

Until the voices started.

Arlo stood still. There was no work to do now. No floors to sweep, no carpets to beat, nothing to mop or plate or wash.

There was only Arlo, and the dark, and the door.

She flexed her ears, straining to find meaning in the persistent susurration that had licked at her steps like the tiniest waves of an incoming tide, until the formless sounds contorted, sliding over each other and at last—at *last*—became words.

Come, they called her, alluring, enticing. *Come, come.*

Arlo thought of the Rossetti poem she still had tucked away in her room, of Laura and Lizzie and the little goblin men. She had the sense, all at once, that whatever lay behind that door was just as fine and rare as the fruits the goblins sought to sell, even though she knew that logically, there was most likely nothing there.

But the voices told a different story.

She approached the door in increments, as slow as if she were wading through chest-deep water. The distance was immense, impossible, every step a battle won, yet she got no closer. Until, all at once, her fingertips grazed against the cool, angular head of a snake, a dull, burnished black in the light of her lantern.

And then, it spoke.

It started as a hiss, the slithering whisper of a thousand reptilian voices that resolved into a single question.

"Do you wish to pass?"

Arlo emptied her lungs in a long, shuddering breath until her chest went nearly concave under the pressure of the question. A small, rabbity corner of her mind scrambled to assign some logic to what was in front of her. Had she eaten a bad egg? Was there some slow leak of gas or air that could be causing the sound? Or would she wake with a startled jerk when Mister Calder scolded her for nodding off over her carpet brush?

She moved her free hand to the arm that held the lantern and dug her thumbnail in, hard. It hurt, so she *had* to be awake. Which meant this was real. Which meant...

"Yes," she said, meeting the snake's shrewd, inky-black eye as its head hovered, bobbing ever so slightly as it watched her.

"You will need three things to gain entrance," it said, drawing every sibilant into a long, luxurious hiss. "The first is something silver. The second, something gold. The third is something you can feel, but never see nor hold."

The snake flicked an iron-dark tongue at her and bobbed its head in a slow, mesmerizing circle.

Arlo stood, transfixed, while the snake pulled back and folded it-self into a sinuous curve, stilling until it was in such perfect harmony with the pattern around it that Arlo couldn't tell it apart from the carving.

Its last words lingered on the air, burning themselves into her mind.

"Bring me what I ask, and you may enter."

In the following silence, nothing moved.

Arlo waited a breath, another, then turned and bolted for the stairs, nearly tripping on her way back up to the house.

Her heart jangled in her chest, kicking like a terrified animal while her breath came in short, sharp gasps.

The door had moved. The door had *spoken*.

It shouldn't be possible, but she hadn't imagined it.

This was exactly the kind of story she loved to read, but she never thought she'd be in one. She trembled with a frantic thrill of delight as the clangor in her chest became the first thin strains of a brass band marching toward her.

If she could find the three things the snake wanted, it would let her through. But she'd have to work fast—Mister Calder would return tomorrow, giving her only tonight to conduct her search.

Something silver, the snake had said. Something gold. And some-thing else that she could feel, but never see nor hold. That last one was troubling. How could she feel something without touching it? An emotion, perhaps, but how could she hand *that* over, and what would a snake even *do* with it?

She shook her head. Leave that for now; focus on the tangibles.

Something silver, something gold.

Easy enough.

Arlo started in the butler's pantry. Mrs. Hollister never bothered to lock it, and there was bound to be some silver in there. Although, now that she thought of it, she'd never had to polish any. Didn't silver need polishing all the time?

She entered to find the countertops bare, but every drawer whispered an invitation. At first, she didn't mind not finding the silver. In a room with this many drawers and cubbies and cabinets, who knew where it might be hiding?

But with each drawer she opened, Arlo crept closer to the realization that there *was* no silver at Calderwood. Mister Calder used the same utensils she and the housekeeper did, plain steel with bone handles, and apparently, since he never had visitors, there was no reason to keep anything more elaborate.

"Damn it," she said, closing the last drawer, defeated. Well, so he didn't entertain. But he spent most of his time in the library. Perhaps there was something there she could use?

Arlo closed up the pantry and crossed to the other end of the house, her bobbing lantern casting erratic shadows as she hurried down the hall. Thunder growled outside, warning of an oncoming storm that fell just as she reached the library door. Rain hissed and splattered against the conservatory glass beyond the library, turning the gloomy space into an underwater otherworld, timeless and strange.

She could almost hear the door's song in the noise. Although the conservatory had nothing in it but bare pots and potential, she had the sense that the room—the whole house—was somehow *alive.* It was singing to her, wanting to be heard.

She closed her eyes and swayed on her feet for a moment, not quite dancing to its music, until a peal of thunder cracked the sky, making her jump. The spell of the moment fell from her like snow from trees in a true-spring thaw, and Arlo returned to the task at hand.

Mister Calder's desk was the tidiest she'd ever seen it, the papers tucked away, pens cleaned and set in an earthenware dish. The lamp key and drawer pulls gleamed in her lantern light, but they were brass, not gold. There was gilding on some of the books, pressed into decorative scrolling on the leather covers, but Arlo suspected that a thin shaving of gilt wouldn't be enough to satisfy the requirement. She pressed a fist under her nose and thought.

Why hadn't she noticed this before? Calderwood had many lovely things: fine bone china, exquisite wood carvings, statues and busts of marble and stone, even some whales' teeth with tiny scrimshaw pictures. Mister Calder's inkwell was blown glass, and his collection of books had to be worth a fortune. But for all that wealth, there was no silver cutlery, no candelabras, no trinkets in any precious metals.

Perhaps he carried his wealth on his person? But no; Arlo had watched him at work in the moments before he noticed her arrival with his meals, and his hands had never flashed with jewelry of any kind.

She sat with a frustrated sigh in his chair and chewed her thumbnail as she thought.

Where else would he keep all his wealth?

Then, she saw something. Directly across from her employer's desk was a large fireplace with a painting hanging over it. She'd seen it before, in passing, but she'd never actually *looked* at it. She looked now, wondering what about the drab still-life seemed suddenly so captivating.

It took her several minutes to realize that it wasn't the painting at all, but the fact that its frame didn't quite line up with the terminus where years of afternoon sun had lightened the wallpaper several shades.

Maybe it had gone crooked? Or maybe... Arlo's breath quickened at the sudden rush of possibility. Maybe it was designed to move.

She stood and hurried over, lantern in hand, and slipped her fingers behind one corner of the large frame. She could barely reach it on tiptoes, but she could at least find out if there was a safe back here, the key to the secret of Calderwood's missing wealth.

Hope beat its wings in her chest for one wild moment before she lifted her light.

"No," she said, half groan, half shout. "No!" There was nothing there but smooth wall. She put her lantern down and fetched over the footstool from the chair by the fire, standing on it to check again. But it changed nothing. There was nothing here.

Arlo put the footstool back and sat on it, chin in her hands, huffing with frustration.

There was nothing here. And Mister Calder didn't *use* any of the other rooms in the house, none except—

She sat up, ablaze with a sudden possibility.

You will never, never *set foot in these rooms. Is that clear?*

She took the stairs by the library two at a time, following them directly up to her employer's bedroom door. The rain nearly shouted here, slapping the roof like it bore a grudge. Arlo tried the doorknob, but wasn't surprised when she found it locked. Mister Calder locked the door while he was *here,* never mind when he wasn't.

She pounded on the door with the side of her fist. It boomed in answer, but didn't budge. She closed her eyes and bleated a short, frustrated moan. There was no way she was getting in, not unless she was willing to break it down or attempt to pick the lock. But even if she did manage to do it, there was a chance that she wouldn't find what she needed on the other side of the door.

If she couldn't get the three things tonight, she'd have to stay here and bide her time until she could come up with another idea. That wasn't likely to happen if she gave her employer reason to throw her out.

Arlo steepled her hands and tapped her two forefingers together, thinking. She wouldn't be able to see anything through the keyhole, not in the dark. But if she waited for another flash of lightning, then maybe—

She got on her knees, pressed her face to the keyhole, and waited for her chance. Seconds limped by, the sound of the hall clock lost in the roar of rain on the roof, until lightning sizzled across the sky with a crack of thunder right behind it. Arlo's heart thrilled as the room lit up, and she cast her gaze around for one frantic instant.

Nothing, there was nothing.

The illumination was too brief, there and then gone.

"Please." She could barely hear her own whisper as she scrabbled like a trapped cat at the place where the door fit into its opening, her soft human fingernails useless against the wood. She grabbed the doorknob and twisted until friction bit at the pads of her palm just below her fingers.

Then she stopped all at once as the pain caught up with her, one hand on the knob, the other on her forehead.

What the hell was she doing?

Was she really kneeling in the hallway outside her employer's bedroom door, waiting for lightning to show her whether the man might be hiding treasures? She rocked back on her heels, chest convulsing with silent laughter that turned, before she knew it, into sobs.

Her hand carried a vague whiff of brass from the doorknob as she scrubbed hot tears off her cheeks. Lord, she didn't even know why she was crying. But it was late. She hadn't eaten supper. And it was obvious, now, that she wasn't going to find her way through any locked doors tonight. Arlo leaned one shoulder against Mister Calder's door while her sobs resolved into slow, steady breathing.

She could do this. It didn't have to be now.

The snake hadn't given her a time limit, so any urgency she felt—no matter how insistent—was completely self-imposed. And perhaps this was a blessing in disguise. Mister Calder hadn't wanted to leave her alone here, but when he came back and found everything just as it should be, maybe his fears would relax. He'd travel again, eventually, perhaps for longer than overnight, and Arlo could use the time until then to come up with another plan.

One that, if possible, didn't involve stealing from the man who'd offered her a job and a home when she had none.

She stood up with a sigh and trudged all the way back to the other end of the house, where her narrow bed waited for her. Her eyes flashed in the tiny round mirror above her washbasin, their red rims making her pale blue gaze look more vivid than usual. Nowhere near as deep as Mister Calder's eyes, of course, and she bit her lip with longing even as she scolded herself for it so soon after crouching outside his door like a common thief.

She took a deep breath, then cleaned her teeth, used the chamber pot, and stripped off all but her shift before crawling into bed. Sleep, that's what she needed.

No matter how tight the door gripped her imagination, there was still the real world to contend with, and she'd need to be at least a little rested to do her work tomorrow.

In the stillness after the storm had passed, every plip of dripping rain and creak of settling floorboard seemed to echo, coming from everywhere all at once. Arlo found herself thinking, too late, that perhaps Tristan had a point about being alone in this house at night. Though her room was nowhere near his, the knowledge of his presence down the hall had been a comfort. Now, the dark she thought she was used to took on a more sinister texture.

The door clicked, making Arlo's shoulders jump until she realized she'd forgotten to lock it. She got up to turn the bolt and slipped back into bed, shivering a little despite the evening's warmth until sleep finally took her.

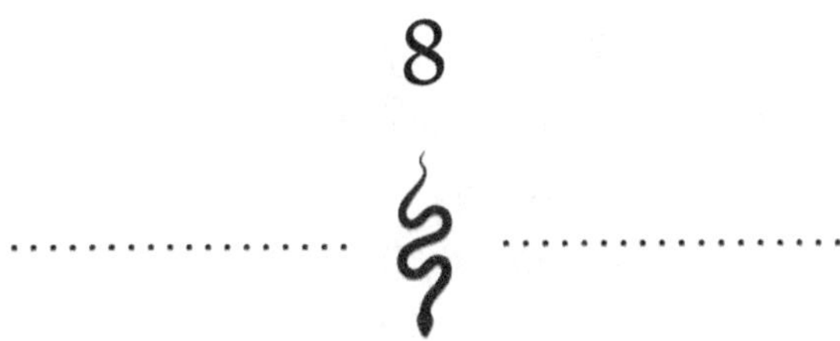

MISTER CALDER RETURNED AFTER lunch. It was earlier than he said he'd be back, but Arlo had at least had time to rise and dress and look something close to human after her late night.

"Did you have a good trip, sir?" she asked as he stepped down from his carriage, overnight bag in hand. Jonathan clucked to the horse and rolled off toward the carriage house and stables.

"Yes, quite." Mister Calder stepped around a puddle from the night's rain and walked past her into the house. "Any trouble?"

Arlo shook her head, keeping her face averted to hide the worst of the dark circles under her eyes.

"None, sir. Just the storm."

He put his bag down in the foyer and turned, looking at her.

"Where's Hollister?"

"Not here, sir. We didn't expect you until later in the evening. She'll be back tomorrow."

"Ah, yes," Mister Calder said. He shrugged out of his coat and hat and handed them over. "Please bring tea to the library in an hour."

"Of course, sir." Arlo hung up his hat, then took his coat to the courtyard and brushed off the small mud splatters by the hem before putting it away. She stoked the kitchen fire and filled the kettle with fresh water, but it was too early to set it to boil. Arlo thought for a moment, then hurried up the servants' stair to her room.

She still had her borrowed copy of "Goblin Market," but she wasn't going to read it again. There was no need for fiction about something trying to entice her, not when the door in the cellar haunted her reality. She slipped the little volume into a pocket of her apron and went back downstairs to prepare the tea.

When she opened the door to the library, there was her employer, as secure in his chair as though he'd never left it. Arlo had never noticed before, but the room seemed somehow more complete with him there. It wasn't just that an empty library felt like such a sad thing: a waste of potential, a place unable to fulfill its purpose. There was that, certainly, but there was more to it.

Last night, she'd despaired at the lack of precious metals in the room. Now she could see that, with Mister Calder here, they were unnecessary. The space seemed made to offset him, as if the library was a jewel box, and he the jewel. His skin glowed against the dark wood of the shelves that wrapped every wall, and the dark pine-green blotter on his desk set off his hands and the deep, cool blue of his eyes in rich contrast.

Arlo startled when he looked up, realizing he'd caught her staring.

"Tea, sir." She bustled over with the tray to cover her fluster. He made space without a word, keeping his gaze on her the whole time. "Also, sir," she said, reaching into her pocket. "I wanted to return this to you." She held the book out.

He took it and ran his fingers over the cover.

"Did you enjoy it?" he asked, without looking up.

Was it her imagination, or did something in his voice sound a little strained?

Come buy, come buy. The goblin men's refrain danced in her memory, overlaid with the song of what she'd come to think of as the snake-door. It tugged at her even now: ghostly fingers in her hair, the sense of an arm around her waist. Gentle, insistent. *Come, come.*

"Yes, sir," she said. "I think Lizzie was very brave."

At this, Mister Calder's gaze seemed to lose its cool, flinty cast. "Oh?" he asked, leaning a little toward her. "Not Laura?"

Laura, who was the first to follow the goblin men. She'd plunged into the unknown, wanting to taste forbidden fruits more than anything else in the world. More than reason; more than sense. She'd gone even when Lizzie had tried to hold her back. And she'd paid the price, wasting away for want of another taste when the goblins deserted her.

It had been Lizzie who'd saved her, saved both of them from the cruel fate to which the goblins had laughingly enticed them.

Now that she thought of it, Arlo could see the lesson there.

She didn't know what was behind the snake-door. What if, just like Laura, she would get her heart's desire only to find herself bereft forever after? But that door was part of this house; it was built into the wall, a piece of the foundation. Mister Calder knew, he *must* know what the snake-door was, else why would he be so cautious of letting anyone get near it?

How *much* did he know? Only that it was there? Or was he aware that it could speak? Did he know it could be opened? The lack of precious metals anywhere in Calderwood loomed in her mind like a sudden shadow in a doorway, sending a shiver down Arlo's shoulders.

Was that lack mere coincidence, or was it an indication that Mister Calder not only knew about the door but also knew its price?

She wished she could just ask him. But if she did, she'd give the game away. He could easily dismiss her for insubordination, for snooping, for any number of things. He could do it for no reason at all. It was better to keep her secrets, bide her time. And it was possible that she could find answers without asking him a thing. This library was large, with some very old volumes. Mister Calder had already told her she was welcome to borrow things. Maybe there was some record here, some explanation of what the snake-door was, or where it led to.

She could go prepared; not a Laura, but a Lizzie.

"No," she said, firm, decisive. "Laura couldn't help herself. But it was Lizzie who tricked the goblins into giving up their fruit *without* getting caught in their snare."

Mister Calder pressed his lips together, but his eyes were smiling.

"I see," he said with a nod. "Very sound reasoning."

Arlo beamed at him, partly for the compliment and partly because, as they talked, something about him seemed to soften. Well, and no wonder. He never had friends or associates here. Apart from his occasional travels, she wondered who he talked to about the things that interested him. He was always scratching away at documents, some of which had to be letters, but they could only stand so much in place of real human interaction. Arlo, at least, had Mrs. Hollister. But when he was at home, Tristan seemed to have no one.

"Thank you," she said. And then, realizing both that she'd thought of him by his first name and dropped the honorific, added a hasty, "sir."

He looked at her for a long moment, then cleared his throat.

"Well," he said.

Arlo bobbed. "Well," she echoed. "Excuse me, then."

She left him to his tea and crossed the house to begin preparations for delivering his evening meal. As soon as she closed the door that separated the kitchen suite from the main house, though, she had to pause, her heart thudding so hard she could hear it in her ears.

That smile; those eyes.

Arlo had to admit that she had more than one reason to prolong her time at Calderwood as much as possible. Whether or not she'd ever give voice to it, she was absolutely taken with Tristan Calder, propriety be damned.

She stood there, breathing deep and steady until her heart slowed to the tiniest of flutters. And when she passed the hall with the door that led to the cellar and all its mysteries, for once, she heard nothing at all.

If she didn't know better, Arlo might believe Mister Calder never left the library.

In the five days since his return, he'd ceased his habit of following her around the house and watching while she worked. She found the development both reassuring and disappointing in equal measure.

Reassuring, because it meant she'd earned his trust: a fact that left her a little guilty, since she was hoping to capitalize on that faith at some point in the future and do exactly what he trusted her not to do.

And disappointing, because she had to admit that while it was strange to look up and see him just standing in the doorway, watching her, the view from her end was not unpleasant.

Besides, it was just the two of them here, apart from Mrs. Hollister. But the housekeeper didn't live here. She didn't spend her nights held up by groaning floorboards, listening to wind rattle the windows and moan over the hills. She wasn't here when darkness rolled like a sigh into every corner, when the slow drain of light made every smell and sound and change in the air stand out like a shout in the gathering night.

Only Arlo was here for that. Arlo and Tristan. It felt special in a way she couldn't begin to articulate, an intimacy that his increased presence the week before had served to enhance. Without it, she felt strangely bereft. But at least she always knew where to find him.

Unfortunately, his near-permanent residence in the library made researching Calderwood and its mysterious, snake-covered door more challenging. After all, she didn't want him to see what she was looking for. And after four nights of sneaking downstairs in the wee hours only to find him still at his post, she was getting discouraged.

On the fifth night, there he was again. Arlo stifled a frustrated sigh when she spied him through the cracked-open library door, hunched over his desk as usual. But after almost a week of being thwarted, she wasn't ready to let this attempt go entirely to waste. Research aside, she was dying for something new to read. Mister Calder had already invited her to borrow a book once. Maybe he'd do it again.

Arlo laid her fingertips on the door to push it open, then stopped when she saw that, for once, Mister Calder wasn't writing. He was looking at something small and rectangular cradled in both his hands. She could just see the dark, shining eyes and bright ovals of two faces almost floating above the background in a way that told her it wasn't a painting nor a photograph but a tintype. Despite being too far away to make out any detail, there was something almost magnetic about the picture, something that drew Arlo into the library before she realized she was moving.

Mister Calder must have heard her step, even on the double-carpet of the runner strip. He started and closed his hands over the picture, whipping his head up to shoot her a glance that was both alarmed and accusatory.

Arlo bobbed a reflexive curtsy. "Good evening, sir."

Her employer laid one hand over his eyes and dragged it down, inhaling as he did.

"Miss Reade," he said, glancing at the clock. "Is everything alright?"

"Yes, sir," she said. "But I couldn't sleep. And I thought..." She gestured broadly to the shelves of books. "I wondered if it would be alright—"

"To borrow something?" Mister Calder asked. "Of course. Did you have anything in mind?"

Arlo let her gaze roam over the dark spines racked neatly on the shelves and heaved a sigh that turned into an embarrassed chuckle. "I wouldn't know where to start," she admitted.

Her employer put one hand under his chin and rubbed it thoughtfully as he looked at her. "You said you enjoy detective stories," he said. Arlo nodded. "And you've read Poe?"

"Oh, yes, sir," Arlo said.

"So you're not opposed to stories that are...a bit on the dark side?"

The question was as delicate as a cat's first step into fresh-fallen snow, and Arlo had to press her lips together to keep from laughing.

"No sir," she said, keeping her smile tucked into the furthest corners of her mouth.

Mister Calder lit a candle from the lamp burning on his desk and stood up, beckoning for Arlo to follow. She did, padding silently after him over the carpet until he stopped at a shelf toward the back of the room.

"Here are some of my favorites." He held up one hand in a gesture of presentation, his mouth twitching around the beginnings of an excited grin. "Does anything strike your fancy?"

Arlo leaned in, taking a closer look at the titles on display. One stood out for its slimness among the thicker volumes, and she hooked a fingernail behind the headband of the spine, tipping it out.

"Strange Case of Dr. Jekyll and Mr. Hyde," she read.

"Ah!" Mister Calder exclaimed. "Do you know it?"

Arlo shook her head. "I've heard of it," she said. "But I haven't read it."

The room went perfectly still for a fraction of a second, as if even the spiders that scuttled in dark corners were holding their breath. Then Mister Calder swooped in, snatching the book from her with an astonished look on his face. He came so close that, for just a moment, Arlo caught a whiff of some crisp, woody spice that made her want to melt into the warmth of his skin. But then he was gone, shaking the book in the air between them, his storm-blue eyes wide and demanding.

"Never?" he asked, incredulous. Arlo shook her head again. "My *God!*" he exclaimed. "Miss Reade, it is a fascinating exploration of the duality of the self, and one man's loss of control!"

"Duality of the self?" Arlo asked.

"Good and evil, warring within us! It's the story of a doctor named Jekyll. Well, it's mostly told by John Utterson, his lawyer friend." He started to pace in front of his desk, hands in the air on either side of his head, the fingers of his free hand splayed as he gesticulated his enthusiasm.

"A record of strange happenings in London, where the story takes place. But at its heart is Jekyll." He stopped and put his two hands together, with the book between them hooked under one thumb. "A man convinced he can separate the good and evil parts of his nature so that his good self can go on being good, and his wicked self can indulge in the worst of behaviors." At that, he pulled his hands apart, separating them. "And neither will stain the other with its influence."

Arlo gasped. It was impossible, unbelievable. And yet, what was she witnessing now but the separation of two sides of a man's nature? Before this moment in the cocoon of the night's darkest hours, she would never have believed her employer could be so animated, so enthused.

"And does he?" she asked.

"He does!" her employer exclaimed. "He formulates a drug, a potion that lets him effect the change." He opened the book, riffling through pages until he found what he wanted. "The most racking pangs succeeded," he read, holding the book out with one hand while clutching at his chest with the other, as if acting the scene in a stage play.

"A grinding in the bones, deadly nausea, and a horror of the spirit that cannot be exceeded at the hour of birth or death." His voice soared and dipped with theatrical agony and he hunched suddenly forward, hair falling into his eyes, his free hand curled into a dramatic claw.

He looked up at Arlo from under his mess of loose, dark curls, and what she saw on his face nearly stopped her heart. She had seen him look calm, and frustrated, and even afraid, but never once had she seen him smile. Not like this.

This was the smile of a man who could fall in love with the whole world, the infectious joy of someone who wanted to share a thing they loved with everyone, freely and simply *because* they loved it, wanting nothing in return but that others might love it, too.

This wasn't Mister Calder. This was *Tristan.*

Arlo's chest felt like a ship dashed on rocks, her heart crashing into her throat with the force of a yearning for something she didn't dare name. He went on staging the narrative, oblivious to her silent ruination.

"And then the pain wears off, and he feels younger, lighter, happier in his body, disordered and sensual," he recited, barely even glancing at the page, his eyes fever-bright, "and tenfold more wicke—"

He stepped closer, one hand outstretched as if he would grasp hers, then stopped all at once and snapped the book abruptly shut with an alarmed look on his face.

"More what?" she asked, barely breathing.

But the moment was gone. Tristan took several steps back, leaning against the front edge of his desk. He tapped the small volume like a fan against his fingertips, then raked his hair back into a semblance of order, all the wild, wonderful mirth gone from his face as completely as if it had never been there at all.

"Ah," he said. "Well, I'd hate to spoil it." Then, with a rueful smile he added, "any more than I already have."

"No, sir," Arlo said, eyes wide, shaking her head slowly. She held out both hands, fingers reaching for the book. "It sounds wonderful. May I?"

He held it out to her. She took it and squelched the impulse to clutch it tight to her chest.

"Of course. Perhaps we can...talk about it," he said, with a self-conscious clearing of his throat and a glance away. "After."

Arlo forced herself to breathe, to slow the galloping of her runaway heart.

"I'd like that, sir. Thank you."

"Well." He stepped away with a stiffness that Arlo nearly wept to see, knowing now what lay hidden underneath. "It's gotten quite late. Best off to bed, eh?" His tone was awkward, jovial in a way that felt distant and forced. "Good night, Miss Reade."

She knew a dismissal when she heard one, though despite the late hour, she doubted whether she'd get much sleep tonight.

Not after that.

"Yes, sir," she said, with a reflexive curtsy. "Good night."

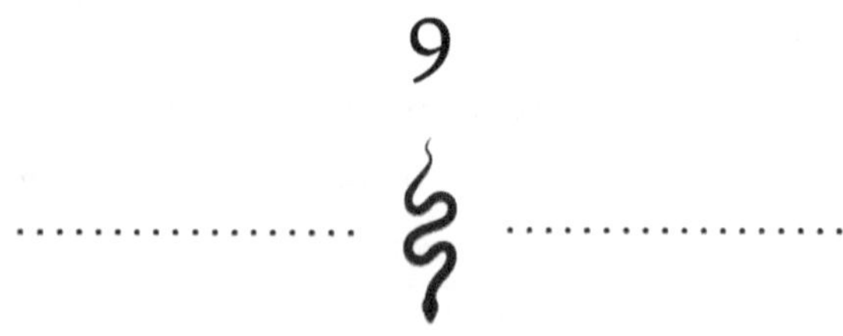

9

ARLO STAYED UP UNTIL dawn reading the *Strange Case of Doctor Jekyll and Mister Hyde*. It was told in vignettes, an outsider's view of a good doctor's descent into the company of an evil man and his inexplicable faithfulness to that relationship even when it clearly cost him dear.

And then—the twist—Jekyll *was* Hyde! One man, transformed by a potion, the two sides of himself constantly at war with each other. Arlo re-read the final section several times, the account of what happened from the doctor's own point of view, recalling how Mister Calder had acted out the transformation, hunching and clawing and clutching at his heart.

And that had been before she'd read the book. She caught herself licking her lips at the thought of his dark tumble of curls, the way his chest heaved as he'd acted out Jekyll's agony. What else might he do, now that she knew the story too? The thought of him acting again for her alone sent a pleasant sizzle down her bones, but it was the possibility of his meeting her eyes, of him turning the full power of that smile on her again that sent her truly quivering.

She all but raced downstairs in the morning, hair barely tucked under her cap, to make it out to the chickens and back in time to bring him an early breakfast. They wouldn't be able to talk with Mrs. Hollister here, and it was nearly a week 'til Sunday, when the woman would be out of the house for the day.

But when Arlo arrived in the library with Mister Calder's tray, he was nowhere to be found. She set down her burden and doubled back, leaving the library and heading up the stairway at the conservatory-end of the house to his bedroom door.

"Mister Calder?" she called, knocking gently. She pressed her ear to the door, listening for any sort of shift or mumble, but none came. "Sir?" she tried again, a little louder this time. As a last resort, she jiggled the handle. It was locked, of course. Like always.

Arlo sighed and headed back downstairs. He couldn't have gone to the kitchen; she would have seen him on her way to the library. She peeked in through the library door again when she passed, but his seat was still vacant. Shaking her head, Arlo started back toward the kitchen. Mrs. Hollister would be here soon, and the chores wouldn't do themselves.

As she passed the hall that led to the terrace door, she noticed a figure out on the hills walking toward the house. She took a few steps closer, peering out. The man wore dark trousers, with a matching jacket draped over the rolled-up shirtsleeve of one arm. His waistcoat buttons flashed in the early light. He could be anyone, but Arlo knew those dark curls lifting around his head in a morning breeze.

Though she couldn't make out his expression from here, his tension was clear in the taut line of his shoulders and the way he tapped the thumb of his free hand against his fingers in a restless, repetitive motion. She'd never known him to take walks on the grounds, although, to be fair, she'd only been here for a little over three weeks. It felt longer, somehow, and like no time at all.

She watched him, a little smile curling one side of her mouth as he shook his head, facing into the wind to get the hair out of his eyes. He really should cut it, but it felt so much a part of him that Arlo couldn't imagine him with the neat trim and combed fashion of the men she'd seen before leaving the city. Something about his gentle dishevelment was so uniquely *Tristan* that it drew his name out of her in a fond whisper.

The sound settled like dust into silence, and in the quiet of the empty house, other whispers rose to take its place.

They seeped up through the floorboards, thrumming in Arlo's feet with the urge to *come, come, come.* The force of it made her sway, and she thrust a hand against the wall to keep herself from falling. Her breath thundered in her ears as she drew gasp after ragged gasp into her lungs, so loud that she didn't hear the terrace door open.

"Miss Reade?" Something in the *s* lingered as strong arms reached out to support her. Arms with the shirtsleeves rolled. Arlo's vision swam a bit as she swayed into her employer's embrace, so that when she looked up, she had the overwhelming sense of blue before it resolved into his concerned eyes looking down at her. "Are you quite well?"

Arlo's mouth hung open for a moment, soundless. The woody, spicy scent he wore curled around her like a second embrace. She closed her eyes and tipped her head back. Her tastes tended more toward the macabre than to stories of romance, but in this moment, the simple act of breathing filled her with a brazen desire that almost made her swoon again. She fought the urge to clutch at his shirt, his chest, to pull him down toward her, to close the distance between them.

It was completely inappropriate. She never wanted it to end.

She opened her eyes again, and the moment shattered. Her employer's arms stiffened, his face a parade of expressions from shock to uncertainty as he finally realized the position they were in. Arlo watched him, frantic and hopeful, until a very brief flash of horror in his eyes pierced her heart like a sliver of glass.

She drew as deep a breath as she could manage, swallowing the lump in her throat and blinking away the tears that shimmered at the edges of her eyes. It reminded her of that trip to the seaside, when she'd stood in the sand while the outgoing tide did its best to cling to the shore.

Pulling away from him in this moment came with that same sucking sensation, the dizzying dichotomy of standing still while some inexorable force stole the earth out from under her feet. She blinked fast several times, smoothing down the front of her dress and apron as she took a few steps back.

"Apologies, sir." She didn't—couldn't—look at his face, not just now. Not when she didn't know whether she'd see regret there, or relief. "I seem to have lost my balance for a moment."

With her eyes downcast, she saw Mister Calder's hand dart forward and pull back in almost the same instant, fingers splayed, as if he wanted to reach out again but didn't dare.

"If you're sure." The uncertainty in his voice nearly undid her. She bobbed a short curtsy, enough for propriety without going low enough to risk her balance again, but try as she might, she couldn't fight the urge to peek up at him through the fringe of her lashes.

"Of course, sir. Breakfast is in the library."

He pulled a watch from his waist pocket and frowned a little.

"Isn't it a bit early?"

Arlo drew the inside of her top lip between her teeth, worrying it with their sharp edges as she fought a bleak little laugh at how different this morning was from what she'd been expecting when she woke. She tried to recapture the enthusiasm that had kept her up all night and found it as cold as three-day ashes, though frustrated fury rose valiantly to take its place.

Not six hours ago, he'd been so excited about the book that he'd acted out a scene, then pressed it on her and invited her to discuss it after she'd read. But the man in front of her now seemed like an entirely different person, transformed by daylight into someone distant and austere, not at all the eager young man she'd glimpsed the night before.

If she didn't have the book in her pocket right this second, it would have been no effort at all to believe the whole thing had been a dream. She had never been prone to shouting, but in this moment Arlo wanted to scream. Instead, she bit her tongue and took another deep breath.

"I saw you walking, through my window, and thought you might like to eat when you got back in," she lied. "If you'll excuse me." She curtsied and spun, turning before he could see the tears pricking her eyes, and all but fled toward the kitchen.

"Goodness, child," the housekeeper said, entering through the courtyard door just as Arlo arrived in the kitchen. "You look feverish. Are you ill?"

Arlo shook her head. "No, Mrs. Hollister. I just had...a bit of a dizzy spell." Technically, that was true. She wasn't about to mention the *cause* of the spell: the house's whispers, beckoning her toward the cellar.

And while it was perfectly acceptable for Mister Calder to have caught her in her swoon, the idea of saying out loud that she'd been in his arms made Arlo's cheeks and the tips of her ears burn. She settled on telling the same lie she'd told her employer.

"I saw Mister Calder through my window when I woke up, so I rushed downstairs to get his breakfast ready for when he came inside," she said. "I think I...may have moved too fast."

Mrs. Hollister laid the back of one hand against Arlo's forehead and clucked. "Sit," she said, pouring a cup of tea.

Arlo took it and breathed the fragrant steam, closing her eyes as something inside her shifted just a little toward calm. When she lifted the cup to sip, it barely shook at all.

"Thank you," she said, looking up at the housekeeper. "Very fortifying."

"I can see you haven't eaten," Mrs. Hollister added, with a meaningful glance at the empty sink. She plucked a piece of toast from its fork by the fire and laid out a small pot of jam alongside. "Get something inside you. We can't have you falling down on the job."

Arlo nodded. The jam knife clinked against the pot as she scooped out a glistening orange marmalade, bright as sunshine. The tea smelled wonderful and tasted better, and the everyday sounds of Mrs. Hollister bustling around the kitchen chased the darkness away and made Calderwood feel, just for a moment, like a place of comfort.

But the feeling splintered in the rasp of the jam knife against her toast, an eruption of hisses that jerked Arlo's mind downstairs so forcefully, goosebumps rose on her skin at the memory of cool cellar air. Tingles seized her scalp and raced down her neck, making her head twitch to the side with a sharp inhale.

In the hall outside the kitchen, she thought she could just see—but no, it was a shadow, nothing more. Not Tristan. *Mister Calder,* she scolded herself. Last night was one thing, but this morning, *Tristan* had never felt further away.

She took another breath, slower and deeper, and slouched a bit in her chair.

"Better?" Mrs. Hollister asked.

"Much," Arlo said, because there was nothing else she could say. She finished her breakfast, washed her dishes, and put them away while the housekeeper went over the day's agenda.

"It's laundry today," she said, though Arlo hardly needed the reminder. Yesterday they'd collected Mister Calder's clothes and bedding from where he'd left them outside his locked bedroom. They'd been soaking all night in two tubs in the scullery, one for white clothes and bedding, and a smaller one for dark.

"Run upstairs," Mrs. Hollister said, as she fed the scullery fire to boil a huge pot of water. "See if there's anything last-minute to add before we get going."

Arlo nodded and went out through the kitchen, holding her breath as she passed the pantry and the hall with the cellar door, not letting it out until she'd gotten all the way up the narrow stairs to the upper floor of the house. She slid open the door between the servants' space and the main house and, sure enough, saw a shirt bunched on the table outside Mister Calder's door.

Something about it sent a surge of anger through her. The casual way it had been discarded, perhaps. She knew how that felt, after all. She snatched it up into a rough bundle and stomped a few steps back down the hall before traces of his cologne wafted up, crisp lavender and bright citrus and some kind of wood with a hint of spice, all mingled with the trace of his natural body odor.

It was like being in his arms all over again. Arlo was torn between the urge to bury her face in the bundle and weep, and the very real impulse to throw the whole thing out of a second-story window. She brought it downstairs, though, and added it to the whites to soak.

She'd just made it through hanging them outside to dry and boiling up a new pot of water for the dark clothes when the clock chimed the noon hour.

"His luncheon tray is ready," Mrs. Hollister said, leaning her head into the scullery. Arlo wiped sweat from her brow and felt a stray hair slick across her arm. There were no mirrors in here, but she knew she'd be a sight after a summer morning spent stirring a boiling cauldron, her golden curls in a lawless corona around her heat-flushed face.

Not that it mattered, she reminded herself. Mister Calder had made that plain. So who cared if she brought his luncheon looking like some untamed thing blown in off the hills? He could barely stand to look at her; he probably wouldn't even notice.

She picked up the tray and marched down the length of the house, not bothering to knock at the library door.

"Luncheon, sir," she said, pushing it open. She very pointedly did *not* look at her employer, setting down his tray with barely more than a nod and picking up the breakfast things from where he always left them.

On her way out the door, he said, "Miss Reade?" and Arlo's heart nearly beat through her chest. She turned, her gaze finding his as sure and fast as a moth finds a flame. Something sparked in his look, his eyes searching her face for the barest moment before his expression went entirely impassive, distant as the depths of the sea.

"Send Hollister, will you?" he asked, looking away.

Arlo pushed the tip of her tongue slowly between her teeth and breathed as quietly as she could through her nose, collecting herself in a moment that felt like it stretched for hours before she answered.

"Of course, sir," she said, and left on her errand.

Her gut roiled as she tried not to storm down the hall. Her cheeks and forehead and the back of her neck blossomed with heat that seemed to flash off her, leaving a chill in its wake. And all the while, the hissing whispers curled up through her mind, hooking misty fingers into the roots of her soul.

Come. Come.

She swallowed against the sudden tight dryness of her throat and knuckled tears from her eyes before stepping into the kitchen.

"Mister Calder wants to see you," she told the housekeeper, too angry and lightheaded to remember her sirs and madams. Guilt followed hard and fast, making her flinch, but Mrs. Hollister barely looked at her before she pointed one finger hard toward the servants' stair.

'Upstairs," she said. "Now."

Arlo blinked at her. "What?"

"You look like you're about to fall over," the housekeeper said, making low shooing motions with both hands. "You're no use if you can't even stand. Go lie down. I handled things before you came here; I'll handle them tonight."

A long, still moment passed before Arlo nodded and turned for the stairs. She clung to the railing as she climbed, every step heavier than the last, until she finally made it to her bed, flopping face-down without so much as removing her apron.

Come, the voices hissed around her, inside her. *Come.*

She let the tide of them carry her away into sleep.

When she opened her eyes again, it was dark. She jerked her head up, mumbling a "hm?" into the shadowy room. Her hair stuck to her forehead and neck, and her clothes felt clammy, slightly damp and sticky against her skin. She made a small, disgusted noise and stripped off her apron and dress, hanging them outside her small wardrobe to air by the window. Then she staggered to the washstand and sponged away the film of dried sweat from her neck, face, and armpits.

It was then she realized how hungry she was. She hadn't eaten since that spot of tea and toast this morning. Her stomach squelched as if to underscore the thought. She slipped into her nightgown and unpinned her coiled hair, scratching at where the pins had been. The sweat had made her scalp feel prickly, and she'd just had her weekly bath three nights ago.

Well, maybe she could find a moment to rinse her hair under the pump, at least. But that could wait. It was late, and food was more important. She stood, then paused as a footstep sounded in the hall.

Arlo had gotten used to the groans and creaks of Calderwood, the wood making its tiny shifts in the night. But this wasn't that. This was a step, clear and sharp and just outside her door.

Her body went absolutely still, every bit of her tense and listening as her heart skittered into a headlong race. It was Tristan, it had to be. Tristan Calder, outside her door in the middle of the night.

Had he come to apologize? To check on her? Or had he come for something else, something that would be easier with the mantle of night lying thick over the house and no one else around?

She had a vision of him striding into the room, his eyes hungry, his hands outstretched, pushing her against the nearest bit of wall he could find and kissing her until both their mouths were ruined.

He couldn't, of course; not with her door locked.

But he could knock, and she could let him in.

Seconds stretched as she waited for the rap of his knuckles on the wood.

It never came.

After a few breaths, she crossed the room on tiptoe to lay one ear against the door. All she heard was silence.

"Tristan?" she whispered, laying one trembling hand against the door. Her stomach tightened with equal parts want and embarrassment as she wondered how he'd react to her using his given name. There was no answer from the hall; only the rustle and hiss of leaves as the wind picked up outside, blowing a susurration across the night.

Or...*was* it the leaves? It sounded like other voices. Darker voices. Arlo laid one hand high on her chest, pressing against her collarbones as she tried to pick out which sound was which; which sound was real.

She took another breath and braced herself to call again, louder this time.

"Tr—Mister Calder?" As much as she liked the sound of his name on her lips, she couldn't quite bring herself to call it at volume. But her words dropped into silence, no answer forthcoming.

Except—was that the scuff of a shoe, a step retreating?

Arlo shook her head and turned the bolt before she quite realized what she was doing. She threw the door open, ready to shout, to ask him to stop, to beg him to talk to her the way he had in the library, when he'd almost seemed a different person.

No one was there.

Poking her head out into the hallway, she saw that the pocket door separating the servants' upstairs quarters from the main house was open just a crack. The only reason an upstairs door existed between the house and the maids' quarters was to make it easier for the lady's maid to attend her mistress. But Calderwood had no lady. There was no reason for this door to be open, unless he'd opened it.

So where was he?

Arlo took a step into the hall, looking down the long corridor. Moonlight diffused through the four tall windows of the two-story great hall at the front of the house, giving just enough light to make the shadows look darker.

It didn't reach the far end, where her employer's suite sat as if behind a shroud.

Apart from a huge mirror in an ornate frame, the wall beside her was a row of closed doors. Each of the disused bedrooms had an empty name plaque posted outside, forlorn reminders of dances and dinners and hunting parties long gone by. The other side of the hall was open, nothing but a balustrade separating the upper level from the great hall below.

She paused, putting her hand on the rail and leaning just slightly over to see if he'd taken the grand staircase down, but the hall was as empty and silent as a new-dug grave.

The only sound was the hissing whisper, the trees outside.

All was still within the house. Arlo let go of the balustrade and turned to go back to her room, when something moved at the corner of her eye.

She jumped and spun, searching the hallway with frantic eyes, her hands buzzing, her heart trying to leap out of her mouth as she groped for someone, some*thing* to pin the movement on. There it was again! She watched, and watched, and then thanked all the angels that Tristan *wasn't* in the hallway to see this, because no one was there at all. No one but her.

She lifted her hand from the balustrade and put it down again, just as she'd done before, and watched her silvered reflection in the mirror do exactly the same.

Arlo laid both her hands along her cheeks, grateful for their grounding coolness, and closed her eyes. Of course it had just been a trick of the moonlight.

Anyway, it was silly to think that Tristan would walk these halls like some kind of ghost, haunting his own house. Why would he, when everything he seemed to care about was down in the library? That's where he would be, if he was anywhere. Either that, or she'd just heard him going to bed.

That had to be it. The sound that woke her hadn't been a footstep at all. Maybe she hadn't closed the sliding door properly when he'd come to ask for breakfast, and there had been some kind of draft when he'd opened his door down the hall that caused the panel to thump and slide from its pocket.

Whatever the reason, Arlo found her appetite gone, replaced with a heavy exhaustion that flowed all at once like syrup through her limbs.

There were still a few hours left before daylight. She should get some proper rest. She trudged back to the servants' wing of the house and slid the pocket door closed, making sure it was secure in its spot before closing her own door and falling back into bed.

10

ARLO BOLTED AWAKE WHEN she realized that the light behind her eyelids wasn't a dream; it was the sun. She tore off her nightgown, scrambled into her unmentionables and donned yesterday's dress. It smelled a little sour, but at least it was dry now. Her hair went up into a hasty coil, and she was still shoving pins into it when she burst into the kitchen, apologizing to anyone who could hear her.

"I'm sorry, I'm so sorry, I—" She stopped, looking around. The fireplace was out, the stove unlit. She peeked into the scullery, which was likewise quiet, and then into Mrs. Hollister's office.

"Hello?"

A flash of movement caught her eye. When she turned, she saw yesterday's laundry flapping on the lines in the courtyard. But was that—she peered, craning her neck forward, narrowing her eyes. Between the dancing white sheets, she glimpsed the outline of a dark figure coming toward the house. Alarm shot in a frisson down her spine, an echo of the fear she'd felt the night before, right before the figure stepped around another sheet and resolved into the house-keeper.

"Ah," the woman said as Arlo opened the door. "You're awake. Just a tick." She bustled past Arlo and into the house to take a large woven basket from under a table in the courtyard lobby, then back out again. Arlo followed her out to the line, reached up to take down a sheet and swayed, knees nearly buckling. She shot a hand out to catch her balance on one of the anchor poles and took a deep breath to steady herself.

Mrs. Hollister looked her up and down, mouth twisted in a moue. "Are you feeling any better?"

"I—think so." She took the towel the housekeeper handed her, folding it into the basket to be put away. "But why is the kitchen cold? Doesn't Mister Calder need breakfast?"

"No, child, Master Tristan was called to the city last night." She pulled down a shirt and handed it over. "I would have told you, but I'd already sent you upstairs."

Arlo clutched Tristan's shirt close to her chest, breath catching in her throat as all her comforting logic from the night before unraveled.

If he'd been called to the city, if he'd already left, then who—

"He left early this morning," the housekeeper said.

Arlo wobbled again, this time with relief. *That* must have been why he was moving around the house so late. He'd been preparing to leave on an unexpected trip to the city. Her cheeks burned with wondering what might have happened if she'd called his given name loud enough to hear.

Mrs. Hollister must have seen the color rise, because she clucked and laid her fingers under her chin in a concerned gesture.

"I wouldn't normally come by while he's away, but we can't leave the laundry out and you were feeling poorly."

"Oh," Arlo said, helping the older woman fold a bedsheet. "I'm sorry."

"No need. Are you well enough to bring these in and put them away, or would you like some help?"

"Please don't trouble yourself." Arlo picked up the basket and anchored it on her hip. "I can manage."

The housekeeper favored her with a long, skeptical look.

"If you're sure." It was almost, but not quite, a question.

"Of course."

"As you will. But lie down when you're done," the woman advised, in a tone that brooked no disagreement. "The house will keep for a day, and you might as well get all the rest you can before Master Tristan returns tomorrow."

"Yes ma'am." Arlo ducked her head, not wanting to attempt a curtsy with the heavy basket in hand.

The housekeeper gave a curt nod, then brushed her hands down the front of her dark dress and turned back the way she'd come, walking toward the village.

Arlo watched her go, shifting her weight to better support the heavy basket. As she moved, one of the sheets shifted against the fabric beneath it with a gentle sigh. The sound lingered in her head for much longer than it actually lasted, curling like a beckoning finger around her senses.

Come, come.

She waited until the housekeeper was out of sight, then went inside and dropped the basket on the floor, sipping quick, shallow breaths as she fought to subdue the sudden trembling in her hands. Her thoughts were a drunken flock of birds, darting all at cross-purposes.

He had left without telling her! Granted, he was her employer, and she was basically a glorified scullery maid; he didn't owe her a thing. But hadn't it meant something, that moment in the library? That revelation of the self he hid behind a stuffy exterior?

Which Tristan was the real one?

Then another thought rose from the depths like a serpent uncoiling, tasting the air.

Mrs. Hollister had said he'd return tomorrow.

That meant Arlo had another night alone in the house. She could try again. Maybe the snake would give her more information, another clue, a different way to satisfy the riddle that didn't require her to keep chasing after things she couldn't find in this house. She licked her lips, then strode straight past the larder and kitchen and pantry, every step a thud that mirrored her heartbeat as she approached the cellar door.

This was it.

This was it.

This was—locked.

Arlo stared agog at the new padlock in the cellar door's latch, a brass oval with a keyhole at its center staring out like a dark, malefic eye. She rattled it in the vain hope that it might slide open, but it held fast, gleaming like an accusation. Her face flamed as she realized what it meant, and she barked a sound that wasn't quite a laugh.

Was *that* what he'd been doing last night? How foolish she'd been, thinking she'd earned his trust. She slapped the door once, hard, her open palm against the wood sending a sharp crack to ring against the walls.

Son of a mongrel bitch.

She laid her forehead against the door with a sigh. Of course. Of course it wouldn't be that easy. What the hell was she doing here, working for a man who ran hot and cold, alone in this creepy old house, enthralled by a door she couldn't even open?

Maybe it would be better to leave. Perhaps they needed a barmaid in the village. She'd lose her lovely room and she'd probably never see Mister Calder again, but surely anything was better than feeling like a baited fish on the end of an indifferent angler's hook.

But what if there wasn't work available out here? She couldn't go back to the city. She wouldn't.

She took a deep breath and sighed against the door. Mrs. Hollister had told her to lie down, but maybe it would be worth taking a walk to the village and inquiring. The worst they could say was no, and then at least she'd know for sure.

She walked out from the narrow hall, thinking about which of her two shirtwaists to wear to make the best impression, when she saw the dumbwaiter across from her. Her eyebrows lifted slowly, mouth opening in an O of delighted surprise before spreading into a grin.

Why hadn't she thought of it earlier?

Arlo opened the door that covered the small moving cabinet and tugged on the counterweight, smiling even wider when it slid along the rails. She pulled until she couldn't anymore, then locked the brake to hold the car in place on the upper floor. Its absence revealed the same rail-and-plank support structure that she'd seen in the cellar, hugging the walls of the shaft like makeshift ribs.

She looked down.

Empty blackness yawned at her, a warning, an invitation.

She glanced up toward where the car hung suspended, remembering Mrs. Hollister's comment about losing fingers. Should she lower it all the way, so it wouldn't fall on her? It wasn't large, but she still wouldn't want to be in its path if the ropes somehow slipped free from the locking mechanism while she was climbing.

But no, that wouldn't do. The only way in and out of the dumbwaiter's cage was through the opening where the car would sit. There was plenty of vertical space between the top of the car and the floor above, but the support planks connecting the rails meant that with the car in the cellar, she'd need to wriggle out and back in again through a narrow space. What if she got hurt, or stuck?

No. She'd move faster if she kept the car out of the way entirely and used the larger opening at the bottom of the shaft to get in and out.

Decided, she checked once more to make sure the car was locked in place before sitting at the edge of the hole and taking a deep breath. Her shoulders and scalp effervesced with the heady lift of cautious hope as she slid her feet questing gingerly into the dark. Her toes tapped air until she found one of the support rungs below.

Little by little, she inched further into the shaft, ducking her head and testing the rung with more and more weight until she was fully inside. She paused for a moment, stiffening as if for the worst, but the bracing held her. Another second, just to be sure, then—"ha!"

The shout escaped before she could stop it, as loud and sharp as a gunshot, sending dust up in gentle puffs from the wall nearest her mouth. A wild fancy seized her, curling her lips with a prelude to mischievous laughter: no wonder Mister Calder needed additional help, if Mrs. Hollister couldn't even be bothered to dust the inside of the dumbwaiter shaft. What *would* the neighbors say?

Demented merriment seized her shoulders, making her giggle and sway, a release that was delicious right up to the point that she nearly reeled too far. She grabbed at the long vertical rails and held them, swallowing hard, instantly sobered.

That had been too close. It was a long way down to the cellar floor, and falling was not an option. She didn't want to sustain an injury. She didn't want to lose her chance to go through the door, and she *certainly* didn't want to have to explain what on earth she'd been doing to have such an accident.

Her skin tingled, and she clutched the rails until her knuckles ached.

When she was ready, she resumed her climb with a good deal more care, focused on feeling her way in the dark with both feet and only one hand, holding the lantern with her other.

As soon as she touched the floor, a thrumming pulse surged up through Arlo's feet. She followed it across the cellar, almost compelled, until the elaborate carvings came into view.

"Snake," she said, her voice sounding small in the empty space. Nothing moved in the breathless silence, and Arlo's hands began to shake. After all this, after everything else, she couldn't have hallucinated the events of her last visit down here.

Could she?

Shadows danced in the door's dark layers, restless and erratic as her lantern trembled. And then, so subtle she almost missed it, a narrow, delicate tongue flicked as a diamond-shaped head lifted itself from the relief.

"You seem to lack the keys," the snake said, drawing out the hiss on each spirant syllable.

Arlo's initial jolt of helpless pleading flashed into angry indignation, hot and bright against the dark.

"There's nothing in this house," she snapped, flinging her free arm back toward the stairs. "No silver, no gold."

"No?" the snake asked, bobbing its head.

"No. And what does it even mean to feel something but never see nor hold it?"

The snake rippled with a nonchalant shrug.

"It'sssss your riddle to solve," it told her, its tone cool and distant and utterly unconcerned. "Come back when you have."

Arlo gritted her teeth. "How do I know it's even worth it?" she asked, leaning closer. "What's behind there?"

The snake's hinged mouth quirked in the tiniest hint of a smile.

"Only one way to find out."

Arlo's lamp flickered. When she looked again, the snake was back in place among the carvings. Damn, damn, damn. Well, it was back to her original plan, then. Mister Calder would be gone until tomorrow. The only place she hadn't looked was in his rooms.

"Right," she said, turning on one heel. She climbed the dumbwaiter shaft back to the main floor and spent a few moments brushing cobwebs and dust from her dress before marching up the servants' stair, pulling pins from her hair as she went. Surely she could just wiggle them around until something clicked. Tristan's rooms were their own mystery: a forbidden space, closed off to her. But maybe she could learn more about who he was, which personality was the true one. And if he had even a little bit of jewelry...

Could she take it? She paused, hands poised with hairpins half-stuck in the keyhole.

If she broke into his rooms and there *was* jewelry there, it would buy two thirds of her passage through the snake-door assuming he had silver *and* gold. But she'd still have to figure out the final part of the riddle, and she'd have to do it tonight. Because if she didn't, or if she got into his rooms and there *wasn't* jewelry there, she'd still be stuck here, only now she'd have to explain why she'd broken into Tristan's private quarters.

And say she did find all the things she'd need to open the door. Who knew what was on the other side? Was this even a risk worth taking?

She rubbed her mouth with one hand, staring thoughtfully at the lock. If she did this, she would have to leave Calderwood either way, through one door or another. She would never see Tristan's smile again, nor the joy on his face in that moment when he'd truly relaxed around her. He didn't seem the type to often let loose, which made it all the more remarkable, perhaps, that he'd done so around her. He must be awfully lonely here, with no family and hardly any servants.

What on earth had happened, to make him live like this? And why did the house have no silver, no gold; none of the usual trappings of a man of his station?

She remembered then what Mrs. Hollister had said about Calderwood having seen its share of tragedy. For the first time, Arlo wondered if Tristan might be in danger of losing it. Perhaps his trips and the paperwork he constantly toiled over were in an effort to hold onto his family home.

Arlo pulled the pins out of the keyhole. She couldn't do this. Tristan might come from a completely different world than she did, but maybe they were more alike than she'd realized. Even without knowing the details of his past, she knew that something had made him choose to live all alone in this big house. But Mrs. Hollister had mentioned parents, grandparents. There had been a whole clan of Calders once.

What had happened to them? Had he lost his family, the way she'd lost hers?

And what would her parents say, if they were standing right here, watching this scene? Arlo could almost see the disapproval on her father's face and, what was worse, the disappointment on her mother's. She pressed the heel of one hand under her chin, heart twisting with a grief as forceful as if it were fresh again, and shook her head.

There was no telling where she'd get silver and gold if not here, but she couldn't do this.

She straightened and let her head fall back with a frustrated groan. Her hair shifted, scalp itching to remind her that she still hadn't rinsed after all that sweating, and now she was dusty, too. Well, at least with Mister Calder and Mrs. Hollister both away, no one could scold her for taking the time to have an extra bath.

She stopped by the servants' linen closet to take a flannel and a towel before going downstairs and out to the water pump, deciding she'd heat just enough water to have a sponge bath and wash her hair. No point in using the hip bath; it was just one more thing she'd have to clean up.

Water plinked and splattered against the tin bucket as she filled it. She lugged it inside, then stoked the scullery fireplace where embers still glowed from the day before. She poured water from the bucket into the kettle to heat.

When it sang, the water went back into the bucket with a handful of flaked white soap from the pantry. Then Arlo took the kettle out to the pump for a little more water before she went back inside.

There was no point lugging this upstairs to the more private maids' quarters when no one was here to see her. So she stripped out of her dress and underthings right in the scullery, lathered her washing cloth in the soapy bucket, and started scrubbing.

Afternoon sun poured in through the windows, warming the room so that Arlo wasn't the least bit uncomfortable in her altogether. Body done, she unbound her long hair and dipped it into the hot, soapy water, massaged her scalp clean, and rinsed with the fresh water in the kettle.

After dressing and dumping everything out, she went upstairs for her comb and returned to the scullery to sit in the sun while she worked out the tangles. As she pulled stroke after stroke, her hair dried and bounced back to its usual curls, shining golden in the light.

Arlo stared at it.

Something gold.

A good night's sleep did wonders for Arlo's mental state, and the knowledge that she was suddenly a third of the way toward solving the snake's riddle sang in her heart like the first birds of spring, so bright and sharp it was almost shrill.

She attacked her tasks with a will the next day so that, after Mrs. Hollister's early departure, she'd have plenty of time to pursue her more clandestine goals.

The timing couldn't have been more perfect—with her family visiting, the housekeeper was only here in the mornings, leaving Arlo with glorious swaths of time in which to conduct her search for the remaining two items. Mister Calder might not have any silver himself, but this house was old. Maybe something had gotten lost between floorboards or misplaced under the edge of a long-disused rug.

After breakfast, she ran her fingers along the edges of the upstairs hall carpet and reached through the narrow gaps beneath the locked bedroom doors, her nimble touch alert for any spare bit of forgotten metal. If only she could get inside those rooms, to see what might have been left behind. But they were locked, their contents beyond her.

She also emptied, cleaned, aired and refilled the upstairs linen closet, earning a "well done" from Mrs. Hollister though, alas, she found no rings or stray cufflinks lost in a folded sheet or pillow cover.

She did find a sack full of dried lavender and cedar chips shoved in at the back of one shelf, ostensibly for making sachets to deter moths and the like. It wasn't something she could use for the door, exactly. But it gave her an idea.

The next day, Arlo spent the afternoon cleaning and airing the coats and shoes in the hall closet. There was no need for it in the middle of June, but she'd stayed up the night before making a few sachets from the larger sack she'd found. Looping them over the hanger hooks and nestling them inside the coats gave her the perfect excuse to root around underneath them. She'd already decided not to steal from her employer, which included not removing anything from his garments. But perhaps there was a fallen silver button or a long-forgotten coin lurking in one of the far corners.

On her knees, hands sweeping the farthest reaches of the closet, Arlo paused to inhale the traces of Tristan's cologne mixed with the well-loved woolens. The closeness and warmth of the space, of that scent, almost made up for the lack of precious trinkets lurking in the corners.

She sighed, backed out of the closet, and shrieked when she looked up to see Tristan—Mister Calder—leaning against the wall, watching her. Arlo stood up so fast her head went muzzy.

"Mister Calder!" She wiped her hands on her dress, disgusted at the sudden sweat that had broken out in her palms. "I didn't hear you there!"

His mouth didn't quite smile but his eyes did, all appraisal and amusement in equal measure. It was criminal, what that look on his face did to every part of Arlo from neck to knees. He flicked his glance from her to the closet and back again.

"What are you doing?"

Arlo blinked at him, speechless, while her mind ran as fast as a spooked mouse. He'd seen her kneeling, reaching into the back of the closet. Thank God, thank *God* she'd come prepared. She pulled the small drawstring bags out of her apron pocket and held them up.

"I noticed that your coats have no deterrents." The words came out as fast as a knee responding to a doctor's hammer. Why did he always make her tumble over her words, as if she couldn't say them fast enough? "It's a small thing, but moths come out in force in the summer, and your things are so lovely. I—"

He held up a hand.

"That's very thoughtful." He captured one of the pouches between thumb and forefinger and squeezed it, rubbing the contents together to release their scent. His eyes closed as he inhaled, and the quirking corner of his mouth blossomed into a full-on smile. When he opened his eyes again, his gaze was on Arlo's face. "Thank you."

He let the sachet go and pulled his lips into his mouth briefly, his expression going thoughtful, as though he wanted to say something but wasn't sure he should.

It was all Arlo could do not to lick her lips as she waited. There was so little space between them. His hand had nearly touched hers just now, a fact that sent her heart skittering against the cage of her chest.

"You've been working so hard, these past few days. I'm, ah... I'm glad to see you're feeling better."

Arlo paused, all her nervous whir going still. "Sir?"

He looked away, and was that—? No. No, that couldn't be a *blush* tinting his ears. Arlo's eyes went wide before she looked down, undone at the possibility of what that flush of color might mean. He rubbed at his chin and bit his generous lower lip. His breath squeaked between it and his teeth, a precursor to speech.

"Would you, ah...like some help?"

Arlo nearly gaped. Help? Him? Granted, he'd been stepping in to do certain chores that were her job. But this time it didn't feel like he was pushing her out.

It felt like he was trying to pull her in.

But it was only when his expression fell and he took a step back that she realized she'd taken too long to respond. He lifted a hand, one finger half-extended, turned halfway away, then back toward Arlo, though he couldn't quite look at her.

"Don't push yourself too hard, in any case. I would...hate to see you fall ill again." Both arms swung by his sides as he seemed caught between staying and going. Finally, he decided. "Well then. Carry on."

He turned on one heel and strode away. His footsteps echoed on the hallway floor, beating in perfect sync with Arlo's heart. She let out the stale breath she'd been holding in a long whoosh and took in another, fragrant with his scent from where he'd been standing.

If she called after him, would he come back?

"Tristan."

The word came out a whisper. Its only answer was the soft click of the closing library door.

11

On the third day after finding her 'something gold', Arlo still hadn't managed any progress toward the rest of the solution. Worse than that, she'd run out of places to look. The bedrooms were locked; the ballroom and drawing room likewise.

In the evening, after making sure the library door was closed, Arlo tested the music room door, the only one she hadn't yet tried because she had little hope it would hold anything useful. To her surprise, the room wasn't locked. What it was was empty, except for a harpsichord hulking under a dust cover in the far corner. Arlo wondered who was the last person to play it.

She slid her fingertips under the cover to press a key and flinched when it bleated a tight, discordant sound. Arlo shot a glance over her shoulder at the door and breathed a relieved sigh when Mister Calder wasn't there.

Come to think of it, where *was* he? Arlo hadn't seen much of him since yesterday, an interlude she still flushed to think about.

She slipped out of the music room, closing the door silently behind her, and walked back to the kitchen. Her evening meal was a sad affair: the heel of yesterday's loaf, toasted to mask the creeping staleness, and a boiled egg left over from the collection this morning.

It was strange to even have an evening meal, but most households had a staff and a cook, and ate a large dinner together in the early afternoon to fortify them for the rest of the day. Arlo and Mrs. Hollister occasionally sat down for tea, but no more.

And it wasn't Mrs. Hollister she missed. She stared at the chair at the head of the table where the housekeeper usually sat, where Tristan had once taken breakfast, eating right there as if it was the most natural thing in the world, and sighed.

Arlo was setting her dishes by the sink to dry when she caught a reflection in the darkness beyond the window. She assumed it was her own, until she moved, and it didn't.

She froze, startled, then took a few steps closer to peer out and realized it wasn't a reflection at all.

It was...Mister Calder?

She stepped out into the courtyard and, sure enough, there he was, though he was no longer looking toward the kitchen. Now he stood with one hand on the high brick retaining wall that separated Calderwood's terrace and gardens from the servants' entrance and the path to the stables and chicken coop. There was, of course, a door in the wall; how else would the servants magically appear with food and drinks for a garden party or charity event?

Mister Calder leaned by that opening now, his face tipped up toward the night sky. As Arlo watched, he pushed away from the wall and ambled a little unsteadily into the gardens.

She couldn't say why she followed him. Something forlorn in the way he looked, maybe; or perhaps it was simple curiosity. She'd seen the hills behind the house, but she'd never been inside Calderwood's garden.

It swept down a gentle slope from the terrace that ran the length of the house's back side. Its builders had laid a series of paving stones to make a path down from the terrace door, so the family and visitors could walk among carefully cultivated hedges and flowers. It was all overgrown now, choked with climbing weeds.

The whole place had a forgotten, melancholy air to it. Not unlike Mister Calder himself. What might this garden look like if he were as open and joyful all the time as he'd been in that one fleeting glimpse she'd had?

She was so focused on the daydream, she nearly walked into him.

"Oh!" She stopped herself just before the collision.

He turned, surprised. "Miss Reade! Is everything alright?"

"Yes, sir," she said, bobbing a curtsy to buy herself time. Despite having followed him in here, she hadn't been prepared to actually talk to him. Her heart still fluttered at the thought of their interaction the day before. What was she supposed to do with the way he'd smiled at her? What could she say?

But now his eyes mirrored the desolation of this place, something raw and lonely crying out in the dark, and Arlo couldn't stand the thought of not saying anything.

"Are *you* alright, sir? In yourself, I mean." She felt a blush rising, and was grateful that the dark would hide it. "I know it's not my place to ask, sir, but I thought...you're all alone in this house, and who else is there to ask you?" She bit her tongue as soon as the words were out, her gaze fixed on the tips of his shoes.

He didn't speak for a long moment. Then he sighed and muttered something that sounded very much like "this house." The sweet, smoky-apple scent of brandy was plain on his breath, and Arlo wondered how much he'd been drinking.

"Forgive me, sir." Now that she'd started, something about the dark made it easier to go on. "But...why are you all alone here? Why not go somewhere else?"

He took a step back, as if the question had shocked him. "Don't be ridiculous. It's my family's estate. Where else would I go?"

"You travel to the city often enough," she said. "Why not go there?"

"Of all the—" He shook his head, clearly lost for words, then turned and stalked away from her.

Arlo cringed, her whole torso trying to curl in on itself in embarrassment. Why had she spoken? Why come out here at all? This wasn't her business. *He* wasn't her business. She started to retreat when, to her surprise, he turned back and stood in front of her again, an imposing shadow under a three-quarter moon.

"Miss Reade." He stood so close that she could smell his spice-and-wood cologne under the alcohol with every clipped word he spoke. "When you took this job, I trust you noticed the peculiarity of the appointment?" Arlo nodded. "And when Mrs. Hollister took you on, what did she say?"

Arlo thought back. "She...told me this house had seen its share of tragedy. But she wouldn't say what it was."

Mister Calder turned half-away from her again.

"Tragedy," he said, nodding. "Indeed. Since the day it was built, a hundred years ago." His voice had a sad sort of smile in it, though Arlo couldn't see the details of his face in the shadows. "I wasn't around that whole time, of course." Then his voice changed, losing even the ghost of mirth. "But the most recent was my..." He hesitated.

Arlo blinked at him, wide-eyed in the dark. What would he say? His father? His mother? Is that why he was all alone here?

He sighed, resigned, but the word came out strangled, as if it wanted to stay unspoken.

"My brother."

It was Arlo's turn to take a step back, dark surprise scuttling over her features. She didn't even know he'd had a brother. Mrs. Hollister had never mentioned one, only parents and grandparents back to the Calders who'd built the house.

"Your brother?"

Mister Calder gave a single tight nod, but seemed disinclined to elaborate. Arlo's cheeks and neck burned with a surge of curiosity, an urge to crawl under his skin and unearth all his secrets, to understand him in a way he seemed determined to prevent, even as the very thought of it horrified her.

"What happened?"

Her employer looked at the sky for a long moment before he answered.

"He ran away. Almost fifteen years ago, now. He was the elder, set to inherit. But one night he just," he paused to make a *poof* motion with the fingers of one hand, "vanished into the hills. It shattered my mother, of course. My father sent out search parties, put word around for miles. But they never found him."

Sympathy reached like fingers around Arlo's heart and squeezed.

"Is he...alive?" She asked, even as she feared the answer.

Tristan moved his head as if he were going to shake it, then shrugged and sighed.

"I don't know. We never heard from him after that. I like to hope, but..." He looked up, as if he might find some message in the stars.

"This is our family home, the last place he lived. If he comes back one day, I couldn't…I can't bear to think of him returning after all this time only to find it empty." The soft leather of his gloves sighed as he wrung his hands slowly in front of his chest. "Or worse, to find it in someone else's possession. Someone has to be here."

He shrugged, then brought his gaze down to meet hers, his eyes flicking as if searching for something in her face.

"It's my house. It's my responsibility."

Arlo's eyes began to well. She clenched her fists to keep from reaching out to him.

"Sir," she started to say, but he interrupted her. His voice had something light in it again, but it wasn't mirth this time. It was the sort of forced airiness that comes from skirting the edge of a precipice filled with tears.

"I don't know why I'm even telling you this," he said, though Arlo had a suspicion that it may have owed something to the alcohol on his breath. "These aren't your concerns. It's just that…" His shoulders slumped as he turned away from her again. "Forgive me, please, but…your eyes looked so much like his just now. I quite forgot myself."

Arlo blinked, taking a moment to catch up with the abrupt shift in conversation. "My…eyes?"

Mister Calder nodded. "His eyes were like yours, such a light blue they were nearly clear. But in the right light, under the moon, they look…almost silver."

The words sent a jolt all through Arlo's body. Partly because he'd noted the color of her eyes, which meant he'd been *looking*. The evidence of his careful attention sent butterflies tumbling in her stomach, a thousand unsaid words and unasked questions, a million daydreams coalescing into heady delight.

But he'd given her an even greater gift than that, because now, she had one more piece of the puzzle.

Something silver.

"If you'll excuse me," he said, with a sharp, small nod. He walked away, his long legs eating the distance to the place where the garden opened to the hills beyond, leaving Arlo gaping behind him.

So there *had* been a family here. Two boys, their parents. Fifteen years ago, the younger Mister Calder couldn't have been much more than a child. How awful, to have his elder brother run away. No wonder they'd abandoned the place. But not him. He'd stayed on the off chance his brother might return, so he'd come back to a place that was still home.

Was that why he walked in the hills so much? Looking out for a brother who might even now be coming back?

It broke her heart a little, but Arlo couldn't deny that the idea was also unbelievably romantic. She blushed, thinking for a moment what it might be like for him to lavish that kind of devotion on *her*.

And it was impossible to say what made her feel lighter on her feet as she practically danced up to bed: the daydream of Tristan Calder's affection, or the fact that she now had two of the snake's three things.

Fantasies carried her quickly to sleep, half-formed scenarios involving Tristan's hands, his eyes, that charming quirk of his mouth just before smiling, but Arlo woke a few hours later with the sudden, absolute certainty that something was wrong.

She couldn't tell what it was at first. The sky was still fully dark, nowhere near dawn. Something had pulled her out of sleep, but she had no idea what. A sound? A step? Perhaps, but this house had fooled her before. It was probably nothing.

Still, she sat up and reached for her matches. The snick and whoosh of the match head were like small explosions, and suddenly Arlo knew what was off.

It wasn't a sound that had woken her. It was the absence.

The air held absolutely still as she lit her candle, not a flicker to be found in the flame nor the branches of trees outside. The house, for once, emitted no creaks or grumbles. Even the bugs had all quieted, leaving Arlo at the center of an uncanny silence. It was like having her head under blankets, under water, an isolation that set her teeth on edge and twisted her familiar bedroom into a place that felt dangerous and strange.

She strained to listen beyond it, every part of her attention heightened, while time crept with the slow roll of molasses almost poured.

Nothing changed, nothing moved until she did. She slid one cautious foot off the bed's edge and onto the floor, followed by the other, and stood. As she did, a sound caught her ear, so tiny she would never have heard it if not for the stillness. Her gaze darted, looking for the source of the noise—a mouse, a moth?—and finally saw movement on top of her dresser. She tiptoed closer, holding out her candle to see that her small pile of hairpins was ever so slightly trembling.

A moment later, she felt it in the floor: a low rumble, beyond hearing, that grew in intensity like the growl of some creature about to attack.

An earthquake?

She groped for something to hold onto, to brace herself against greater tremors, but as soon as she touched the wall the shaking stopped. Her shoulders went absolutely still as she flicked her gaze around, anticipating another wave. The very floor beneath her feet seemed to gather, as if pulling back to generate even greater force, and Arlo's bones shook in her skin as the rumbling crescendoed to the roar of a storm in the trees, the howl of a man in agony.

She sat bolt-upright, both hands clutching her sheets, chest heaving as she gulped terrified breaths. Her candle sat unlit on her bedside table, while from outside drifted the gentle sound of the nighttime chorus.

A dream.

She pressed one hand to her heart, her wide eyes turned on the ceiling, seeing nothing.

Then another scream sounded: the high, anguished shriek of a vixen somewhere out in the hills. Arlo's whole body flinched into a tight ball, the covers pulled high above her head. For the first time since she could remember, she wished for her mother in the pure, unthinking way of a frightened child.

With midsummer just past, it was almost six years since her mother had died. Arlo had been seventeen; old enough to remember her smile, her laugh, the smell of her cooking. But what Arlo remembered most were her songs. She sang one now, breathy and halting, with none of her mother's skill or grace. The tune scooped Arlo's chest hollow with a fierce, deep longing to feel her mother's hands one more time, smoothing her nightmares away.

The sheets brushed against her hairline and her eyes welled with tears. She would never see her mother again, never hold her or be held, or...

Wait.

Arlo went very still. Not long ago, the task the snake had set her seemed impossible, the riddle unsolvable. But she'd been looking for solid things, material things, when all along the answers had been in plain sight, hidden in what she already had yet had never thought to consider.

Golden hair; silver moonlight. And now, her shallow breaths stretched little by little into long wheezes of laughter as she realized that here was the final key, the last thing the snake had asked for.

All she needed now was a chance to use it.

12

"MISS READE, ARE YOU quite alright?"

Arlo jerked her head up from where she'd been watching the dancing reflections in her teacup and fixed her startled gaze on Mrs. Hollister. "What?"

"Your leg, child."

As if to underscore the words, Arlo's knee bumped the table where they sat for tea, sending a gentle clatter through their cups and saucers.

"Oh!" She pressed her foot down hard against the floor and flashed what she hoped was a natural smile at the housekeeper.

"Are you well?" the woman asked, one eyebrow lifting.

"Quite well, Mrs. Hollister," Arlo said, though it wasn't true. She was waiting, itching, *dying* for Mister Calder to leave again. It'd been days since Arlo had collected all the things the snake required. Every moment she couldn't race to the cellar scratched at her like a frayed seam against her skin, until just the thought of it made her squirm.

The clock chimed eleven, signaling an end to their tea. Mrs. Hollister stood and began preparing their employer's lunch, leaving Arlo to clean up the dishes for both of them. She watched the housekeeper work, noting that she brought out a wine glass but no bottle.

"Wine?" she asked, eyeing the glass.

"Won't be a tick," Mrs. Hollister said, pulling up the shiny new key on the ring she always wore at her belt.

Arlo pounced on the opportunity.

"Why did Mister Calder lock the cellar?" she asked, trying to sound casual. "Did he say?"

"He did not." The housekeeper sniffed, her lips tightening into a moue. "And it's not our place to question."

"No, no." Arlo waved one hand, loose and dismissive, as though it didn't matter to her in the least. "Of course not. I was just curious." The teacup she was washing nearly slipped out of her hands as she moved to place it on a towel to dry. She caught it with a gasp and a sigh of relief.

"A little less curiosity and a little more diligence, my girl," the housekeeper said with one eyebrow raised. "Get the flatware, will you?" She lit a hand lantern and bustled downstairs, leaving Arlo alone in the kitchen.

When Arlo came back from the butler's pantry, flatware in hand, Mrs. Hollister was removing the cork from a dusty bottle. One last squeaking turn brought the cork free. The kitchen filled with a sharp, earthy scent and a hint of dark fruit, like a blackberry patch after sudden, hard rain.

For a moment, Arlo's head was all vines and snakes and secret underground places.

Come buy our fruits, come buy.

"This won't fit on the tray," Mrs. Hollister said, breaking the spell. "We'll need to go together."

Arlo nodded and followed her down the hall to the library with the tray in both hands.

"Master Tristan?" the housekeeper called, knocking at the door.

"Mm?"

They went in. Mrs. Hollister's tongue clicked as she took in the mess on her employer's desk.

"Master Tristan, you really ought to eat in the dining room. Your papers would be just where you left them when you came back."

It was the closest thing Arlo had ever heard to a scolding in his direction. Envy burned like acid at the familiarity between them. She thought back again to that night in the library and, more recently, in the garden. The way he'd looked at her; the softness in his voice. But in the days since then, he'd gone back to maintaining his distance. It was as if night in this house was some kind of parallel time, existing next to the day but not linked to it. The things that happened in the dark stayed there.

"Don't be ridiculous, Hollister," Mister Calder said, looking up. "Why get the whole dining room fancied up when everything I need is already here?" He gestured to take in the whole room and nearly knocked over the wine bottle by its slender neck, grasping it at the last moment and righting it with a slosh. "Ah. I do need to leave, though," he went on. "Saturday."

"Another overnight in town?" Mrs. Hollister asked. Mister Calder nodded. "Very good, sir. I'll inform Jonathan."

"Thank you, Hollister."

Arlo barely heard their exchange for the roaring in her ears, a cacophony like several thousand snakes in celebration, a long, drawn-out *yesssssss*. She had only to survive the next few days, and once Mister Calder was out of the house, she could present her keys to the guardian at the door.

Saturday morning dawned bright and clear, the fullness of July sun kissing Calderwood with a golden glow. It permeated the thick greenhouse glass, making frail seedlings strive up from forgotten pots, hungry for life despite their lack of resources. Arlo's excitement nearly vibrated her out of bed well before sunrise. She dressed to the sounds of the dawn chorus, then went out to the chicken coops to feel the early sun on her face and breathe the wet, wild scent of the misty hills.

Some madness seized her mind as she watched the endless green roll on, an impulse to let her hair stream loose, to run shouting through the country, rousing every creature and spinning with her arms flung wide until the world lurched beneath her like a ship at sea. She contained it, only just. But the exhilarated buzz stayed with her, lightening her steps to and from the sheds.

Today was the day. Today was the day. Today was the day.

By the time Mrs. Hollister arrived, Arlo had already swept the great hall and set out Mister Calder's preferred traveling coat to air.

"Stand ready," the housekeeper said with an approving nod. "Jonathan's coming around now."

Arlo heard the clatter of hooves beyond the open front door just as Mister Calder came downstairs, leather valise in hand.

"Ah," he said, taking them in. "Good morning."

Arlo and Mrs. Hollister both curtsied.

"Is there anything else you need, sir?" the housekeeper asked.

Mister Calder shook his head. "Nothing." He swept past them with a nod and handed his luggage off to the coachman. The women followed him out. "I return tomorrow evening," he said, stepping into the coach.

"Very good, sir." Mrs. Hollister handed his coat up to him.

Arlo didn't say a thing as she watched her employer fold his coat across his lap. He looked so fine in full daylight. The sun called out a dusting of freckles across his nose and cheeks, a hint of some vigor blooming under his usual pallor. What might he look like, she wondered, if he spent less time in the library and more time in his garden?

His eyes met hers, holding her in their blue depths for a moment that stretched to forever before he nodded and looked away. To her surprise, though, Mrs. Hollister didn't take her usual seat on the bench. Jonathan snapped the reins, and the carriage rolled away with both servants watching.

"Don't you usually take a ride to the village?" Arlo asked, when they were alone.

"I do, but I do inventory on the first Saturday of every month. I'll need to survey all the house stores before I go back."

"Ah," Arlo said. "Well, let me know if you need anything."

The housekeeper peered past her shoulder. "I think you'll need to do the great hall again. Jonathan's tracked dirt all over."

Arlo followed the woman's gaze in through the open front door and sighed. The coachman had indeed left souvenirs of his work on the broad tiles Arlo had just cleaned.

Well, there was nothing for it. Mrs. Hollister would be here at least all morning, and it wasn't as though Arlo could hurry downstairs with anyone else in the house. Besides, she wouldn't be able to get the final key until tonight, when the moon was up. She might as well get the cleaning out of the way.

She scrubbed the great hall floor until it shone, then brushed the library runners until they looked next to new, collecting all the dust in a pan that she emptied beyond the courtyard. If only Calderwood had silver, so she could sit and polish it in the kitchen, in view of the locked cellar door. It wouldn't make time go any faster, but having the door nearby would make her feel like she was closer to what waited behind it.

She kept it in her sights as she went about her chores, crossing back and forth past the servants' stair and the short hall alongside it more times than were strictly necessary. The padlock gleamed in its shackle, bright against the faded green of the cellar door, a silent declaration that no one could pass. Every time she looked at it, she couldn't help but smile.

No lock could keep her out.

It took Mrs. Hollister most of the day to complete her survey, though full summer meant it was still light when she left. Arlo stood and waved until the woman was out of sight down the road toward the village.

And then, she was alone. The mouth she'd kept so carefully neutral all day spread into an impish grin. She ran for the courtyard door, slamming and locking it behind her with a delighted, breathless laugh, then went immediately to the green-painted door to the cellar.

The decorative scrollwork in the ornate lock Tristan had hung reminded her of the snake door below. It seemed to writhe as her gaze went soft and hazy, though it snapped back to its proper place as soon as she focused. Her desire to see beyond that mysterious door was like a second person standing behind her, two hands at the small of her back pushing her forward. But she couldn't go yet.

Not until dark.

She brushed the dust off her apron and went down the long hall to the library. There were hours yet before night would fall. Perhaps she could find out something about the door while she waited. Finally, after almost an hour's search, Mister Calder's shelves yielded a dusty corner filled with historical records of the house. Arlo traced her way to the oldest, which had CALDERWOOD: PLANS stamped on its spine.

The book opened with a dusty crack, stiff glue snapping along the spine. Its pages, slightly yellowed at their furthest edges, were purest white at their centers, as if the book had been bound and shelved and promptly forgotten. Arlo pored through the pages, diagram after diagram of rooms and plans, of fireplace specifications and the names of stonemasons and carpenters long dead.

It was obvious that someone had *loved* this house, even in its conception. The Calders of old hadn't just commanded some builders to erect a domicile; they'd invested in the creation of a home, where Tristan and his brother had eventually been born.

How awful it must have been for him to lose his brother at such a young age, to so uncertain an end. It was obvious his grief weighed on him. He'd barely seemed willing to bring up the subject that night in the garden, and once he had, it hadn't escaped Arlo's notice that he'd never once said his brother's name.

She wondered what it was, though she might not have to wonder for long. If she could find it anywhere, it would be here, among the family records. She put down the book of plans and traced her finger across the other books on the shelf, looking at the dates inked on their fabric spines. There was a new volume every handful of years, from the house's completion in 1723 through…well, that was strange. The last volume showed an end date in 1861.

She scanned the neat row of spines again. Each had two dates in a careful hand, each volume marked as ending right before the next one began. They had kept meticulous records until thirty-four years ago.

Why had they stopped?

Arlo's gaze fell on the bust of a veiled woman next to the last volume. It sat nestled on the far-right side of the bookshelf in the corner of the room, its blank eyes downcast, secrets locked behind stone lips. She followed its draping lines with absent eyes while she turned over dates in her head.

Tristan was thirty at most, so it couldn't be a case of his doting parents suddenly being so busy with raising their boy that they'd fallen off the thorough recordkeeping of their forebears. They would have had nannies, anyway, in a place like this, and it hardly seemed likely that a family who'd kept such careful records for so long a time would suddenly stop.

But Tristan was the younger sibling of a brother he could barely bring himself to talk about. Had they stopped keeping records with the advent of their firstborn son?

Arlo glanced at the other side of the corner, hoping that the line continued there. Spines stood like patient soldiers on the corner-facing shelf, but the titles were all in Latin and Greek, indecipherable. Arlo pushed her lips out, frustrated. Then she looked at the bust again.

She followed its gaze down, grabbing the edge of the shelf for balance as she crouched to scan the titles there.

1881-83. 1883-

The handwriting was different from the ones before but the books were otherwise the same, picking up as if nothing had happened. The family hadn't stopped keeping records, but someone had moved a handful of them. And it wasn't coincidence, it couldn't be, that the missing volumes were from dates between when Tristan's brother was likely born and the date, fifteen years ago, when Tristan said he'd run away.

Those volumes would have had everything from Tristan's childhood—his parents, his brother. Happier times, now gone. A heavy grief, indeed.

And Arlo knew exactly where the missing books would be: under lock and key in the master suite. They *had* to be; she'd seen them nowhere else in the house. Her initial flash of irritation at the lack of an answer gave way to fresh pity for Mister Calder, who missed his family so much he kept them close in the only way that was possible in this desolate place.

Arlo sighed and went back to the book she'd abandoned, flipping slowly through the pages that marked the earliest plans for the house she now lived and worked in. Finally, there: a full floor plan. There was the kitchen, the scullery, the halls just as she knew them. The next page held the same shape, but with the upstairs rooms. She had her first glimpse of Tristan's rooms this way, and saw that what she'd thought of as one room was actually three: a large sitting room, a bedroom, and a dedicated bath.

No wonder he kept most of the house closed off. Between his bedroom suite and the library right below him, he had everything he could possibly need within easy reach.

Arlo flipped back and forth a few pages, until—there! There was the cellar, finally picked out. She saw the coal bin, the cold storage for meats, and the wine cellar at the bottom of the servants' stair.

As she'd suspected, the wine cellar opened on two ends. The room was more of a vaulted hall that ran the length of the great hall above it, opening out to a room marked "recreation" that was accessible only from the stair tucked in next to the library at the opposite end of the house.

The other side of the house was one large room marked "LUMBER," a place for spare furnishings and decorations to be kept until season or need brought them into the light. But apart from a bleak realization that the Calders' disused lumber room was bigger than any place she'd ever lived in, the chamber didn't interest her. Not when she was on a quest for something else.

She swung her gaze to the North end of the house, the rectangle of space under the hub of servant life. Apart from the doors that opened to spaces under the main house and the chute for coal, the walls were bare, unmarked. There was nothing under the kitchen but open space. No windows in the foundation, no other enclosed storage spaces.

No doors.

She flipped one more page, looking for some greater detail, but found nothing. The rest of the book was given to more detailed drawings, window specifications and door designs and the like. But the one door she cared most about appeared not at all.

Arlo traced her finger over where she knew the door sat in its dark frame and wondered. What had kept them from marking the door in the plans? It would have had to be part of the foundation. But perhaps the Calders had some great treasure, some secret they needed to keep hidden.

Far from fear, it was curiosity that thrilled in Arlo's breast at the thought that, very soon, she'd solve the mystery once and for all.

She shut the book and slid it back into its place just as her stomach rumbled a demand at her. A glance at the clock told her it was nearing supper time, though the afternoon still poured light into the room. If it was winter, it would be dark by now, but summer took its own sweet time rolling out the carpet of night, and waiting was torture like nothing Arlo had ever known.

She didn't want to eat; didn't want to do *anything* but go through that door. Every tick of the clock was a hammer blow to her soul, every space between heartbeats an endless void of terrible waiting.

But wait she must. She couldn't complete her set of keys until the moon rose.

She scraped together a meal that she barely picked at, watching the sun sink through the wide, high scullery window until dusk turned the sky the same deep blue as her employer's eyes.

Finally.

Arlo crossed the room on shaky legs. She opened the doors that hid the dumbwaiter, then hauled on the counterweight and locked the car in place on the floor above her. The darkness below was like an old friend, the whispering voices a siren song. Her body buzzed with impatience to climb down, to *jump* down, to close the distance between her and the waiting door.

But she had one last thing to do. She opened the courtyard door to watch the fat, full moon make its slow procession over the hills, distant and regal, impossibly bright, while Tristan's words from their encounter in the garden echoed through her memory.

In this light, they look almost silver.

She hoped *almost* would be good enough. But there was a magic in this, wasn't there? A trickery, of sorts, just like in all the old fairy tales she'd grown up on. Talking snake-doors shouldn't even *exist*. The door in the cellar led outside the foundation: to nowhere. Impossible.

But if it was *magic*, then Arlo knew how the stories went.

The answer had been there all along, just waiting for her to be clever enough to see it.

When the last of the moon's curve hung in the sky, Arlo stared for a long moment before shutting one eye tight and locking the courtyard door behind her. She scratched a match to life and lit her lantern, then climbed down the bones of the dumbwaiter's cage until her feet found solid ground. Her heart lashed at her ribs, blood so loud in her ears that she couldn't hear her steps on the floor beneath her.

"Well, child?" the snake asked, uncoiling. "Can you serve me what I seek?"

Arlo threw back her shoulders. This was it.

"I've been looking at the moon," she said, her tone defiant, bravado hot against the fear that somehow this wouldn't work, that it was real gold and silver the snake required. "You can still see its light in my eye." With that, she opened the eye she'd kept screwed shut, and for just a moment she *swore* she could see the snake in greater detail under some ghostly silver illumination.

"Something silver," the snake admitted in a grudging tone.

Encouraged, Arlo pulled the pins out of her hair. She ran her hands through her golden curls until a few strands came free, and held them out to dangle at her fingertips.

"Something gold," she said, letting them float to the floor.

The snake flashed its tongue at her, eyes widening. "And the last?" The sour, waspish boredom was gone from its voice, replaced with surprise and the barest edge of anticipation.

Arlo chewed on her lip for a moment. Then, she started to sing. She sang the song her mother had sung to her whenever she was sad, or afraid, her eyes drifting closed as she remembered her mother's arms, the warmth of her touch, the safety of her love. Tears slid down her cheeks, silent tracks of memory.

When she opened her eyes, the snake's beady black gaze was mere inches from her own.

"I would have accepted heat or cold, or a puff of breath," it said, after a long silence. It darted forward, flicking its forked tongue at her cheek to taste the salt there before pulling back. "But your sorrow is so much sweeter." Its jaw fell in a gaping smile, and it bobbed its head toward the center where the double doors met. "Enter," it said.

The door creaked open.

13

ARLO STEPPED THROUGH THE door and blew out her lantern. The acrid scent of its smoking wick filled her nose as she stared around her in wonder.

This was no storage room, no root cellar. Of all the things she could have expected, all the things she could have dreamed, this had never even crossed her mind.

The room she was in was the one she'd just left, with one noticeable difference: light. Candelabras of various heights lined the walls, each glowing with candles that bathed the room in a soft, golden illumination completely counter to the Stygian darkness she'd left behind. From inside this cocoon of gentle radiance, Calderwood might as well not be there at all. It was as if she'd been born at the center of some dark flower, and was only now entering the world.

The walls were a uniform stone, the same variegated gray she'd glimpsed with her lantern on the other side, except for a deeper hue staining the threshold between the two rooms. She peered at it, stepping closer, when a footfall sounded behind her.

"Ah," a man's voice said. Arlo froze, but her shoulders began to relax almost as soon as she flinched, because the man's tone wasn't disappointed nor affronted. No; he sounded...*relieved*. Expectant.

He confirmed it with his next word, a breathy utterance whose harmonics twined through Arlo's consciousness and provided a balm to her soul that she didn't know she'd needed.

"Finally."

She turned, abandoning the dark stain on the sill for an even greater fascination. Who on earth could be down here, and why did he sound so grateful to see her? He must be mistaking her for someone else, though her dusty maid's uniform could give little illusion as to who she might be. Arlo readied an explanation, but when she saw the man at the opposite end of the room, all words abandoned her.

He was tall, with shoulders that were obviously strong without being overly broad. His straight hair was as light as Tristan's was dark, so pale it was nearly white, caught in a black velvet ribbon to cascade down his back in a straight, fluid fall, and his eyes were so deep a black that Arlo couldn't see where the pupil ended and the iris began. The strong angle of his jaw exuded powerful masculinity, but the languid movement of his mouth as it slid toward a smile belied an almost feline grace as he took her in.

Arlo started to bob, the reflexive curtsy she used so much upstairs. She knew nothing about this man, but his pristine formal dress and the casual coolness of his manner told her that whoever he was, he was wealthy, and likely had been for a long time, though he didn't appear as though he could be much older than she was.

"My dear." The smooth, low thrum of his voice sent Arlo writhing in a way that put her immediately and embarrassingly in mind of some of her more lurid dreams of her employer. She sank deeper to hide the heat that flushed her face like scarlet ink blooming through a glass of water, but stopped when she saw he'd reached a gloved hand out toward her.

"I've been waiting for you."

She looked up to see a grin as bright and dazzling as polished mirror-glass.

"Me?" Her voice nearly squeaked with the first word she'd said since entering this place.

"You," he assured her, breathy and slow, and it was all Arlo could do to keep her knees from melting. "Please," he said, inching his hand just a little more toward her. "Won't you join me?"

"Join...you?" Arlo felt as though her brain wasn't working, as though the world had broken and she couldn't even see the pieces, let alone pick them up.

She saw the hand in front of her. She heard this man's voice, smelled the sweet beeswax of the candles all around. This was a real place.

But how could it be?

The man had entered from the opposite side of the room, which meant there had to be at least one more room beyond this one—a room, no less, that would give this beautiful man occasion to wear a tuxedo. Was there a whole other house here, adjacent to Calderwood?

It was certainly strange that the foundation of the property should somehow abut another residence, or a passage thereto. There was no other house in sight of Calderwood; nothing in the direction this door pointed but the village.

If this man, whoever he was, inhabited these halls, did he do so entirely underground? Was he some kind of prisoner here, despite his elegant manner and fine attire?

Was *that* what the Calders didn't want known?

Arlo tried to think of Tristan being the sort of person who could keep a prisoner, and failed. Stuffy and awkward as he might be, he had also proved to be kind and thoughtful. Surely there had to be some other explanation.

The same hunger that had driven her down here now compelled her to want more. She had thought that opening this door would give her satisfaction. On the contrary; this was only the start of the puzzle.

She hesitated a moment longer. But she'd come so far. Her solving of the riddle had been a triumph, a satisfaction bordering on joy, the first she'd felt in...she couldn't remember how long. What point would there have been in any of what she'd done if she refused to go on from here? She took a deep breath and touched the stranger's hand.

He bent, the barest brush of his lips on her skin sending tingles through every inch of her before he straightened and smiled again. Perhaps he'd never stopped.

"Call me Lucien," he said.

The lack of a family name left Arlo fumbling. How should she introduce herself? No one but her family had ever called her by her given name. In her position as a servant, her employer and Mrs. Hollister only ever called her Miss Reade, as was appropriate. Lucien was clearly at least equal to Mister Calder's station, if not above it, so it followed that he should call her Miss Reade, too.

He seemed to sense her struggle and gave her an opening.

"Miss..."

"Reade."

"Miss Reade."

Arlo's stomach danced with relieved butterflies, but their wings beat faster when Lucien leaned close. He smelled of amber mixed with the bright, mineral and vegetal tang of rain falling on parched earth, so thick she could almost feel it settling on her tongue.

"And is that the name you'd like me to call you?" he asked, radiating gentle amusement. "Or would you prefer to become...better acquainted?"

His invitation danced over the skin of her neck and shoulders and down her arms in an avalanche of shivers.

"Arlo," she said, barely more than a breath.

"Arlo." He lingered on her name, his mouth wreathed in playful smiles, and extended his elbow toward her. "Please, come in."

A part of her clamored an appeal to reason: they were underground, in a place that shouldn't exist, behind a door that had cost her three very strange things to pass. This shouldn't be happening. It couldn't be real.

But the mystery of this place plucked at her with insistent fingers, drawing her ever onward.

Come. Come.

She slid her hand into the crook of Lucien's elbow, shivering a little at the contrast of the smooth, velvety jacket with hard muscle underneath. She'd seen plenty of muscled men working in the city, but where they'd had an obvious strongman look about them, Lucien's strength was lean and sinuous, hidden until it was close enough to touch.

Her fingers tightened, a reflexive gesture that earned the slide of his dry, smooth hand over hers. She glanced up at him, a startled blush searing her cheeks, but his gaze was fixed on the door opposite them. Only the dark glitter of his eyes and the scythe-edge of a smile gave any indication that he knew exactly what she'd felt, and just what her reaction had been.

She followed on weak knees as he guided her across the candlelit room. There was a structure near the far wall. Arlo blinked with a touch of vertigo as she realized it was the dumbwaiter shaft.

But it couldn't have been the one she'd climbed down. Could it? She'd just left Calderwood.

Hadn't she?

Lucien led her toward a staircase that looked likewise familiar. It wasn't until they passed through the door at the top of the stairs that Arlo realized why she recognized it.

This was Calderwood. They'd just been in the cellar, which she hadn't recognized because she'd never seen it lit before. And this was the hall just next to the pantry. Except...

"Come." Lucien tugged on her arm, steering her left and into the main hallway of the house.

Arlo closed her eyes, fighting a sudden wave of dizziness. It was a *right* from that hall to get to the main house. Wasn't it?

The thought wriggled like a fox in a trap for the barest moment before music swept in, arresting her attention. Beyond the open ballroom doors danced a glittering crowd of the most beautiful people she'd ever laid eyes on.

Their skin ranged in color from palest marble through true ebony. Every face was a sculptor's dream; some were narrow, some wide, but each one was chiseled just so and accented with artful cosmetic splashes in bright yellows, rich scarlets, earthy browns and vivid, striking greens. Gowns in materials Arlo had never seen returned the light of a thousand candles to make the room a scintillant rainbow, dazzling and fine.

Arlo slid her free hand against her thigh and pinched herself as hard as she could through the drab, sturdy black cotton of her working dress. She winced, but didn't wake up, and a shiver traveled up from her shoulders to the hairline at the base of her neck.

This was *real.*

Lucien shifted beside her, making Arlo look up. "Shall we dance?"

Arlo looked to the far corner of the room where musicians played on a small stage. Their syncopated waltz made her heart stutter and jolt to try and keep up, a problem the other partygoers seemed not to have as they whirled and laughed and tucked themselves into pockets of shadow for more intimate exchanges.

Until a few weeks ago, Arlo had spent all her life in the city. Though she'd never moved in moneyed circles, she'd seen the wealthy leaving theaters and dances. As a child she'd even run with others to peek through ornate fences at the passengers alighting from fine carriages at aristocratic parties, to swoon over their elegant silhouettes and refined manners.

What might it be like, she'd wondered, to live in that world? But it had never been more than an errant daydream.

Now here she was, standing on the threshold in her shabby maid's uniform, on the arm of a man with whom she'd not even exchanged surnames, who nonetheless seemed entirely willing and possibly even eager to while away a glittering evening with her by his side. She looked up at him again through the fringe of her lashes.

Among his guests, Lucien was the only one not decorated. His tuxedo was spotless, his skin as pale and perfect as fine ash, almost as white as his hair, but he wore no color, no cosmetics. His simple, understated elegance made him stand out more, not less, amid the riot of colorful guests, and it was clear that Arlo wasn't the only one who'd noticed. All eyes were on him.

And—consequently—on her as well.

Arlo gulped. Her host bowed his head toward her with an attentive, inquisitive expression on his face.

"I shouldn't be here." Her whisper was a frantic moth against the shell of his ear.

Lucien turned his head to brush her eyebrow with the edge of his smile.

"Don't be silly," he assured her, low and gentle. "You're exactly where you should be."

Arlo's spine tingled with delight at his closeness, at how natural, how *right* his attention felt. Lucien was behind the door that had called to her all this time. Did that mean it had been *him* reaching out somehow, inviting her to find him? That made her an invited guest, which meant that she *did* belong here. With him.

Whoever he was.

And she couldn't deny that despite her obvious incongruity here, his attention and steadfast assurance made her feel like a lady. A princess. A queen.

But she couldn't shake the feeling that the others judged her wanting. And why shouldn't they? She'd cleaned like a demon all day, battling heat and the dust of century-old books, then climbed down the bones of a dumbwaiter and through the dark to come here. Her forehead itched, and her stomach and spine seized with the sudden realization that she was probably covered in dust and cobwebs.

If she belonged here at all, it was only in the way that a jester belonged: to be laughed at.

She curled her hands into anxious fists and felt the prickling sting as the flex pulled open the cracks that several weeks of harsh soaps had carved in her knuckles, no matter how much lanolin she rubbed in.

Lucien touched her hand, his fingers gentle, with no sign of disgust at her rough, damaged skin. On the contrary, he lifted her hand to his lips and took a deep breath in through his nose, eyes closed, a steadying moment that grounded Arlo, too.

He drew her into the swirling mass of guests just as the musicians struck up another tune and, to her surprise, she danced as though she'd been trained to it from birth, following him like a flower follows the sun. There was no thought, no effort required. Lucien's lead made dancing as natural as breathing, and everything in his dark eyes shouted that she was welcome. She was wanted.

When Arlo was small, her mother had filled their tiny home with music and laughter. Eugenie's voice had been as light and clear as lark song, so inviting that even her father sometimes joined in, adding a pleasant gravelly bass to round out her mother's brightness. He'd called her his flower, his angel, his dove. Some of Arlo's earliest memories were of toddling up to them, so obviously in love with each other and with her, to be swept up and sung to and cuddled until she fell asleep in the warmth of their affection.

Both her parents had cherished her, then. But when Death came too soon to take Eugenie's hand, he left a broken home behind. There were no more songs or stories after that, no more hugs, and the more Arlo grew to look like the tintype they had of her mother, the less her father could stand to look at her. He never said so, but she knew. Each was all the other had left, but without Eugenie they drifted apart until Arlo felt like an orphan even with one parent still living.

She'd been long used to feeling unwanted, out of place even in her own home.

Yet now, here she was. Not just with a man who made her feel lightheaded and bold, welcome and wanted, but who could bend an entire host of others to do the same. Because there was something about the way the guests watched him that told Arlo this was Lucien's place; his party, his house. He was a king here, and—for tonight, at least—she seemed to be his queen.

"Come," he breathed in her ear, leaning down again as they ended another in a long string of dances. "Let's get some air."

Arlo nodded. They giggled like children darting among their elders, though Lucien never had to dodge anyone. He engaged in another, subtler dance, where every guest had a sense of him and moved to let him pass, leading Arlo out to the hall and down toward the other end of the house.

The sight of the library door sent a galvanic current rocking through Arlo's heart. *Tristan.* But no, he wasn't here. Tristan was traveling. The real question was, would she see him here if he *was* in residence? Perhaps she'd crossed into some dream world, some shadow of the past. Perhaps, if he was here, Arlo could watch Tristan like a ghost staring down the ages.

Lucien drew her gently away, down the hall between what were, in Calderwood, the music room and drawing room. Here, the music room boomed with laughter while the drawing room let out only low, murmuring tones and a heavy cloud of sweet-smelling smoke that writhed against the ceiling with an oily sheen. He passed it all, bringing her to the terrace door and out into the night.

Arlo inhaled the clear air, then caught her breath when she saw what lay before her. Below the terrace, the garden rioted with life. The full moon picked out leaves so dark and lush that Arlo felt sure it would be like getting lost in the jungle to go down there without a guide, and everything smelled of night-blooming flowers and rich earth.

"Oh," she said, a wordless expression of wonder. Lucien stepped closer, spreading his hand on the small of her back. She arched like a cat, pressing into his touch. She knew it was the height of wickedness to behave this way with a man she'd just met, but that was in her world. Those concerns seemed awfully far away from wherever she was now.

She thought back to the fairy tales her mother used to tell her long before Arlo had developed a taste for the penny dreadfuls. In this world below the house she knew, she felt just like one of the twelve dancing princesses, escaping the strictures of her life above for the magic of a revel in another world. The princesses in that story visited the underground kingdom many times.

Perhaps Arlo could come back, too.

Lucien let out a contented hum. Arlo smiled. Perhaps she'd never have to leave at all.

"It's beautiful," she said, gazing out over the silvered garden and the endless hills beyond.

"Yes," Lucien said. His breath was so close on Arlo's neck that she flinched toward him, only to find that his lips were a mere whisper away from hers. She shied back, surprised, but her host only gazed into her eyes and said, "beautiful."

His bright hair and fair skin made him look like a sliver of moonlight that had gotten lost. He took a step closer.

"Arlo," he said.

And then, the horror: Arlo's stomach squelched too loud with a reminder that she'd eaten almost nothing since that morning. She pulled her lips between her teeth and bit down on them, holding back a little scream of abject humiliation, but Lucien only smiled.

"Come," he said, dark eyes flashing. "Let's get you something to eat."

She smiled an apology and followed him back down the hall, past the smoke and the laughter, past the glittering ballroom and across the hall to the dining room.

In what Arlo had come to think of as the daytime world, the table was always empty here, the sideboards bare. But here, in the moonlight world, every surface groaned under the weight of the most sumptuous foods she'd ever seen.

Tiny birds roasted whole in pastry baskets with a gleaming white sauce sat beside pancakes smothered in thick whipped cream and glistening caviar, plates of miniature cakes topped with candied cherries, and platters on which pomegranate seeds winked like jewels among sliced cheeses and slivered figs.

Arlo didn't realize she'd paused gaping in the doorway until she felt Lucien's hand driving her gently forward.

"What would you like?" he asked, already filling a small plate with the most beautiful of the offerings.

"I—" Arlo took the plate, but didn't move to eat anything. Something niggled at the back of her head, something she felt like she should remember, but it dissolved in the scent of warm sugar wafting up from the board.

"Here." Lucien plucked a cherry from the top of a cake and held it gently against Arlo's mouth. She started a little, but didn't move away this time, letting her lips part around the fruit. For the barest moment she tasted the warm salt of his finger behind the sweetness, and blushed as he put that same finger to his own lips and smiled. She barely noticed the cherry bursting between her teeth, caught as she was in the spell of his eyes.

"Do you like it?" he asked, taking the plate and setting it down on the table beside them.

Arlo nodded as he drew closer, inhaling as he put one hand on her shoulder, the other under her jaw.

"Arlo," he said, then stopped, whipping his head toward the door as, somewhere, a clock chimed four times.

"What is it?" Arlo asked.

Lucien turned back toward her with sadness in his smile.

"Morning already. I didn't realize the night had flown so fast." He leaned in again, close to her ear. "I wanted much more time with you."

Arlo's heart twisted, torn between the lift of hope and the crush of disappointment.

"What do you mean?"

"You must go." Lucien took her hand and led her back toward the kitchen, the hall, the cellar stairs. She stumbled after him, struggling to keep up with his ground-eating strides and nearly barreling into him as he stopped abruptly before the door she'd entered through.

"Lucien—"

He grabbed her by both arms and turned her to face him, his grip so tight it almost hurt as he stared into her eyes.

"Come back to me," he said, pleading. "Tomorrow."

"I—"

"Promise me." He looked so wild and fierce, so earnest, and Arlo knew she would move heaven and earth to get back to him, to spend more time in this magical world of his, wherever, whatever it was.

But...tomorrow?

Mister Calder would be back tomorrow. She still hoped they could discuss poor Jekyll's experiment and Hyde's rampant evil, but even if they didn't, she still had to return the book to him. Of course, Tristan—or more likely Mrs. Hollister—would eventually find it in her room if she disappeared, but she wouldn't feel right if she didn't return it herself. Even if he didn't want to talk about it with her anymore, even if he was determined to pretend that the moments between them had never happened, he had trusted her with one of his precious possessions, and she owed it to him to return it with the respect that trust deserved.

And, not least, Arlo found her entire body suffused with a sick dizziness at the thought of leaving Calderwood without saying goodbye. Of leaving Calderwood at all.

She shook her head, coming back to the moment.

"Not tomorrow."

"Soon, then." Lucien caught her hand in his and pressed it to his mouth, breathing her scent as though he might never see her again and had to remember. "Promise me."

Arlo nodded. He planted a kiss in her palm before shoving her through the door. The space between them closed until the candles disappeared completely, leaving Arlo in utter darkness.

Air rushed from her lungs in an involuntary sob as she hunched forward, heart pounding, chest squeezing, breath heaving against the coming of tears.

"Soon," she said, stumbling back toward the dumbwaiter. She turned back to look toward where she knew the door stood, though she couldn't see it. "I promise."

She climbed up the dumbwaiter shaft back into Calderwood, where morning hadn't quite begun to reach its fingertips over the horizon and bathe the house in its meager light. Arlo had made it halfway up the narrow stairs to the servants' quarters before she realized she'd left the dumbwaiter car on the top floor, and went back to lower it before trudging up once more to her narrow, lonely bed.

She fell asleep with the taste of cherries in her mouth, and it wasn't Tristan she dreamed of.

14

"MISS READE!"

The voice had the exasperated quality that comes with repetition. Arlo blinked blearily awake to Mrs. Hollister's face, which twisted with a reddened expression somewhere between frustration and fear.

"Saints preserve us, child, are you dying?"

"Wha—" Arlo tried to sit up, then fell back on her pillow when the movement proved dizzying. At some point during the night someone had swapped her tongue for a wad of cotton, or so it felt.

"Master Tristan comes back today," the housekeeper reminded her with a huff. "I came directly after church expecting to find you downstairs, yet here you are still abed. What has gotten into you?"

Promise me.

Arlo closed her eyes. What *had* gotten into her? Lucien, that's what. She could still feel the soft brush of his lips on her palm, the firm skin and juicy pop of the cherry he'd fed her, the heavy gaze of all those glittering dancers as she turned about the room in his arms.

Had it even been real? Surely a night like that was too perfect to be anything but a dream.

"And your dress," the housekeeper said, picking up Arlo's uniform from where she'd left it crumpled on the floor. "Look at the state..." She trailed off, brushing away dust and a lone, long strand of cobweb that defied gravity, floating toward Arlo like a beckoning arm.

Come, she heard the dancers beyond the door call to her. *Come.*

"Sorry?" she asked, aware that Mrs. Hollister had asked her a question, but not what it was.

"I said, what were you doing yesterday?" Her eyes narrowed as she glanced at the haphazard pile of corset at the foot of the bed. "You weren't...exploring dark corners with a beau, were you?"

Arlo's shoulders rocked a little. Though Mrs. Hollister wasn't correct, not in the way she thought she might be, the accusatory subtext hit a little too close to home. Arlo knew the rules of employment—there was no romance allowed in houses like this. But, technically, Arlo hadn't been in the house.

At least, not *this* house. Besides, the housekeeper was probably picturing Arlo with her back pressed against the pantry wall, skirts around her waist and some village swain grunting into her ear. She shuddered to even think of it, especially in comparison to what she *had* been doing. The memory of Lucien's fingers nearly in her mouth sent a low throb through her belly.

"I don't know anyone around here, Mrs. Hollister," Arlo reminded her in a gentle, cautious tone.

"Ah," the housekeeper said. "That's right." She slapped the dress once more with a flourish and slid it onto a hanger from the narrow wardrobe. "Well, there. That will do for now. Are you well enough to come downstairs? Master Tristan will be back in," she checked her watch, "two hours or so."

"Of course." Arlo shuffled her feet to the edge of the bed and let her heels hit the floor, wincing as something pinched in her lower abdomen. "I'm sorry you had to find me like this. I...had some trouble sleeping."

"Well, nothing like a little hard work to set you right again." The housekeeper bustled out, leaving Arlo alone to wash her face and get dressed.

Her hair took the longest, resisting every pass of the brush with snarls and elf-knots that yanked at her scalp. She finally got it braided and pinned, then examined her reflection. Purple shadows had crept in under her eyes overnight, a faint bloom that echoed the sky in Lucien's world, and her lips were the red of fresh blood against her newly wan skin. She pinched her cheeks to bring back a semblance of vigor and sighed at the mirror.

It would have to do.

Come back to me.

Her heart tried to pull her chest-first back downstairs, through the door, back to Lucien, but Arlo shook her head, fighting against the impulse. There was nothing she wanted more than to return. Before, she'd wanted to stay for a chance to solve the mystery, but she'd at least considered whether it might be a good thing to seek employment elsewhere. Now, the thought of leaving this place, of leaving *Lucien,* twisted her heart to the point of actual pain.

A very small part of her wondered why. In the cold light of day, everything that had happened last night seemed like a dream.

Who was Lucien, and why was his house tucked behind a door hidden in Calderwood's cellar? There had to be another way in, for all those guests to come and go. But Arlo hadn't seen another house for miles. There was nothing but the carriage road between Calderwood and the village.

Arlo bit her lip and swore she tasted a hint of cherry, a flavor that rocked her right back to that moment with Lucien's hand touching her lips as he fed her. Her promise rose in her mind, along with the unabashed need in his eyes as he'd extracted it from her. There was no question—she *would* return. But she had to be smart about it. Bide her time. She was fortunate that Mister Calder traveled so much, and he hadn't mentioned her staying at the inn overnight since that first time.

Another opportunity would come, she was sure of it.

She could only hope it would be soon.

She slapped both cheeks hard and stood up. No amount of wishing would get the chores done, and the last thing she needed was to be dismissed for daydreaming and shirking her duties. Not now that she knew what was at stake.

It didn't stop her, though, from seeing reminders of Lucien *everywhere.* His smile flashed in the light that reflected in mirrors and other glass. Every shadow was a glimpse of his tailcoat, every sliver of white door trim an echo of his hair. And always came the whispers—*come, come*—enticing her with the invitation to run downstairs and disappear into his arms.

She didn't notice she'd paused in her work until the clatter of hooves and carriage wheels in front of the house brought her out of her daydreams. Her knees prickled from prolonged contact with the library carpet, and she had to stand slowly to avoid falling over as her head went light. It didn't help that she'd had no breakfast, and though she knew it was her own fault, it had still stung to find the kettle deliberately cold and breakfast conspicuously absent when she'd finally dragged herself downstairs.

Mrs. Hollister may have let it go this morning, but Arlo was learning that the housekeeper wasn't a woman to cross.

If only Mister Calder would go away for more than an overnight. If Arlo could just have the house to herself for a little longer at a stretch, she wouldn't have to worry so much about the state she'd be in come morning.

She arrived in the great hall as Mister Calder stepped down from the carriage, giving her just enough time to fall in line beside the housekeeper, head bowed. His steps echoed on the tiles a moment later.

"Hollister," he said, acknowledging the housekeeper.

"Good afternoon, sir. Will you dine in the library tonight?"

"As always."

Arlo had grown accustomed to her employer's solitary habits, and yesterday, she wouldn't have batted an eye. But now she contrasted his lonely choices with last night's spectacle: a house full of people and candles and music, with every surface in the dining room offering a sumptuous feast. Lucien would never eat alone in the library. The thought of him drew a whisper of sound from a flutter in her throat, the barest hint of a fond hum. She didn't realize it had even been audible until she saw Mister Calder's shoes stop in front of her.

He stood there for a long breath. Two. Finally, Arlo looked up to see her employer looking at her. She tried to keep her expression neutral, but fear clanged behind her careful composure. Did he know? Could he tell? Could he sense traces of Lucien's house on her like the rainbow sheen of oil on water?

And, though it had never occurred to her before, a new thought seized her now—how would he know, unless he'd been down there himself, another guest at the underground revel? Had he danced in Lucien's world, eaten his food?

His expression remained as impassive and unreadable as ever, but something burned in his eyes for the barest moment before he dragged his gaze away and headed inside.

Arlo's heart quavered as she fought not to follow him with her eyes. As Mrs. Hollister fell into step behind their employer, asking if he'd like hot water sent up, Arlo diverted her gaze instead to a small mirror hanging inside the entry hall and cringed. She'd done her best to smooth away the signs of her sleepless night, but her face still looked pale, her under eyes dusky with purple shadows. She pinched her cheeks again and hurried after them.

Tristan turned toward the library while Arlo and the housekeeper made for the kitchens. Arlo knew without being asked that she'd be the one to take the hot water up to him, though more accurately, they'd send it in the dumbwaiter. She'd meet it on the upper floor, and then she'd only have to carry a boiling kettle down the hall rather than up the narrow stairs.

The thought of the dumbwaiter made her smile. Such a useful little device. The car traveled up and down the house, and no one would ever suspect that its presence could be used for...other pur-poses.

She grinned to herself when she was safely outside, alone at the water pump. Somewhere below her feet, Lucien waited for her.

In the kitchen, though, it was Mrs. Hollister waiting. She'd set a large, black kettle on the stove and stood up from stoking the fire. Arlo poured the water into the kettle without a word. When she stepped back, her abdomen throbbed again, and she had a sudden sense that it might be wise to remove herself for a moment.

She excused herself and found her suspicions to be correct. Her monthlies were on her for, she realized, the first time since coming to this house. Not that she'd had any concerns on that front—despite what Mrs. Hollister might choose to suspect, Arlo hadn't had any of the sort of congress that would result in an interruption. Her cycle had been longer than usual, though that was hardly surprising with the major change in her life and all the strangeness she'd experienced since coming here.

She fetched and arranged her napkin and belt, then went back downstairs.

"Feeling better?" the housekeeper asked.

Arlo nodded and flashed a wan half-smile.

"The curse is on me." She noted the easing of Mrs. Hollister's expression and turned her head to hide her mouth as it spread into a grin. Take *that,* madam, for all your scurrilous assumptions!

"Well, that explains it," the housekeeper said. "Do you need—"

"I'm well set up," Arlo said. "Thank you."

Mrs. Hollister nodded, then stood as the kettle whistled, pulling it from the stove with a thick cloth and placing it on a sturdy tray.

"Two fresh towels and a face cloth from the closet upstairs," she said, transferring the tray to the dumbwaiter. "Tray on the table by the door."

The reminder stung a bit—as if she'd ever forget *that* instruction again. But Arlo just curtsied, then went back upstairs to fetch the linens and wait for the steaming water.

"Mister Calder?" she called with a gentle knock when she'd set the tray on the little table. "Your water."

She started to walk away, then stopped with a jolt when she heard the door open behind her. After the last time, she thought he'd wait until she was gone. She turned. Her employer had his shirtsleeves pushed up over his elbows, his unbound hair falling in dark waves to brush his shoulders. In the shadows under his opened collar, she could just see the faint line of a healing cut over what looked like the tight, pink track of an older scar along the underside of his left collarbone.

"Thank you," he said with a glance at the table, before she could get a word in.

"Sir." The sliver of exposed collarbone tantalized her, and her mind jumped with almost violent suddenness to wonder what it would taste like if she pressed her lips to the hollow at the base of his throat. She bobbed and turned to go before he could catch her fluster, but he stopped her again.

"Are you..."

She turned back to see him with one fisted hand shaking gently in front of him, as if he'd just caught something and held it back. He cleared his throat and tried again.

"I'll be right back," he said, picking up the kettle. "With this."

Arlo bobbed again. "Of course." He disappeared back into his rooms, and she heaved a huge breath as soon as she was alone. Where had *that* come from?

She could admit, if only to herself, that Tristan had featured heavily in her fantasies over the past several weeks. But last night—both in the real moonlight world and in her dreams of it, after—it was Lucien who'd taken center stage. Lucien, who was attentive and charming where Tristan was standoffish and awkward, who'd given her a glimpse of what Calderwood could be like and made her feel wanted, rather than just barely noticed.

Mister Calder appeared again, opening the door just enough to put the kettle back on the tray and take the towels. He fixed Arlo with a long, opaque look before he nodded and withdrew. She stood there for a long moment, nervous and kinetic, as though she balanced on a knife's edge before a yawning precipice.

If he could somehow sense Lucien's world on her, would he say something? Or was this the prelude to the sacking she'd managed to avoid before?

Fingers tingling with an uncertainty bordering on panic, Arlo took the tray back to the dumbwaiter for the journey downstairs. She didn't see him again until supper time, when he surprised her once more.

"A moment, Miss Reade," he said as she turned to leave after placing his tray in its usual spot on his desk.

"Sir?"

"Are you...well?"

The words stopped Arlo's heart. Not just for the invitation, the opening of a conversation where he was usually so closed, but because of his tone. His tentative voice betrayed a cautious caring, delicate as a flower bud seeking the sun. Even as her body yearned to run back to Lucien, something inside her rejoiced. Here, *here* was a hint of the man she'd glimpsed that night, the man who'd given her permission to borrow from his library, the man with an unexpected capacity for compassion and a smile that could light up whole worlds.

Not that he was smiling now. His expression was one of concern, as though he feared her answer but couldn't help asking.

"It's just," he continued when she didn't answer, "you look pale. I..." He drummed his hands against the desk, casting his gaze toward the far wall as if some useful words might be written there. "I know Calderwood is a bit...strange. If it's too much for you..."

Cold realization trickled down Arlo's spine like the slow, creeping trail of a half-frozen egg. He knew where she'd been. He knew, and he was going to send her away.

"Please, sir," she said, curtsying again to hide the panic she felt contorting her face. She got it under control before she looked up at him. "I've been feeling poorly, but I'm better now. It won't happen again."

"It's not—" he started, then stopped and started again. "You're my responsibility as long as you're in my home. I value your service, but I wouldn't blame you if you wanted to seek employment elsewhere. I can even help you, I'm sure—"

"No!" Arlo said, and gasped as she realized she'd just shouted at him. She scrambled to cover the faux pas before he could say anything else. "That is, I like Calderwood very much, sir," she continued in a more schooled tone, though she couldn't keep her voice from quavering around the edges. "I don't want to go away."

From the corner of her eye she saw his chest rise and fall as he took a deep breath.

"You aren't in danger of losing your position," he said, quiet and low. "I don't...want to send you away. I only thought...well. Good night, then."

Arlo looked up to see his inscrutable eyes locked on her face for a single, questing moment before he picked up his fork and looked down at his tray, signaling an end to the exchange. Color flooded all the way to the tips of her ears, and she whipped off the fastest curtsy of her life before retreating, her stomach in knots and her heart poised for flight.

Arlo barely slept that night. Her body's exhaustion, profound though it was, couldn't contend with the absolute tumult going on in her head. Every time she fell asleep, a dream would send her rocketing awake, pulse racing with some new unrest.

Mister Calder was suspicious of her. He'd said he wouldn't dismiss her, but she couldn't forget the look in his eyes when he'd come back, as if he *knew* she'd gone through the door and was just waiting to catch her out.

She might never get back to Lucien, might never feel the grace and poise she enjoyed in his arms, nor taste the fruit of his table.

"Fruit of his table" turned into a euphemism in her mind, flushing her cheeks with warmth even as his face kept changing from Lucien's to Tristan's and back again. Cold returned as she remembered Tristan's words—*I wouldn't blame you if you wanted to seek employment elsewhere*—yet he'd seemed reluctant as he'd said them.

None of it made sense, and it left Arlo dizzy to think about. She flopped her arms down by her sides and stared up at the ceiling, breath heaving out in a gust.

She could be certain of only one thing: sleep seemed less and less likely as the minutes ticked by.

Sheer determination saw her through the following morning, a forced cheerfulness that even she could tell was shrill and too bright. Mrs. Hollister kept shooting strange looks when she thought Arlo couldn't see her, though Arlo, who by this point was used to feeling watched, sensed every glance like a brush on her skin.

She was able to keep her energy up until luncheon, when the cart arrived with Mister Calder's meals for the afternoon and evening. Arlo took the food inside and waved Mrs. Hollister away toward the village. Once the woman was gone, Arlo just...stopped.

She had to bring Tristan his luncheon tray. It was right there. But when she lifted a hand, the food seemed too far away to reach. And the plates. The plates were still in the butler's pantry. And the flatware. And the napkins. And...

Arlo's hands shot out to grab the table as her body swayed, already halfway to sleep. The shock of nearly falling jolted her awake, though after a few steps across the room she started to slow again. She blinked, her lids heavy. Tristan was always so busy at his desk. Surely he wouldn't notice if she sat down, just for a moment.

She was still sitting when she heard a footstep outside the kitchen door. Her head jerked up, eyes barely opening, to see Tristan's face go from puzzled to concerned.

"Ar—Miss Reade!" He rushed to her side, bracing one hand on the back of the chair as he knelt beside her. "Are you ill?"

"I'm perfectly well," she insisted, though even she could hear the words slur as she said them.

Tristan snorted. "You certainly are not. Stay there."

He glanced at where Arlo had left the food, still covered, with nary a plate in sight, and stood up, crossing the kitchen to the butler's pantry. A moment later he returned, not with one plate but two, and two sets of flatware.

He was doing her job again. "Sir—"

"Hush." He uncovered the dishes from the inn and began to move the food to the plates only to stop with a frown. "Hm."

"What's wrong?"

"It's gone cold."

Arlo laughed once, a soundless burst from her chest. She started to rise, looking at the pans hanging by the stove. If she could get to them—

"Sit." Tristan's voice was strong; not angry, but forceful. He followed her gaze and took one of the pans down, hovering his hand over the range to make sure it was hot before he lay the cast iron on the burner. "Butter?"

Arlo gestured over her shoulder, to the larder. Tristan returned a moment later with the butter dish and cut a huge golden slice into the hot pan, where it sizzled and smelled divine. Arlo nearly swooned, though she knew that the food smelled better than it would taste.

That was something she'd noticed after coming back from Lucien's world. Everything she ate was as bland as porridge and left her starving. Granted, it often *was* porridge, or toast or the like. But perhaps, with enough butter, it would be different.

Tristan moved the food to the pan to warm while he fetched water from the pump and set the kettle on another burner. The next thing Arlo knew, he was setting a plate in front of her, along with a steaming cup of tea.

"Please eat," he said, nudging the plate a little closer to her. "You look halfway to death's door already."

Arlo looked blearily from her plate, up his arm, and down the other arm to where he held his own fork poised above a matching plate.

"I hope you don't mind," he said. "I thought you might benefit from some company. I know I would. This house, it's...lonely." He moved a few things around on his plate, but didn't lift anything to his mouth. "It must be quite a change from living in the city. Did you grow up there?"

For the second time in as many days, Arlo felt as though she'd somehow walked into a dream. Was she truly sitting with Tristan Calder at his kitchen table, sharing a meal and talking about her childhood? Was this reality? Or had she never actually managed to get out of bed this morning?

But his eyes were so attentive, so earnest. He hadn't just asked to fill the silence. He was waiting for her answer.

"I—yes." She poked at a heap of boiled small potatoes, nudging one back and forth.

"And your family?" He put a potato into his own mouth and chewed, watching Arlo with a focus that made her shift slightly in her seat.

"I have no siblings. My mother took in sewing and laundry. My father was a laborer." She winced, knowing how base that must sound to someone with Mister Calder's money, but he showed no evidence of judgment.

"Which one loves reading?" Arlo looked up at him, surprised. He smiled. "At least one of them has to, for you to enjoy it so much."

She returned his smile, remembering. "My mother did."

His face went still. "Did?"

Arlo's breath hitched as she realized that Tristan had no idea about her background.

"She died, almost four years ago now. And my father, a few months past. It's just me left." She shrugged and smiled, but couldn't stop the sniffle as she held back the urge to cry.

The gentle good humor fell from Tristan's face, seizing Arlo with the abrupt need to steer the conversation to something else as soon as possible.

"What about you?"

Tristan tilted his head. "What about me?"

"Your family must love stories too."

He nodded, expression soft with fondness.

"Both my parents do. Winters in the city, my mother and her society friends would go to plays all the time. The next morning she'd regale us at breakfast with all the theatrics we'd missed. It was..." He stopped, his gaze going sad, and his next words were quiet. "It was fun."

He looked down at his plate and took a large bite of food, too big for politeness and certainly too much to talk around.

Arlo couldn't help but think that was on purpose. She pressed her lips together. What a pair they made, these two and their sadness. It danced around them like ghosts at a ball, swooping in to take their hands when they least expected it. She inhaled slowly, then perked up as a thought occurred to her.

"I wonder if I ever saw her," she mused. Tristan looked up. "Your mother, I mean. I—when I was younger, sometimes my friends and I would walk over to the theater district and watch the highbrow audiences leave the shows, just to get a glimpse of their dresses. They were bright as birds," she said, with a little laugh. "And about as noisy."

Tristan's mouth spread slowly into something approaching a grin.

"Maybe you did, at that. I'm sure she would like you."

Arlo blinked. "Me? Sir, I'm a servant. I don't think she'd notice me."

"Why not?" He speared a potato, watching as the tines of his fork pushed slowly into its flesh. "I do."

His gaze stayed fixed on his plate, giving Arlo plenty of time to stare at him. He spoke again without looking up.

"All I mean is that...despite the unfortunate circumstances that prompted you to leave your home..." He fiddled with his napkin, rolling one corner in on itself. "I'm glad you're here."

He smiled, then looked down at his plate and ate in silence. Arlo followed suit, the only sounds in the house the quiet companionship of a shared meal until the clock bonged once.

"Ah," Tristan said, pushing his plate away. "I should get back to work." Arlo started to stand and reach for his plate all in one movement. Tristan stopped her. No more than his fingertips touched her wrist, but even that scant contact sent a tremor shivering up her arm and down her spine. "Don't," he said. "You should go get some rest."

"But Mrs. Hollister will scold me if—"

"I'll take care of this later. Mrs. Hollister will never know."

Arlo's body sagged under the weight of almost seventy-two sleepless hours, but this wasn't his to do. "Sir," she said, "I really—"

"Please." The word fell as light as snow between them, though its power rippled through Arlo several times.

She nodded. "All right. Good afternoon."

Tristan smiled. "See you tomorrow."

She plodded toward the servants' stair and trudged slowly upward. In the swish of her skirts, she couldn't tell whether the next word she heard was real, or the beginning of a dream.

"Arlo."

15

ARLO SLEPT LIKE THE dead after her meal with Tristan, an event she still wasn't completely sure had actually occurred, and woke up feeling refreshed. Just in time, too, because Mrs. Hollister's family had gone, meaning that the woman was once again there to oversee every minute of Arlo's day. She worked Arlo to the bone for the next two days which, in a way, was a good thing.

Idle hands, as her mother used to say.

But there were plenty of other places for the devil to play.

To begin with, no matter how hard she scrubbed, her feet still itched to run back downstairs. The knowledge that the door was open to her now, that Lucien was waiting, was almost too much to bear. Especially now that she knew Tristan's attention was out of concern, not the suspicion she feared. But, oddly enough, it was Tristan who kept her from racing back down to Lucien's world.

Even as every nerve in her body screamed for a repetition of that night in Lucien's moonlit world, every glimpse of Tristan made Arlo flush with a heat that reached from the tips of her ears to the places she'd never shown another person. She felt galvanic, *alive*, a sensation that danced like sparks over her skin and made her squirm with unspoken desire.

One sunny afternoon in early July, a few days after her foray through the dark door, Arlo stood in a shaft of brilliant light coming through the library window. Her feather duster twitched absently over the books on their shelves while she made a careful study of how the tendons moved in Tristan's hands as he wrote, bent so far over his desk that his unruly dark curls nearly brushed the paper he worked on.

"Are they that bad?" Tristan asked.

Arlo startled, nearly biting through her lip.

"What?" she asked, sucking at the sore spot.

"The books. You've been dusting for ages." He gestured with his pen to the shelf, and her cheeks heated. But he didn't look annoyed. It was worse. He looked amused, almost indulgent, his twilight eyes sparkling, his mouth turned up with a barely-hidden smile as his gaze met hers.

Arlo scrambled desperately for something to say, but he beat her to it.

"By the way." He set his pen down and steepled his fingers, elbows on the desktop. "We haven't talked about the Stevenson. What *did* you think of poor Doctor Jekyll and his diabolical counterpart? Please." He stood to fetch the footstool from the chair near the fireplace, then set it next to the desk and gestured vaguely between it and the feather duster in Arlo's hand as he sat down again. "Sit."

She stared at the stool for a moment. At how little space there was between it and him. Bees droned outside the open window, adding texture to the silence. But Tristan didn't move, didn't take back the invitation.

He just waited. For her.

Arlo put the duster down on the floor and brushed her hands against her apron before approaching, then sat facing her employer.

Her body surged with two opposing forces. On one hand, even after their last conversation it was still awkward to sit in his presence and converse informally. Tristan gave every indication that he enjoyed her company beyond the relationship of employer and employee, leaving Arlo's toe clawing at the line that separated mild transgression from blatant impropriety as her curiosity raged.

What might his mouth taste like?

How would his hands feel pressed to her ribs in a crushing, desperate embrace?

She stayed perfectly still, hands clasped so tight in her lap that her knuckles mottled red and white.

"Well?" he asked.

Arlo swallowed. "I think the account leading up to it was interesting, to see the story as if Jekyll and Hyde were two men. But my favorite part was the doctor's own account, the revelation of what he did, and why."

Mister Calder said nothing, only watched her, so she went on, talking to her hands to avoid the intensity of his attention.

"I thought it was interesting that his baser thoughts caused him so much shame that he felt the need to remove them entirely, rather than admit them and repent and move on."

Those thoughts were a part of everyone, after all. Her own were racing right this moment under the relentless intimacy of her employer's steady gaze. She babbled on toward safer territory.

"And it was terribly sad, that he spent so much time looking for more of the chemicals he'd used in their purest form to reverse the change, only to discover it was some unidentified, unrepeatable *im*purity that caused the singular effect of his experiment."

Mister Calder stayed silent for so long that Arlo finally risked looking up, only to find her suspicions correct. He stared at her, his gaze so intense it seemed his eyes were lit from behind with some internal fire, his mouth hanging slightly open so she could just see the ridge of his teeth.

"Sir?"

He shook his head, breaking their gaze.

"Forgive me," he said. "This is going to sound terrible, but I had no idea you'd be so bright, in your position."

It was absolutely an insult, and it stung like one, to have him assume that because she was a maid she couldn't also be clever, though there was balm in the tacit admission that he'd been wrong. Besides which, the assumption worked to her advantage. After all, if he'd taken her intelligence for granted, he wouldn't have stopped at a lock on the cellar door.

"I agree with you, though," he went on, resting one elbow on the desk and his chin in his hand as his mouth spread into a true smile that nearly stopped Arlo's heart with longing. "That's my favorite part, too."

They stayed frozen there: him leaning toward her, her sitting rod-straight, the heavy wood of his desk beside them but not between them.

If they wanted to, they could close that distance easily.

Even as Arlo watched, the cant of Tristan's upper body deepened as though he yearned to be closer to her just as much as she wanted the same. Then he stood, an abrupt motion that came with much clearing of his throat.

"Well," he said, walking over to the shelf they'd taken the Stevenson from. "What would you like for the next one?"

The next one. Had a phrase ever been so musical? *The next one* wasn't just a book to read; it was the promise of another shared experience. Another conversation. Another moment like this, drenched in an afternoon as bright and sweet as lemon cake, just the two of them in a world of their own.

Arlo licked her lips and swallowed, trying to work moisture into a mouth that had gone suddenly dry with anticipation.

"You choose."

He made a thoughtful hum as he surveyed the shelf, his finger hovering slowly over the titles. Arlo caught *Dorian Gray* and *Otranto* in glimpses before he settled on a volume and pulled it free.

"Do you know *Frankenstein?*"

"What's it about?" Arlo knew of the title, but her family had been unable to afford the subscription fees at the circulating libraries near their home, so she'd spent more time with penny dreadfuls and other short, cheap publications than with books of any length.

He smiled and held the book out to her.

"You read it, and tell me."

Arlo turned the book over in her hands, considering its form.

"This is much longer," she said. "It will likely take me—"

"Take as long as you need."

Six words. But the meaning beneath them turned every heartbeat into a bird beating hectic wings in her chest. Not three days ago, he'd offered to help her find employment elsewhere. But a man who was about to send her away wouldn't tell her to take as long as she needed in borrowing one of his books. She could stay, could share this with him. And even as she cherished the thought, another part of her seized on the possibility that, with enough time, she was sure to get another chance to see Lucien again.

She looked up to find Tristan staring—not at the book, but at *her*, his gaze locking with hers the moment her face was upturned.

Time hung suspended between them, a lifetime in the spaces bounded by every tick of the clock. Then the dinner hour struck, the heavy bong of the hallway case-clock shaking them both from their shared reverie.

Arlo stood, slipping the book into her apron pocket where it just barely fit, straining against the seams.

"Excuse me," she said, fetching the feather duster from where she'd let it lie before bobbing a curtsy by the door. She made for the kitchen, only to find Mrs. Hollister coming down the hall with Mister Calder's tray.

"Where have you been?" the woman asked.

"Don't admonish her," Mister Calder said. Arlo looked back to find him standing in the doorway, one shoulder against the open frame, arms crossed in front of him, with a comfortable smile on his face. "We were talking about books."

The housekeeper gave a breathy harrumph before sweeping past Arlo and into the library. Mister Calder's glance flicked to follow her, then focused again on Arlo. He winked—*winked*—and rolled his shoulder away from the door and back into the library where Arlo could just hear their voices, but not what they said.

She pressed her lips together in a secret smile that barely held back a giggle and ran upstairs to deposit the book in her room while the housekeeper was distracted.

That wink burned in her consciousness for the rest of the evening, its pull on her almost as strong as that of the door in the cellar.

Almost.

16

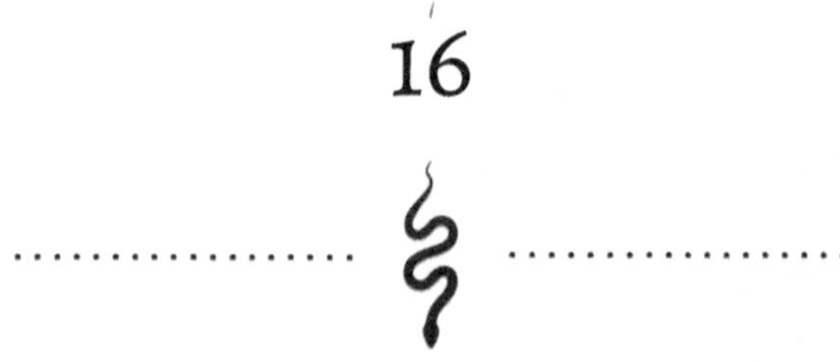

FRANKENSTEIN KEPT ARLO BUSY all that week. She was barely in bed each evening before she had the book open, following the journey of Victor Frankenstein and the monster he'd built. On the seventh night, she closed the book feeling thoughtful.

How strange it was that in both of the stories she'd most recently read, men created monsters in some way or another, only for both man and monster to die in the end. But while *Strange Case* focused on a single man's duality, *Frankenstein* delivered a broader message: no matter how logical, how rational, how controlled a person might believe themselves to be, chaos lurked just around every corner.

Both stories were unsettling. But more troubling than the literature itself was the theme in both tales that echoed at Calderwood.

Frankenstein's monster was a killer, but it was obvious that the alienation he suffered as punishment for his crime was also its cause in the first place. And here lived Tristan, alone in his house, estranged from the rest of society except for his three servants and some sporadic traveling. The thought of Mister Calder harming anyone except by some bizarre accident was, of course, hilariously foreign.

But in the dark loneliness of her narrow bed, every pop and creak of the house's long settle into night set Arlo on edge. Even her own stomach turned against her, growling in the dark as it gnawed at her from the inside. She'd eaten, but apart from the repast she'd shared with Tristan, food had lost most of its appeal after a week of meals that never seemed to satisfy.

Everything was so *sparse* here, that was the problem. Calderwood was a place that always left her wanting. Little food, no people. Arlo wondered when Calderwood had last hosted a party, a hunt, anything that would open the doors up to guests, to feasting, to merriment and fun.

She didn't generally consider herself in need of people; by choice, she kept mostly to herself. But the juxtaposition of this place with the other Calderwood she'd seen weighed heavy on her and, little by little, the elation of Tristan's attention gave way to the thrum beneath her feet, the constant call of Lucien and his glamorous guests.

Come. Come.

But Mister Calder hadn't left the house at all this week and, what was worse, had spoken of no plans to do so in the near future. Arlo hugged her knees to her chest as she listened to the hiss that might or might not be the wind in the stand of trees outside her window, but that only reminded her of the whispers that had led her to the door. To Lucien.

The memory of his kiss still burned in her palm, and when she closed her eyes she saw the shape of his lips as he said her name.

She drew her pillow up over her face and groaned into it, petulant non-sobs rocking from her chest and abdomen until her hot breath turned the softness stuffy and damp. With a grunt, Arlo flung the pillow aside. Her head turned with the motion, her gaze landing on the flowing lines of the carved arch over the empty bed across the room. She'd thought the carvings were vines before. But was that a snake's head, peering out from under a broad, curling leaf? Was that a serpent's tail? Were these friezes separate, unrelated, or were they somehow linked with the door?

She shook her head, not quite laughing, her tendons and muscles twitching with the urge to sit up, to stand, to start walking until she reached it: the door. The door. Everything went back to the door.

It would be safer to delay her next visit until she was alone in the house again. But need had etched itself into Arlo's bones so deep that now, in the dark, she couldn't wait a moment longer.

She slipped out of bed and paced, gnawing at the edge of her thumb.

Lucien's door sat in the foundation of the northern wall, at the far end of the servants' side of the house. Tristan almost never left the southwest corner where his rooms and library sat stacked like the tiers of a lonely cake, so even if he was awake, there was little chance he'd venture into Arlo's demesne. Besides, the cellar door was locked. And as far as he knew, there was no way Arlo could get downstairs.

All she had to do was be back before morning. Which meant that time was wasting.

She slipped out of bed, wishing she had a fancy tea gown to throw over her nightgown. But she shrugged into her wrapper, deciding with a glance at her much-repaired corset that it would take too much time to undress and dress again.

She crossed the room, coiling her loose braid into a hasty updo as she went, and reached for her small pile of hairpins only to hesitate just before she touched them. She knew what awaited her—the guests, the splendour—but Lucien hadn't seemed to mind her being dressed as a maid, and perhaps it was best to leave her loose braid falling down her back. After all, if Mister Calder *did* catch her wandering around the house at night, a claim that she'd been sleepwalking would be more believable if she was in her nightgown with her hair unpinned.

She opened her door and listened. The hall was silent of any footstep, and she tiptoed downstairs with only the rustle of her skirts to give her away. The dumbwaiter waited for her at the foot of the stairs. Arlo disengaged the lock that kept the car sitting at kitchen-level, then hauled slowly on the rope, wincing every time the mechanism creaked or rumbled. But eventually, the car sat as high as it would go, and Arlo locked the brake on the rope to keep it from descending.

After a moment's consideration, she removed her wrapper and balled it up with the inside facing out so that the outside wouldn't pick up any stray grease or coal dust. She let it fall down the dumbwaiter shaft, then followed more slowly after it, pulse pounding in her throat, her ears, rocking her chest with every heartbeat.

She had never done this without a lantern before, but it was too risky to shine a light in this endeavor when she wasn't alone in the house, so she made her slow way down, then felt around for her wrapper and got back into it. Turning from the dumb-waiter rails, she made her way straight for the wall where the door waited for her. There was no need to see it; this close, all she needed was the sound of the whispers to guide her way.

Come. Come.

Besides the feeling that got stronger as she got closer, she knew she'd reached the door when the sometimes-carved snake hissed from its perch, lingering on every sibilant in a greeting that seemed designed to make the most of the sound.

"Nice of you to join us again."

It sounded so loud in the silence that Arlo fought an urge to shush it while Tristan's face flashed in her mind. What would he say, what would he do if he knew she was down here? But the door swung open, leaking candlelight into the dark belly of her employer's house, and Arlo's reservations vanished like a shadow at dusk as she felt the pull of Lucien's world sink into her.

The room beyond was just as she remembered it, candles flickering as though she'd been gone only moments rather than days. They seemed to pulse in time to the music that wafted down from above, and she fancied she could catch the scent of the night-blooming flowers in Lucien's garden and the feast that was surely laid out for his guests. Every part of her strained to be there again among that dazzling crowd, on the arm of the most handsome of them all, but she paused in the doorway, looking at the dark stain that spread on the stone below her feet.

Perhaps someone had spilled wine? Probably one of Lucien's guests; Tristan never came down to the cellar and he certainly wouldn't allow visitors down here, if he ever had them. But this room was charming and, more important, it was private. How surprised could she really be if it turned out that this was a favorite hideaway for all kinds of intimate encounters away from the crowds in the main house?

She stepped through the door and looked up to find Lucien staring at her from the doorway at the other end of the room.

"Arlo."

Her name was a whisper, a prayer, a spell. She all but melted as he rushed forward to take her hands in his, her skin buzzing everywhere he touched. He lifted her hands to his lips and brushed a kiss against her knuckles, his deep, dark gaze fixed on hers. Surely he'd balk this time at the rough skin of a maid's cracked knuckles, but he lingered over her flesh as he might admire the finest silk, then pulled her closer, planting one long hand against the small of her back as he guided her toward the space that led to the house.

"Come," he said.

She let him steer her, though walking was a struggle as she forced her thighs together to contain the overwhelming urge to squirm under his touch. They emerged into the hallway of the main house, where a party was once again in full swing. The women tonight seemed even more beautiful, the men more charming, and Lucien shone above them all like a cut gem in a crate of rough stones.

Without a word he pulled her into a dance, sweeping her across the floor and around the room. Despite the dynamic, resplendent assembly in much finer attire, Lucien's focus never strayed from her. Arlo arched her back under the press of his hand, painfully conscious of the fact that in her current state of dress, very little separated them. He seemed to know it, too, as he pulled her just a little closer and grinned as he perceived the lack of corset.

"I missed you," he murmured into her ear after several un-interrupted waltzes, sending a powerful shiver straight down to the base of her spine. Arlo swayed into him, letting him hold her scandalously tight.

"Lucien—" she started to reply, though she had no idea what she'd say. Just the sound of his name was enough, and the smile it pulled from his lips.

"Come with me." He grabbed her wrist and pulled her out of the ballroom, past the great hall, past the library whose door set off a twinge in Arlo's heart, past the drawing room with its curling, greasy smoke, and into the conservatory. The plants here were just as lush as the ones outside, the air heavy with moisture and the heady scent of so many flowers packed in together.

One thing Lucien's conservatory *didn't* have was other people. He pulled her through a maze of plants in pots and on long tables until they reached the far end of the room, where a jutting half-circle gave them a view of open land stretching to the horizon under the burning stars.

They could see out, but there was no one out there to see in, and the flourishing greenery inside the room screened them from the view of Lucien's guests. Humid air coaxed curling strands from Arlo's braid to stand in a halo around her head, tickling her neck, ears and forehead while the waning moon perched above them, its glowing crescent the artful smile of a co-conspirator.

Lucien guided Arlo around to face him. His thumb stroked the tender inside of her wrist as a moody waltz drifted from the other end of the hall. The sound melted into the night around them. Arlo thought she might dissolve, too, into a thousand shivers of delight, a feeling that intensified as Lucien caught her around the waist and pulled her close. Her nightgown shifted against her breasts, her hips, caressing every inch of her into a fuller wakefulness than she'd ever felt. He slid one hand under her jaw to brush his fingers against her neck and cheek until her face tilted up toward him.

Over his shoulder, in the tiny space between two plants, Arlo thought she saw something glimmering and dark. A moment later she picked out wine-red lips parting in a grin, a knowing look from dark-rimmed eyes under heavy lashes. Shadows undulated behind the face, more dark dresses and suits and smiles.

Arlo stiffened, fighting the urge to claw at her ribs as the pleasant butterflies turned into spiders. They were *watching*. Her stomach twisted, tight and sour. The women here were so beautiful, so elegant, in gowns of fabrics so fine that Arlo had no frame of reference with which to identify them. How could a maid with no money and chapped hands ever compare?

Unless she was never meant to. Unease fizzed into panic under her skin, and she started to turn away.

Lucien caught her.

"What is it?" He turned, following the line of her gaze, and his eyebrows dipped, drawing low over his dark eyes. He spoke to them in a language that sizzled like water droplets in a hot pan. Arlo couldn't understand the words, though the tone of command was clear. The lurking guests withdrew beyond the open conservatory doors, though the low susurration of their murmurs and laughter still slunk in through the veiling leaves.

Arlo and her host stood mostly alone again. The air between them now crackled with something tense and disjointed.

He put his hand back under her chin, stroking her jaw. She turned her face away, unable to look at him, hating the hot, ashamed tears that threatened to overflow. Coming back here had been a mistake. She should have kept that one magical night as a perfect memory and quit while she was ahead.

"Arlo," he said, pleading. He stroked the flesh on the underside of her jaw, from the hollow under her ear to just behind her chin, a slow back-and-forth movement that set her quivering even though it no longer felt quite right.

She swallowed hard, the high buttoned neck of her nightgown suddenly too tight to contain the lump in her throat.

"Tell me what's wrong."

A ragged sigh shuddered its way down her throat as she drew breath and the courage to speak, though she held her words until she was almost sure she could say them without sobbing.

"This has been...the most magical experience of my life," she started, her gaze fixed on the subtle glimmer in the cloth of his pristine shirt. "But I—"

"Stop, I beg you," he said, interrupting her. "You sound like you're saying goodbye."

Arlo looked up into his dark eyes. They were huge and shining, otherworldly in the shadowy depths of this miniature jungle.

"What else is there for me to say?" she whispered, her voice catching on every new word. "This world, this place...I don't belong here. You have all those beautiful women waiting on your every word." She plucked at her wrapper with a tearful scoff. "What could I possibly offer you, compared to them?"

His gaze swallowed hers as he drew her close, lining her up so that every part of her body pressed against him and his lips were mere inches from hers.

"Everything," he said, his breath on her cheek almost as hot as the heavy humidity that stuck to her skin. "Arlo, I want you *because* you're not like them. You're so vibrant." He ran one hand down her side, outlining each rib on his way to her waist in a way that made her gasp. "So alive." His other fingers still stroked her neck, but now they went lower, dipping under the collar of her nightgown, pulling the fabric away from her to touch the arching flesh of her neck. She closed her eyes and tipped her head back, lips parted slightly as her breath came in shuddery little pants.

"Your guests—"

They hadn't drawn any closer, but Arlo could still sense them just beyond sight.

"Say the word," he breathed, leaning in so his lips brushed the front edge of her ear. "And I'll send them away."

Arlo startled a little at that, pulling back to meet his gaze.

"Why?" she asked. "They were here first. They were invited. I just...wandered in."

"Don't belittle yourself." He ran a hand up her back, fingers tracing her spine. "My guests are like shadows." His hand spread across the back of her neck, tangling in her golden hair. "But you are light." He leaned in, brushing his lips against the flesh of her neck. "Life."

Arlo fought to keep her wits while her knees gelled and her hips squirmed. As though she could get any closer. It was impossible to think with his hands on her body, his breath on her cheek, his voice ringing inside her head.

He'd said he would send the watchers away if she asked. Did that mean he wouldn't, if she didn't? She'd never known a man... intimately... and the thought of a room full of elegant, worldly guests watching whatever might happen next sent Arlo's foot back in a reflexive step.

The curve of her hip bumped into the short end of a long table covered in potted plants whose broad, glossy leaves rustled together in what sounded like a passionate exhalation. Arlo echoed them as Lucien pressed more firmly into her, pinning her between himself and the table.

The watchers tittered, yanking Arlo's mind back from the want that threatened to drown it. Who were these people? How did they get down here; what were they all doing in this strange, mirrored version of the house above?

Her questions died unasked as Lucien flicked his tongue into the hollow just below her ear. She closed her eyes, her head falling back as he dragged his mouth down to her collarbone.

"You belong here," he said, dropping the whispered words like promises on her skin. "With me." His hands all but raised sparks as they wandered over her arms, her back, the curve of her breasts in a teasing trail. Arlo wanted nothing more than to believe him, to have a place here.

But Lucien and his guests were so elegant, so worldly, so obviously accustomed to wealth and excess, while she...

"I'm just a maid." Her protest came out as a whimper, a whisper, a tremulous admission laced with something like shame.

He shook his head. "You are so much more than that." He pressed his lips to her forehead, then pulled back to meet her gaze again before kissing her cheek, dangerously close to the corner of her mouth. "You are a *queen.*" One finger under Arlo's chin tipped her head back, and his next kiss was on the tender flesh below the corner of her jaw. "You can't speak of leaving." He drew back again, gliding both his hands across her goose-pimpled skin until he cradled her face between them and locked his gaze with hers. "Stay with me," he said. "Always."

Arlo's eyes flashed wide, even as she felt them wanting to roll back with pleasure.

"Lucien," she said, but then his mouth was on hers, one hand tangled in her hair, the other crushing her body to him. She kissed him back, moaning with all the hungry need that had consumed her every step since the last time she was here. He tasted of smoke and sugar, of secrets and the scent of earth.

She slid her hands up the hard planes of his chest and over his shoulders to lock behind his neck under the silky fall of his snow-white hair. His answering sigh nearly undid her. She threw herself deeper into the kiss, pressing herself against him so hard it was almost as though she was trying to climb him, feeling and not caring as one of his hands came around to work at the buttons of her collar while the other splayed over her back, strong and possessive. His hand was electric on her bare skin, sliding over her collarbone to clutch at her shoulder and back before dipping dangerously close to her breasts.

"I want you to be mine alone." He breathed the words into her mouth, never ceasing to kiss her. "Promise me you'll give me your forever."

"Forever," Arlo echoed, but it curled with the edge of a question. Forever was...well, it was forever, wasn't it? Something about this world felt so separate, so strange, that Arlo knew without knowing *how* she knew that staying here would mean staying *truly*. She would never see the other world again.

She would never see Tristan again.

She shook her head.

What did that matter?

Lucien was just as handsome as Tristan—more, in fact—but he was also gallant. Sensual. He paid attention to her in a way no one ever had, and made her feel in real life things she'd only ever felt in her dreams before now.

But...forever.

He seemed to catch her uncertainty, letting his lips linger for one last moment on hers before backing up just enough to look her in the eyes again.

"I know we hardly know each other," he said. He still held her tight, one hand on her back, her body pressed to his as close as possible while they were still dressed. Arlo flushed with embarrassment at how far across the line she was with a man she'd only just met, though she didn't withdraw her arms from around his neck. "There's something special about you, Arlo." He landed a lingering kiss on the place where her pulse pounded in her neck and whispered, "I can feel it."

Why not? Tristan's question echoed in her memory. *I did.*

Stars burst behind Arlo's eyes at the whip-crack force of the recollection. Why was she thinking of that *now,* with this beautiful man in front of her, offering her a future most women could only dream of? She worked her throat, but words deserted her.

Lucien straightened up and met her gaze again. After a long, searching glance, he sighed. Disappointment tugged down the corners of his mouth as he let his arms fall away from her and took a step back. A complex longing eddied in the space between them, her yearning for him and the magic of his world warring with an equal desire to go back. To go home.

He shook his head, looking gracious even under the new pall of melancholy that seemed to overtake him.

"It's near morning," he said, "and I can tell you're not certain."

Heat rushed up from Arlo's belly as Lucien took his hands away. Her skin felt cool, bereft, in all the places his touch had been. Her neck flushed; her head swam.

"I—" she started, not knowing what she'd say, but he held up a hand to stop her.

"Come on." He drew her back the way they'd come, out through the plants into the house. It was still packed with guests, though many had spilled out of the ballroom to cluster in twos and threes along the hallway. Some talked, some kissed, and others just sat, looking dazed from too much wine.

Lucien guided her past all of them, his arm a protective shield around her shoulders, until they'd come all the way across the house and back down into the candlelit room that marked the threshold between their worlds.

He held her by the shoulders, his gaze searching her eyes.

"I want you more than you can possibly know," he said. "But if you stay with me, it must be of your own free will. So I'll send you back tonight, and force myself to be content with waiting." He took her hand in his and held it against his cheek, leaning into it like a cat. His closed eyelids were as thin as bone china, shot with an elegant tracery of delicate blue veins. "If you return once more, it means you accept my proposal."

Faster than Arlo could process the motion, he pulled her close again, kissing her as he walked her backwards toward the opening door. She could barely breathe, but as long as his lips were on hers, perhaps she didn't need to. When she stood just past the threshold, chest heaving, he pulled away and held her gaze again.

"Come back to me, Arlo. Forever."

All she could see with the light behind him was the silhouette of his exquisite form, the tips of his gleaming shoes resting just shy of the dark stain on the threshold.

"Good night."

The door shut between them, its closing like a funeral knell, though the sound of the latch barely dented the silence. Arlo flung herself against it, feeling the cool wood against her cheek, her hands, and the hot tears cutting streaks down her face.

"Good night," she whispered, standing there for a long moment before finally turning and making the eternal climb back to her lonely room.

17

AT THE TOP OF the stairs, Arlo swore she could still hear the party happening far below her, as if nights in Lucien's dizzying world never ended. Her mouth tingled with the memory of his kiss, the taste of his mouth, hot and insistent.

Forever.

He wanted her, forever. She leaned against her door, eyes fluttering closed in a half-swoon as she recalled his words. His question. His *proposal.* She touched her neck, mimicking the way he'd brushed his fingertips against her skin, their bare flesh electric with wanting.

He could have had her. She flushed to think it, but if he'd pushed her up against the wall or onto one of those long tables, she wasn't sure she'd have been able to say no.

She wasn't sure she'd have wanted to.

She stood there for what felt like only a few moments before dawn announced itself through her window, reminding her that no matter how she'd spent her night, Calderwood still had work to be done. Besides, she hardly wanted a repeat of her last "morning after." She had no doubt that Mrs. Hollister would complain to Mister Calder if it happened again. He'd said she was in no danger of losing her place, but the housekeeper had been here longer and clearly had a level of trust with Mister Calder that Arlo couldn't ignore.

She closed her eyes and took in a deep, slow breath, sighing it out through her nose before unbuttoning her nightgown to get dressed for the day. The top three buttons were already open, a fact that sent her into another flash of ecstatic reverie as she thought of who'd unfastened them, his hands burning on her skin, his breath stirring the tiny, fine hairs on her cheek.

She peeled off her wrapper, pulled the half-buttoned night-gown over her head and flung them both to lie across the foot of her bed. Then she slipped into a fresh chemise and drawers, fastening her corset closed and re-lacing it just a little tighter before putting on her petticoat and corset cover.

After her scandalous state of undress last night, the act of donning her everyday layers felt a little like putting on armor. And well she might need it, facing another day of work with an entire night's wakefulness behind it. At least, compared to the factory, Arlo's workdays at Calderwood were blessedly short. Mister Calder didn't need her for anything beyond cleaning up after supper, so she could look forward to an early bedtime.

The one good thing about not having slept was that she beat Mrs. Hollister's arrival by nearly an hour, which meant she was able to eat in peace without the housekeeper breathing down her neck to start scrubbing or brushing or sweeping something.

Breakfast was eggs, as usual. She cooked a portion for Mister Calder, too, along with toast and tea. She'd left *Frankenstein* upstairs, but perhaps he'd still be willing to discuss the book if he wasn't in the middle of something.

A knock on the library door got no answer, and Arlo pushed her tentative way in to find the desk chair empty.

"Mister Calder?" She peeked around into the corners she couldn't see from the door, but he wasn't anywhere. She left the tray on the desk with its plates covered and exited the library, habit taking her steps toward the kitchen before she stopped, one hand to the wall in a moment of vertigo.

It took several moments for her to realize that her disorientation wasn't from lack of sleep, but rather from a feeling of having been cut adrift, abandoned in a familiar place that had turned vaguely sinister.

Another moment's thought revealed the cause—Calderwood was *backwards*. The habit of several weeks had taught Arlo's feet the way around the house without her having to think about it, but her mind was in upheaval as it kept trying to walk the mirrored layout of Lucien's halls.

Which had come first? Had some Calder ancestor admired Lucien's unorthodox home and built another? Or had the Calders come first, leaving Lucien to copy their construction?

Perhaps it didn't matter. But the thought of Lucien brought Arlo back into his arms, just for a moment, and from the corner of her eye something flickered, a movement just enough to attract her attention. She turned and faced the entry to the conservatory, gazing at the door with a hard swallow.

Countless glass panels winked in the dawn light, squares and rectangles and triangles bounded by cast iron framing. Long tables stood empty of everything but the barest smudges of dirt, while spiders made homes in stacks of pots piled against the eastern wall at the back of the house. Arlo ran her fingertips lightly along one table as she followed her footsteps from last night.

This was where Lucien had brought her, in his world. Where he'd praised her, kissed her, called her a queen. She could still feel his hands and the heat of his mouth on her skin. It was so immediate, so real she could almost taste it, while outside the early mist turned the hills into something like a dream.

What was more real? This isolated house with its solitary occupant, or a rich man who threw parties in his lush, elegant estate?

What if Lucien's world was the real one, and this was the dream?

Some of the low clouds swirled and Arlo saw a shadowy figure walking out over the hills toward the dawn, his unbound curls tumbling softly in the breeze. There was no horizon, nothing sure in the distance. Only the hills stretching into the mist, with their single occupant. Arlo's heart squeezed with a sense of vast loneliness as she watched him make his way toward the house, followed by a tenderness that surprised her.

After last night, she should have thought of Tristan only in terms of how best to avoid him, to get back down through the door to her handsome prince. What was it about him that still vexed her so, even in the face of Lucien's attention? How could she think of him while standing in the very spot where Lucien had asked her to spend the rest of her life with him?

Forever.

At that moment, Tristan looked up. Even from here, Arlo fancied she could see the smoldering blue of his eyes. She ducked behind the stacked pots, breathing hard. Had he seen her? She bit the tip of her tongue. Stupid. *Stupid.* What was she hiding from? She was a servant and this place needed cleaning, even if he'd never asked her to do it and Mrs. Hollister had never listed it among their duties.

At some point, heavy pots had been stacked too high against the glass on this side. A stress crack in the pane where they leaned split Arlo's reflection and made the dark circles under her sleepless eyes look positively bruised. She could almost hear the panel's slick, whining creak under the pots' weight until the terrace door opened, obliterating the quiet.

She stood, brushing down her skirts and straightening her shoulders before she did her best to stride out of the conservatory and into the hallway outside the library. He met her where the halls intersected, and Arlo had a flash of memory: a swoon, his bare arms around her, his gaze searching her face with an expression she couldn't begin to read.

Today, she stood her ground.

"Good morning, Mister Calder," she said, with a curtsy.

He stared at her for a long moment, as if he wasn't sure what to say.

"Did you have a pleasant walk?" she asked.

"Ah—yes," he said, nearly stuttering. "Did...is everything well? With you?" He brushed his dark hair away from his face with one hand, while gesturing at her with the other, a concerned look creeping into the corners of his eyes and the set of his brow. "You look—"

"Quite well," she told him, clipped and efficient. "Thank you. Your breakfast is already inside."

He glanced past her through the open library door, then started that way before he stopped and turned.

"What were you doing?" he blurted with a glance toward the conservatory.

Arlo's head jerked slightly back. Then he *had* seen her.

She glanced over her shoulder. "I was just wondering about the conservatory."

"Oh." Tristan wiped with his fingers at a fine sheen of sweat that had collected along his hairline in the warm, humid morning. Arlo pulled a handkerchief from her pocket and handed it to him, then cursed herself for such a familiar act, though he took it without comment and dabbed at his skin. Then he held the plain linen square in an awkward fist, as if unsure whether to give it back.

"Do you..." he asked, wringing it in both hands. "Do you like plants?"

"Do you?" she countered, remembering Lucien's vibrant garden and how much she'd liked what had happened among the plants in his house. As soon as the words left her mouth, Arlo cursed herself an idiot. Tristan had told her he wanted her here, but she'd never been so rude to him. What if he changed his mind? She took a deep breath and called up the way she'd speak to him if Mrs. Hollister were watching. When she continued, her tone was level, demure.

"That is, it's such a beautiful room. It's a bit sad to see it standing empty."

A sad smile tugged at one side of Tristan's mouth.

"No different from the rest of the house," he said. "Except for me, and...and you." He paused, then cleared his throat and strode past her, his hair falling in a curtain between them so she couldn't see his eyes, though she thought for certain she'd caught just the edge of a panicked look before he passed. "You said breakfast is already on?"

"I did," she said, though he was already closing the door. Arlo stood there looking at it for a long moment before she realized he still had her handkerchief. Well, nothing for it now. Perhaps she could get it back when she returned his book.

She met Mrs. Hollister as the older woman was coming in for the day, informed her that Mister Calder had already eaten, and gathered her tools for another day of work. Though her sleepless night wore on her, Arlo's churning thoughts more than made up the difference in energy while she worked.

They assaulted her in a series of images: Lucien's face against the backdrop of lush greenery.

Tristan alone in the mist.

Lucien's hands on her face, her neck, her waist.

The brush of Tristan's fingertips against hers as he'd taken her handkerchief, and the way he couldn't quite look at her.

She scrubbed at the corners of the hall, attacking every mote of dust that dared to defy her. Lucien had kissed her. Tristan had winked.

Lucien had proposed. Tristan ran hot-and-cold enough to drive her mad.

So what was it about her employer that was making her second-guess the desire to throw herself through that snake-door one last time and be with a man who so clearly wanted her?

She brought the full dustpan out into the courtyard and tossed its contents into the air, letting them float away on the breeze. The mist was gone, the hills verdant under the summer sun, though the dense, heavy quality in the air promised a storm later on. Tristan's hills seemed to roll on forever, even without the morning brume to obscure the horizon, nothing to interrupt the view but an occasional solitary bird against the vivid blue sky.

The reclusiveness of this place hit her again as she thought of its mirror below. Lucien had a house full of beautiful, stylish, distinguished people. He had wealth and taste and a thriving social life. Tristan had no one. He lived here all alone except for the ghosts of a past he couldn't release.

Arlo found herself wishing she knew how to free him. For all his awkwardness, Tristan had welcomed her. He'd opened his home and his library; he'd shared a love of books with Arlo that made her feel like she was part of something, even if it was just the two of them in a handful of stolen moments.

In Lucien's arms the rest of the world melted away. But could she ever really be *part* of that world? Could she ever be one of those women? He'd said he wanted her because she wasn't like them, but to become his she would need to move in his circles. Entertain his guests.

Arlo wondered what kind of guests Tristan would welcome, if he ever found himself willing or wanting to do so. Would they be fancy people? Stuffy people? Or might he host bookish people, scholars and poets and guests from far-off, to fill his library with stories and his home with laughter? What might Calderwood be like, brimful of so much conversation that the guests would have to interrupt each other to get a chance to participate?

Her gut twisted as she realized that *that* was exactly what had been bothering her.

Interruption.

Nearly every time Arlo had tried to speak, Lucien had smothered her words with a touch, a kiss, or words of his own.

She knew how the world worked; marriages were arranged more often than not, and love developed over time or not at all. She wasn't the first maid that a rich man wanted to possess, and she wouldn't be the last. Granted, she didn't think the men who diddled maids on the side did so while talking about *forever* or calling them queens.

Yet, for all his apparent adoration, Lucien didn't seem to think that Arlo might have anything to say. He'd pleaded most ardently for Arlo to become his, but he'd never actually asked *her* feelings on the matter.

It was Tristan who listened to her. Tristan who loaned her books and wanted her opinion. He asked her questions. He left her spaces to have a say, and seemed comfortable to wait on her answers.

Arlo watched the last of the dust motes glitter in the sun, unsure of how long she'd stood there before the courtyard door opened.

"Miss Reade," the housekeeper barked.

Arlo blinked. "Coming."

She carried the dustpan back inside and laid it away with the broom, picking up a polishing cloth and working her way up the banister of the grand staircase. When she reached the top of the stairs she saw Tristan's sheets heaped in a pile on the floor outside his room. She collected those and brought them to the dumbwaiter shaft, pulling the car to the upper floor and shoving in both sheets and polishing supplies before fetching new linens from the nearby closet and placing them on the table outside his suite.

As she started to walk away, a tendril of whisper curled around her ear, making her pause. She reached for the doorknob, just to see, but it was locked as always and didn't budge under her hand. She sidled up closer to the door, pressing one ear against it.

For a moment, she'd thought...but no, he wasn't in there. Not during the day. She was being silly, and besides, even if he *was* in there, he wouldn't let her in. He'd made it clear early on that no one was welcome in his rooms, and despite the little ways he'd opened up since then, that rule hadn't changed.

Then the door opened. Arlo jumped back before Tristan, who'd come out with his head down, nearly walked into her.

"Oh!" he said, pulling himself short. "Miss Reade?" In the dark of the hallway his face was especially striking, its almost-gaunt lines cutting sharp angles between shadow and the steely, moody light that reached past the portion of upstairs hallway open to the foyer and its tall windows. Arlo stared at him, utterly captivated and unable to say why until she realized that in this atmospheric half-light, he almost reminded her of Lucien. The illusion dissipated as he stepped forward, shutting the door behind him, though he never took his gaze off her as he did.

Arlo shook her head as if to clear away cobwebs and bobbed a belated curtsy.

"New bedding, sir."

"Oh." Tristan looked over his shoulder at the neat pile of sheets on the table. "Yes. Thank you." He pulled a small watch from his pocket and glanced at the hallway clock, then wound a dial and replaced the timepiece.

Arlo watched his hands the whole time, hypnotized by their movement, wondering what they might feel like dipping below the line of her collar, up her thigh, to—

"Good morning, Mister Calder," she said, barely containing the strangle in her voice, bobbing again and turning without even a glance at him back toward the dumbwaiter. She slid open the wall panel and slipped inside, looking back only when she was mostly behind the wall, but Tristan had already gone. Foolish, foolish. What was *wrong* with her? What did she expect to happen?

A few tugs on the rope slid the dumbwaiter car back down to the house's main level. Arlo met it downstairs a moment later.

"What's this?" Mrs. Hollister asked.

"He left sheets outside his room."

The housekeeper's mouth tightened. "It's not laundry day."

Arlo shrugged. "Perhaps he forgot?"

Mrs. Hollister regarded Arlo closely, narrow-eyed and pinch-mouthed. Arlo nearly quailed under the stare, until she realized what it meant and then almost ruined the moment by laughing out loud. Did Mrs. Hollister think that Mister Calder had occasion to change his sheets off-cycle because of *her*? The very idea of her, making a mess of Mister Calder's sheets.

The very idea of her, making a mess of Mister Calder's sheets...

Arlo poked her tongue at a corner of her mouth, her eyes glazing as the enticing image she'd just shaken off started to form again in her mind, then bit it hard enough to taste blood as she realized she was starting to daydream right in front of her superior. She snatched the rag and bottle of polish from the dumbwaiter and put them in their places before washing her hands and pushing a few stray tendrils of hair back under her cap.

Maybe it was best if she avoided the other end of the house as much as possible today.

It wasn't because of Mrs. Hollister's misplaced judgment. At least, not exactly. There was just too much going on in Arlo's head right now. She needed to think. She needed to *sleep*. She needed to decide what to do about Lucien's proposal with a level head, a state which seemed impossible to achieve when she was anywhere close to her employer.

The humid air would make sweeping and carpet-cleaning a sticky, useless job, so Arlo retreated to the kitchen and then the scullery where she scrubbed and scoured until her body ached and her mind went numb with the repetitive motion.

It worked for several hours, and Arlo thought she might get away with not seeing Tristan for the rest of the day. But the sky had other plans.

"I'm off," Mrs. Hollister said, bustling into the scullery with her hat already pinned in place.

Arlo drew her hands out of the small scullery stove she'd been scrubbing and sat back on her heels, wiping sweat and stray hairs from her forehead with the back of one wrist as she looked up.

"So early?"

"To beat the rain." Thunder punctuated the statement, a low, creeping rumble in the distance. "His supper tray is already set, except for the food warming in the kitchen." The woman glanced over Arlo from head to toe. "Clean up before you deliver it."

"Of course." Arlo bowed a little, the best she could do for a curtsy while kneeling. "Good evening, then."

"Good evening." Mrs. Hollister walked out through the lobby door just outside the scullery. Arlo drew herself up to her feet and watched through the window as the woman's skirt whipped in the rising wind.

She sighed, licked her lips, tasted soot, and rubbed her mouth only to realize she'd probably just made it worse.

When she went upstairs to wash and tidy herself up, the small mirror in the tiny water closet confirmed the extent of her grubbiness. She considered *not* washing—surely she wouldn't be able to entertain carnal or even romantic daydreams knowing she looked like a runaway chimney sweep—but it would hardly be appropriate to deliver food in this state.

She went to her room and dipped her face cloth in the basin, rubbing away the grime until her face was rosy and her hands were clean. The apron...well, that was a lost cause for now. She untied it and carried it downstairs and out to the courtyard, pinning it to the drying line and assailing it first with a wire beater and then with a brush.

In the soupy air, it was a wonder that droplets of water didn't collect on the fine hairs of Arlo's arms just from standing outside. If it was going to rain as much as those clouds seemed to promise, perhaps a good soaking would take care of the rest.

If not, though, she could always wash her apron with her employer's sheets, an entanglement that sent her mind down wanton pathways once again until she forcibly curtailed them.

Sleep. She would deliver his dinner, and then go straight to bed.

Arlo brushed down her dress, then rinsed her hands and face again at the pump and used her wet fingers to smooth rogue curlicues back under her cap, cursing the close, heavy air. She removed his supper from its pan and plated it, covered the dishes, and carried the tray to the library.

A few deep breaths fortified her before entering. She could do this.

She could do this.

When she opened the door he was already looking toward it, toward her, as if he'd been waiting. But he averted his gaze as soon as she stepped through, fidgeting with something on the desk that he slid under a stack of papers as she got closer. She could just see the corner of an image poking out from beneath the pile and wondered if it was the same picture she'd caught him looking at before.

"Good evening, Mister Calder." Arlo set the tray down in front of him and turned to leave.

"Wait, Miss Reade."

Arlo suppressed an inward cringe, schooling her face to careful blankness before turning back to face him.

"Sir?"

"I just...have you finished it yet? *Frankenstein,* I mean." He drummed a restless non-pattern against the edge of his desk. "I was hoping to...to hear your thoughts."

Arlo blinked a few times, fighting the urge to let her mouth fall open. Now? He wanted to talk about this *now?*

"Would you like to sit?" He gestured toward the same upholstered ottoman stool he'd offered last time.

Arlo eyed it. If she sat down, could she stay awake? But she couldn't just walk away from her employer, not after he'd asked her a direct question. She sank onto the seat, hiding her hands under her skirt so she could pinch her thigh hard, the pain helping her to focus what little wakefulness she had left. But even that only took the barest edge off her swimming, looping thoughts.

Where to start?

"I think he was very lonely."

Tristan in this house. Tristan in the mist. Tristan talking to himself, locked away in his rooms. Arlo caught herself just in time and added, "The monster, I mean. Victor may have been lonely, too, but I think his was more a question of wanting to create something. To control. To play at being God. But he was the master of an empty house."

Tristan made a sort of strangled half-sound. Arlo looked up at him, then realized what she'd said and jerked into a nervous prattle to hurry the moment along.

"I mean, the creature he'd built and given life to didn't worship him. It was all for nothing. He didn't want a real person, not a human being with flesh and desires and..."

Damn it, damn it, get away from that train of thought.

"And dreams. He just wanted a living automaton he could show off at parties. But the creature was more than Victor planned for..."

Further words pressed against her tongue, burning the back of her lips. On a bright afternoon, she wouldn't have said them. But there was something about the quality of the light right now, the stormy sky leaching its pewter haze into the silence. It gave the moment a dreamy, underwater quality, and Arlo found she couldn't stop the next thought from coming.

"And there's no controlling the human heart."

The words fell into a soft haze of sound, a patter that took Arlo a moment to place as raindrops hitting the roof and the ground outside. It sounded almost like the whispers from the door, the hushed conversations of Lucien's constant guests. She nearly thought she could hear the music from the ballroom while the musicians played on, waiting for her to return.

Then lightning flashed, a brilliant burst that illuminated the library and drew her back to reality. She looked at Tristan to find him staring at her, fingers soft against his jaw, eyes bright.

"Sir?" she asked, at the same time he said "Miss Reade."

Arlo pulled back, waiting.

"Miss Reade," he said again. "I can't help but notice that you ...that is...I want you to understand that..." He trailed off, looking frustrated. "Blast it, I..."

He looked away, and Arlo followed the line of his gaze to the wall above the fireplace, where she'd once thought a safe of some kind might be hidden. His attention lingered there, gaze fixed as he continued speaking.

"Miss Reade, I've already told you that while you're in my house you're my responsibility. And that's still true, but it's..." He rapped his knuckles on the desk, a hollow thunk in the gloaming, then steepled his hands and pressed them against his lips before he continued, gesturing vaguely.

"I hope you won't think it too forward if I tell you that, despite our differences in situation, I've come to think of you as...as a friend. I've enjoyed our conversations." He took a deep, steadying breath, and Arlo noticed his hands trembling a little on the desktop. He stood, pushing away from his seat to pace the carpet behind his desk.

"You've," he said, drawing vague patterns in the air with his hands. "You've brought a light to this house, Miss Reade, and the fact is, I can't stand the idea of you being hurt or ill because of me and my self-imposed exile."

His back was turned by now, and this time, when her mouth wanted to open, she didn't stop it. She gaped at him, all coherent thought stopped. Above them, around them, the rain roared down in sheets, spattering in huge drops against the windows and the conservatory roof while thunder cracked and rolled above them.

Had she already fallen asleep? Was this some kind of dream?

She stood up on shaky legs, using the edge of the desk to brace herself.

He turned, hearing the motion, and the raw, rapt expression in his gleaming eyes almost made her sit down again. She'd had her share of lascivious fantasies involving her employer, fair enough. But those had been private. Secret. One-way castles in the air that she knew could never come to be.

At least, not until now, when the look in his eyes told another story altogether.

Arlo's heart flung itself into her throat, her back and shoulders erupting with shivers in a strange mixture of terror and cautious, fledgling ecstasy.

"Your supper will get cold," she whispered.

He glanced at the tray, then walked right past it and took her hands in his.

"Miss Reade. This lonely old house is no place for a woman of your intelligence to waste away on menial tasks." Arlo blinked, fast, and he went on. "I'm not sending you away. That discussion has been had. What I mean is that...surely you must know that I..."

Her blood fizzed as he pressed his thumbs into the backs of her hands, rubbing so she felt his touch pass over each ridge of tendon and bone.

She tried to speak and found she couldn't. Only a breath came out, wordless and thin with distress. When she finally managed it, her voice barely dented the sound of the rain.

"Mister Calder?"

He lifted one hand to her jaw, making her sigh as he brushed with barely more than a feather's weight over her skin.

"Miss Reade," he said, his pupils blown huge in the dimly-lit room. "May I kiss you?"

Time hung still as Arlo tried to make sense of what he'd just said. What he'd just *asked*.

"Sir," she began, half expecting him to cut her off, to kiss her like Lucien had done.

But he waited, watching her.

She drew her hands away from his and pressed them to her mouth, her wide eyes locked on his with a heady mixture of shock and all the desire she'd ever felt for him humming in her body, building like a wave that could destroy whole coastlines. His eyes were an answering ocean, and she saw the moment he withdrew before he took a step back.

"Please forgive me." He pressed a palm against his jaw and dragging it back toward his ear in an embarrassed gesture. "I don't know what came over me, I...we never have to speak of this again, if you don't want to. I apologize if I startled you."

Arlo blinked at him, then curtsied and walked away without a word. She'd just reached the door when he stopped her.

"Would it," he began.

She didn't turn, but stayed to listen.

"Would it be too much to ask you to think about what I said?"

She stood perfectly still.

"Ah," he said, after a long silence. "Well. Good night, then."

Arlo curtsied again without turning back and walked away on wooden legs until she reached her room. She shot the bolt, then removed her dress and corset with the most mechanical gestures, letting them fall to the floor as she slipped between the damp sheets with her hair still pinned in whatever was left of her bun after a dank, sticky day.

Rain spattered in through the narrow gap in the partially-open casement while she lay curled in her narrow bed, hugging her knees.

Her breaths came fast, then ragged, then heavy with astonished sobs as the impossible reality of Tristan's words and the look in his eyes replayed over and over in her head. She had no sense of the passage of time, only of the rain's heavy drum tapering to a gentle hissing tap as her breathing evened and the tears dried on her cheeks.

The next thing she knew, it was morning.

18

A FULL NIGHT OF sleep was balm to Arlo's soul, but it did less than she'd hoped it would for her complexion. Plum-deep shadows still lurked under her eyes, which were now red-rimmed and puffy from crying herself to sleep.

Groaning, she splashed her face with cool water at the basin and used gentle fingertips to massage the delicate skin. Her hair was a wreck, too, curse this humidity. She unpinned the long coil of braid and worked her fingers through the strands until it hung loose over her shoulders like a stray beam of sunshine.

You've brought a light to this house.

She swallowed hard and pressed cool hands to the sides of her warming face. Had he really said that? Had he really held her hands, and asked if he could kiss her? She closed her eyes and shook her head, scrunching her face up with a disbelieving smile. Hair tickled the back of her neck, reminding her of his fingers.

Of Lucien's fingers.

Oh, God. Lucien was still waiting for her. And though her body was rested, her mind still whirred with too many thoughts mashed together in a constant, panicked litany, no space for breath between them.

Lucien wanted her. *Tristan* wanted her.

What did *she* want?

Arlo had made a decision to leave the city because she knew what she *didn't* want. The men who'd approached her had done so only when she was at her most vulnerable: newly orphaned, with no family to speak of and nowhere to go. They'd assumed she wanted someone to protect her, to provide for her, though she was smart enough to know the intentions lurking under their words. A wife's debt might be to her husband, but she dared to dream of a relationship that was more than transactional. After all, her parents had found it. But no one who propositioned her the way those men had done were doing it for love.

But now...she didn't know. God help her, she truly didn't know.

Tristan had occupied every corner of her mind before she'd met Lucien. But she couldn't shake the desire to see her mysterious paramour again. Something about him drew her, like a cord in her heart pulling her ever downward. The only problem was, if she went back again, she was as good as accepting his proposal.

She wasn't sure she could do that now.

Come, the door whispered in her feet, in her mind, in the remembered taste of lips and cherries. She slipped her corset over the drawers and chemise she'd slept in, and tugged on its laces. The snug embrace echoed the feel of Lucien's hands crushing her ribs with the force of his need. *Come.*

"Stop it," Arlo whispered, closing her eyes. She brushed out her hair and braided it again, coiling the long plait around her head. She hadn't even finished driving in the last pin before she saw that several unruly curl-ends had already flicked their way free. With a disgusted grunt, she turned away from the mirror and went to the window. When a peek outside proved the road clear of Mrs. Hollister's advance, Arlo wrenched the casement wide and thrust her maid's dress out into the air, giving it a few hearty shakes to relax any wrinkles before putting it on.

Her apron still flapped on the line in the courtyard where she'd left it yesterday, waving a gentle reminder at her. She hurried down to get it and grimaced a little as she wrung out what felt like all the water from last night's storm. There was no way she could wear it today. Best to leave it here and let the sun do its work.

She didn't really *need* to wear it anyway—most maids didn't, she knew, unless they were serving a meal. And Mister Calder hadn't seemed to notice its lack. Part of her thought she really should see about getting another dress, a good working dress, so she wasn't wearing her fine uniform all the time. Then again...

This lonely old house is no place for a woman of your intelligence to waste away on menial tasks.

The memory of his words brought a wry smile to her lips as she rolled her eyes. How like a wealthy man to assume that a working-class girl could haul up her bootstraps and do whatever she liked in the world, just because *he* had that option. Still, she knew he'd meant it as a compliment, and shame burned somewhere under her ribs at the way she'd spoken to him.

He didn't deserve that. Arlo's mind flashed back to that moment: his wide eyes, his warm hands reaching for hers.

May I kiss you?

She shook her head and slapped both her cheeks. Mrs. Hollister would be in any minute, and Arlo didn't want to be caught daydreaming. She couldn't help but notice that the housekeeper had been shorter with her lately, more likely to snipe than praise.

Arlo knew exactly when it had started, too—the morning after she'd spent her first night with Lucien and failed to wake up on time.

She'd thought it was just that the housekeeper wanted to shame her for her apparent lack of work ethic. But yesterday, the woman had all but accused her of canoodling with their employer, and the suspicion in her eyes had told Arlo all she needed to know about the housekeeper's feelings on that point.

She was protective of him, Arlo could see that. He was all alone in this house, with no one but Mrs. Hollister to look after him. Arlo blushed to think what the woman would say if she'd seen her precious Master Tristan last night, then slapped herself again.

"Are you all right?"

Arlo darted her glance toward the open courtyard door to see the housekeeper watching with quizzical, leery eyebrows. She cleared her throat, straightened her shoulders and fixed a pleasant, neutral expression on her face.

"Yes, thank you. Good morning, Mrs. Hollister."

The woman only nodded and brushed past her. It was all Arlo could do not to giggle at the sour expression on her face. Her mirth didn't last, though. She collected a bucket and mop and went to clean the floor in the great hall, though no one had walked there for days. Each step she took put her in mind of the poor Little Mermaid, who'd sacrificed her tail to walk on land for a chance to win her prince, yet was made to feel the whole time as though she was walking on sharp knives.

Arlo's frenetic heart beat itself hard enough to leave her chest, anticipating Tristan around any and every corner.

She didn't know what would be worse—finding out that he'd meant everything he'd said last night, or finding out that he hadn't—and wasn't sure she could bear it either way. Maybe it would be best to get out of this house, to never find out, to keep Tristan as a dream in her most secret heart.

But did that mean going to Lucien?

Could she live always underneath Tristan's house, so close yet a world away, knowing he was near and never being able to see him again? Would Lucien wash her mind of her past, fill her with so much gaiety and excess that she'd never think of her old life again?

The faintest strain of music coiled up from below her, as if to reinforce the reminder that she had a decision to make.

Come. The voices beckoned as she passed the hall to the cellar door. *Come.*

Arlo did her best to ignore it, though Lucien's allure was a barbed thing, drawing her ever back, ever toward him. She avoided Tristan, too; Mrs. Hollister's suspicion was at least useful for that. The woman seemed insistent on handling anything that needed doing in the library today, from delivering meals to brushing the carpets.

Arlo was happy to let her do it. The longer she could avoid Tristan, the longer she could preserve the perfect memory of his confession. If she never spoke to him again, she'd never have to know if his mind had changed.

By the end of the day she was ragged. Part of her wanted to go straight to bed, but Saturday was bath night, and she didn't want to miss her one opportunity to thoroughly wash, especially not after a week that involved cleaning an oven and climbing up and down a dumbwaiter shaft.

She waited until Mrs. Hollister had left the house, then put on the kettle and a large pot of water to boil while she filled a bucket from the pump outside and hauled it inside to the dumbwaiter.

Then she dragged herself upstairs, hauled the dumbwaiter car to her floor, and dumped the full bucket into the shallow tub in the upstairs washroom. She repeated that process three times before the pot boiled, and then she hoisted that, too, all for the dubious pleasure of sitting in a lukewarm hip bath.

When she was done, she dumped out the water, changed into her nightgown and wrapper and sat by the window in her room, combing her long hair out with her fingers.

The cool evening air kissed Arlo's skin and coaxed drying tendrils from around her hairline to brush against her face. She found herself dozing as the shadows reached like long fingers over the hills before dissolving into the greater night, sinking into dreams without realizing the transition.

"Miss Reade," Tristan asked, his gaze a bottomless well of unmistakable need. "May I kiss you?"

Arlo reached for him.

In her dreams, Tristan was confident and sure. He was the man Arlo knew hid somewhere inside, who gave dramatic reenactments of his favorite stories, who seethed and jumped and buzzed with life.

He stepped forward, closing the distance between them, brushing his lips against hers, each light touch a question, an offering. Arlo threaded her fingers into his dark hair and pulled him close, tasting tea and mint and inhaling the woody, spicy scent on his skin.

So nice, the breeze whispered. Surprise.

The words sounded hissed, sharp, out of place in the softness of this moment.

Arlo startled awake. The hissing followed her.

She cocked her head, listening. The wind in the summer trees? A glance out the window put the thought to rest; the breeze was soft, not enough to rustle leaves into sound. Besides, it sounded like it was coming from inside the house, though it wasn't the usual whisper of Lucien's twinkling crowd.

It was something else.

Arlo went to her door, unlocking it and opening it just a crack. There was nothing, nothing. And then, a groan, as of a soul in desperate torment, followed by a muted litany she couldn't quite make out.

Was that...Tristan?

She crossed the hall to the pocket door separating the maids' quarters from the main house and slid it ever so carefully along its rails, flinching at every tiny sound it made. The words unmuffled a little, though they were still unclear. She crept closer through the pitch-dark hall, the moon outside its windows a bare sliver against the velvet sky.

"There's nothing for it," she heard. Tristan's rich, mellow voice was strangled, tight with emotion. A narrow strip of light shone in the gloom.

His door was unlocked. Open.

"The die is cast, I can't take it back. She knows my feelings now." She heard the bell-like ring of crystal on crystal, the glug of a drink being poured and then swallowed.

"But how am I to give her a life?" Another pour; another swallow.

Arlo stifled a gasp. He was talking about *her*.

She inched closer to the door, shuffling on silent feet to peer in through the open crack. Beyond a small vestibule with a shallow corridor branching off to the left, she saw a siting room, well-adorned but showing the subtle, elegant wear of quality furniture that had been used for a long time. Through the narrow gap, she could just see Tristan standing before the fireplace, facing away from her with his forearms braced on the mantel, head bowed, a crystal tumbler half-full of amber liquid glittering in one hand.

"We'll have to leave." He turned, and Arlo shrunk away from the door, hand over her mouth to keep from breathing.

Leave Calderwood? She had a sudden vision of the two of them visiting every lending library the city had to offer, and bookshops and tea houses and maybe even parties, like other people of Tristan's station did. But he should be throwing parties *here*. This was his family home. He paced again, to the other side of the room, and then there was the soft pomf of him sinking into an armchair.

"Surely you understand why we'll have to leave."

Surely...you? Did he have someone in there with him? Mrs. Hollister and her son had both gone for the day, and Tristan never had guests. Who on earth was he talking to?

Arlo put a tentative finger on the door and pushed it a little further open. Tristan sat in one of the plush chairs with his legs splayed, one hand covering his eyes while the other dangled that glass by the fingertips. He sighed. No one went to him. No one spoke.

She widened the gap just a bit further to see if there was someone standing by the fireplace, but Tristan was alone. Unless he'd been talking to the fire, the only other thing there was a portrait of what looked like a younger Tristan, maybe thirteen or fourteen years old. The artist had captured his striking blue eyes, his mop of dark hair, and the same serious, careful expression he wore as an adult, though his mouth seemed to hint at a smile fighting to break free.

There was another dark-suited shoulder just next to his in the painting. Arlo peeked a little more, craning until she saw a flash of long, pale hair, an arch smile curving the corner of a beautiful mouth, and—

"Lucien?" She didn't even realize she'd spoken until Tristan's footsteps boomed like thunder as he rushed to the door and wrenched it fully open.

Arlo startled back with a gasp, heart clanging, hands tingling on the edge of numbness as a sudden rush of fear flooded her.

Tristan loomed over her, a menacing silhouette with the only source of light behind him. Disheveled curls licked at the edge of his collar, which was open almost to the waist, his half-untucked shirt held in place only by his suspenders. This close, the residual warmth from his standing so close to the fire reached through her nightgown to graze her skin. Panic melted as her body surged with wanting, only to be jerked back as the cool curl of underground voices slithered back into her awareness.

Lucien's call was so strong that Arlo swayed under its power, knees buckling, head tipping backward, yet she didn't fall.

Tristan caught her.

But this time there was no holding her close, no circle of his arms. This time it was hard fingers around her shoulders, his grip like talons as he stared at her with the angry embers of his eyes.

"What are you doing here?" he demanded, searching her face.

Arlo whimpered as sense came back to her, the lure of the underground falling away under the heat of Tristan's hands. She squirmed her shoulders, partially to loosen his grip and partially because...now they'd come to it. She'd already been ninny enough to blurt out Lucien's name without thinking through why that portrait might be here, what it might mean. She didn't want to compound the offense, though her heart sank with the realization that it was likely already too late.

Tristan had just been talking about running away with her, she was sure of it. But now, he couldn't seem to whip his hands off her fast enough.

"I'm sorry." She took an unsteady step back into the hallway. Her voice trembled, high and breathy. "I just—I heard you talking, and I thought…" Her mouth flooded with sourness, a bitter combination of fear and shame. If she kept talking, Tristan would know what she'd found, where she'd been.

There'd be no coming back. Not from this.

But there was no other way, not if that portrait meant what she thought it did. She pointed to it, swallowing hard.

"That looks just like—" Was it her, or did the esses in her words linger a little, hissing whispers writhing in the dark? She started to wobble again, eyes rolling back in her head until Tristan slashed a hand between them, cutting off the sound and snapping Arlo's awareness back to him.

"Don't say his name." The words came out through gritted teeth.

"But—"

"You shouldn't be here," he told her, stepping even closer, pushing her out of the space by the door.

Arlo cringed. No, she shouldn't be here. She wasn't allowed in his room; she wasn't supposed to see him so bedraggled and vulnerable. Tristan began to push the door closed. It hissed against the rug, making Arlo shiver for a moment before she stiffened with resolve.

This was it.

"I saw him!" she cried.

Tristan froze, one hand on the door frame, both eyes open wide, incredulous.

"You can't have seen him." His words were clipped, formal, distant as a city across the sea. "My brother ran away."

Brother. So it *was* true. Arlo's heart leaped with a complicated twist. If Lucien was Tristan's long-lost brother, then he hadn't really disappeared. He hadn't gone far at all. He was right here, close to the family home that Tristan had been keeping in case of his return.

Hope dawned, rising like bubbles as Arlo realized what this meant for him. For them.

"But don't you see?" He could relax. He could leave. He could take her away, just as he wanted, because there was no need to stay in the house waiting on the possibility that his brother might be found, or come back, if his brother was already here.

But on the other hand, perhaps he wouldn't *have* to leave. If Lucien's disappearance was what had emptied Calderwood of almost everything but its ghosts, then it was possible that his return could heal it.

"Please," Tristan said, pointing down the hallway before Arlo could articulate any of her racing thoughts. "It's late. Go back to bed, and we...we won't speak of this again."

"But Tristan," Arlo said. She didn't care anymore about the complete impropriety of such familiar address. The *s* in his name held on as she said it, giving way to a wave of whispers that rocked over her, forcing her to clench her jaw as if to keep the secret caged behind her teeth.

Arlo fought it. This was too important to keep to herself any longer, and damn the cost.

"He's *here!* I've *spoken* to him!"

Tristan glared at her, eyes wide, chest heaving with ragged breaths.

"What did you say?"

Arlo wanted to grab him, to shake him, even as she quailed at the force of his outrage. After all this, he still didn't understand?

"The door," she said, throwing caution to the wind. "The door with snakes, at the far side of the cellar. Tristan, he's *there*, he's been right under your nose this whole time!"

"You're lying." His voice whipped out in a venomous whisper, low and dangerous, his face contorted with wrath, though his eyes looked more frightened than furious.

Arlo balled her fists at her sides, her own breath coming hard as her body responded with outrage of its own. How *dare* he accuse her of lying? Granted, her nocturnal forays into the cellar and beyond probably counted as lying by omission, but dammit, this was important to him. Why wasn't he listening to her?

"Oh really?" she asked, her tone taking on the sharp, cunning timbre of someone who knows they're about to play a winning card. Her heart pounded in her throat as she spat her next words at him. "If I'm lying, then how did I get his name right?"

Tristan thrust a pointed finger toward her, but his mouth hung open, wordless. Then he pulled the finger carefully back into a fist and turned, rummaging in a side table. He came back a moment later with some folded banknotes.

"You have ten minutes to pack your things," he said, his voice the sort of calm that belied a volcanic explosion just below the surface. "After which point you will get out of this house. Go to the inn, or farther afield, if that's your desire." He snatched her hand and pressed the money into it. "I still owe your first month's wages, and you can consider the rest a travel stipend."

The fire leaped, splashing his shadow on the wall behind him so that he seemed to loom, dark and terrible.

"I'll be watching the road," he told her. "If you're not on it in the next ten minutes, I'll drag you to the village myself, and that's the last I ever want to see of you. Do I make myself clear?"

Arlo blinked quickly several times, pulling her head back as she stared wide-eyed at him.

Leave Calderwood? He'd said her position wasn't at stake, he'd all but told her he loved her. Now this? Especially when she'd just presented the end to all his problems?

Her heart broke, even as some part of her accepted this as inevitable. Of course he hadn't meant what he'd said to a mere scullery maid. Of course he hadn't really wanted any of the things he'd said, or at least, not with her.

Perhaps it had only ever been his loneliness talking. In another year or two, he might well propose to his housekeeper.

But...

"Go!" he shouted, shocking her into action.

Arlo ran back to her rooms, stripped off her nightgown and wriggled herself into a shirtwaist and walking skirt, not even bothering with a corset. It was scandalous, but he'd given her so little time. She shoved the rest of her things into her bag without regard for their condition, eyeing the black maid's dress through a haze of tears for only a moment before deciding that she would rather leave it here than have any reminder of this place ever again.

She hauled her bag down the servants' stair and fled from Calderwood as though her life depended on it, running without looking back all the way to the village and whatever awaited her there.

19

ARLO STARED OUT THE window at the bulk of Calderwood, alone among its hills.

The innkeeper's wife had taken pity on her when she'd shown up in the middle of the night, bedraggled and dazed, with a single bag and no husband or chaperone to accompany her. The common room was empty and the kitchen cold, but they'd heated soup for her and found her a room.

It hadn't been visible when she'd fallen on the bed weeping in the dark, but in the morning, she found she had the perfect view of the grand old house, majestic in its solitary splendor as the sun rose behind it.

She watched it, retracing the steps she'd be taking right now if she was still there. The kitchen. The hallway. The library.

A knock at the door drew her out of her trance.

"Tea, love?" The innkeeper's wife elbowed in with a tray. Arlo smiled. Yesterday, that had been her. Perhaps they could use some help around the inn. It would be better than going back to the city, where everyone who'd tried to coerce her into marriage after her father's death would see her as nothing but the poor little girl who ran away. And hadn't they told her she couldn't take care of herself on her own in the wide world? Of course she couldn't. She needed a man.

Well, she'd had *two*, briefly, for all the good it had done her.

Arlo sighed and sipped her tea, the calming fragrance ever so slightly gentling the raw edge of her loss. In the space it left behind, a thought hove into her awareness, as slow and gentle as a drifting balloon.

There was something familiar about the look in Tristan's eyes before he'd pulled himself under tight control. It was the same frenzied panic as when he'd first seen her downstairs, just outside the wine cellar.

Several other memories followed, slotting together like pieces of silverware in a velvet box: the refusal to mention his brother's name. The intentional darkness of the cellar, and his volunteering to step in for any chore that required a descent.

The lock on the cellar door.

She already knew he'd been aware of the snake door. Had he known, too, that Lucien was behind it?

Had he been aware of his brother's presence all this time?

If that was the case, why the elaborate charade?

What was he protecting?

But the answer came even before the question was fully formed: Lucien's world was magic.

It was underground, but it had a sky, and the only way she knew of to reach it was through a door in Calderwood's cellar. Imagine what the world would do with something like that, if they knew. Arlo had never gone past the house and its garden, but what else might be waiting beyond the Calderwood estate in Lucien's world?

Surely all those guests and musicians, all that food, all those plants had to come from somewhere.

And if Lucien was Tristan's brother, why hadn't he said anything to her? Told her who he was? He would have to assume that Arlo knew Tristan, if the only way into his world was through the house. Tristan had said that his brother was the elder, set to inherit before he'd disappeared. Wasn't Lucien the least bit upset, knowing that Calderwood should have been his?

But maybe he was happy in the new life he'd found beyond that door. A life that he'd practically begged Arlo to be a part of.

She pictured herself on Lucien's arm at the front of the ballroom, greeting his guests. *Their* guests. With the right hair, the right dress, she could do it. She'd been born into a lower class, but there was no reason she couldn't rise above. Even Tristan had believed she was more than her birth.

At least, he had before he'd banished her from Calderwood. Now she'd likely never see him again, and without access to the house, she couldn't get back to Lucien either.

Now, they were both lost to her.

On her second day at the inn, Arlo rose and dressed early.

The innkeeper's wife looked delighted when Arlo showed her face downstairs for the first time, as though she'd been worried about the poor woman who'd arrived under such mysterious and possibly scandalous circumstances.

Arlo nearly cried at the kindness in her eyes. At least *someone* worried about her.

"Breakfast?" the woman asked.

Arlo nodded and received a plate of ham, eggs, and toast with sunset-orange marmalade. It burst bright in her mouth, so delightful that she almost missed the moment Mrs. Hollister came through the door.

Arlo's eyes bulged with panic, her mind racing with a litany of chastisement. How could she have been so foolish? This was where Tristan's meals came from; *of course* Mrs. Hollister was bound to show up eventually.

She cast around for somewhere, anywhere to hide, but there was nowhere in the room that offered good concealment, and since the common room was almost empty at this hour, standing up would likely draw *more* attention. She settled for bending down at her table, as if she'd dropped something on the floor. Her breath thundered in her ears, nearly drowning out the sound of the innkeeper's greeting.

But what she heard made up for every bit of awkwardness she felt.

"No meals today," the housekeeper said after finishing with pleasantries. "Mister Calder will be out of the house this afternoon, returning tomorrow evening."

"Very good," the innkeeper said. Mrs. Hollister nodded and left.

Arlo sat up slowly, her hands trembling with sudden possibility. Why hadn't she thought of it sooner? Tristan traveled—not all the time, but often enough. And when he did, Jonathan drove him and Mrs. Hollister didn't stay.

When Tristan left Calderwood, he left it empty.

Well. Empty-ish.

He'd lock the house, of course. But Arlo could get past that. She'd bypassed his locks before.

"All right?" the innkeeper's wife asked, seeing the flush in Arlo's cheeks. "Can I get you anything else?"

"No, thank you," Arlo said, standing. "It's such a fine morning, I think I'll go for a walk."

She walked out the front door and stuck close to the inn, peering down the road until she judged Tristan's housekeeper to be far enough away. Then she followed, her green walking skirt swishing gently around her legs as she made her way up the road.

She had to keep just the right amount of distance between them—too little, and Mrs. Hollister might hear her and turn. Too much, and Arlo might lose track of the woman. She knew how to get back to the house, of course. But she'd need to know where Hollister was in order to avoid her.

Passing by the house would be the trickiest part. Should she go around the back, where she could be almost certain Tristan wouldn't see, but the housekeeper might? Or should she risk passing by the kitchen window, where Mrs. Hollister might or might not be looking at the moment, and then by the library where Tristan would undoubtedly still be sitting if he hadn't left yet?

In the end, going around the back was probably the safer choice. All the rooms on the terrace side of the main house were closed off, so as long as she could avoid Mrs. Hollister in the servants' wing, she'd be out of danger as soon as she cleared the garden wall. Her best chance lay in going through the small patch of woods that flanked the house's north side.

She broke off from the main route as she got near the house, holding straight while the path curved right and making her way for the clutch of trees that stood nearby. She tracked the flash of Mrs. Hollister's skirt through the gaps between trunks, moving slowly to avoid any loud noises from the underbrush, until she could see the chicken coop at the back of the wooded area.

Then she waited, knowing that without her there, the housekeeper would have to come back to fetch eggs for Tristan's breakfast.

Anticipation thrummed under her skin, making it almost impossible to stand still. Even the ground seemed to feel it, humming under her feet as if it might surge and lift her stumbling toward the door. It was as though Lucien knew she was close, and was calling to her.

I'm coming.

She watched the path between coop and house. Mrs. Hollister came and went. Once the courtyard door was closed Arlo edged through the wood, staying just behind the tree line until she reached the closet point to the edge of the garden wall. Then she broke, bolting for the garden wall and the safety beyond.

Her skirt nearly tripped her twice, but she made it, gasping with her back thrust hard against the stones. What next?

The stables and coach house were behind the house on the southeast side. She could just see one corner of the closest building from her vantage point, but the overgrown hedges in the garden shielded her from view.

Safety was a slim tether on her desire to run and keep running, to get into the house and back to the cellar, but it held her in place. Only her heart raced, galloping to beat a running horse as she listened, ears cocked for the slightest sign that things were moving.

It came about an hour later: Jonathan's chatting to the horses, and the sounds of a carriage being readied for travel.

Yes. Arlo held her position, listening as the carriage rumbled around the front of the house. It was another several minutes before the carriage rolled off again, but the creaking thunder of its wheels rivaled any other music Arlo had ever heard.

She listened until it faded into the distance, counted another several minutes under her breath, just to be sure, then hiked on trembling legs across the garden perimeter and up the hill past terrace-level to the back of the greenhouse.

It took a moment of orienting herself to find it from the outside, but there was the cracked pane of glass, just waiting to be broken.

Arlo tapped it with a tentative finger. It hissed and squeaked, shifting ever so slightly. After one last look around, she hoisted her skirts as high as she could, drew back one leg, and kicked.

The glass shattered, spilling terracotta pots into the grass and leaving jagged spikes around the perimeter of its frame. Arlo moved the fallen pots and booted all the small pieces of glass out of the frame until nothing was left to slice her, then regarded the pile of shards on the floor and ground with a calculating eye. She didn't have a jacket to put down in this weather, but she'd need to crawl over the broken pane on hands and knees to fit through.

After some consideration, she tore long strips from her petticoat and wrapped them around her hands so that she could creep forward on fisted knuckles while her skirt layers protected her knees. It took what felt like forever, but before long she was standing in the conservatory. Her breath came hard, more from nervousness than exertion, but she'd made it.

She was inside.

As soon as her feet were within the walls, something felt...different. It wasn't just that Tristan wasn't here—she'd experienced that before. But back then, as an employee of this house, she'd had a right to be here.

Her illicit presence now sent a thrill down to the tips of her toes. Or was that the ground trembling again, demanding her return?

She obliged, striding down the hall toward the kitchen and all the secrets beneath it. In her blouse and walking skirt, she could almost fool herself into thinking she belonged here, that she was the lady of this house, not a maid. She reached the service wing, passed the servants' stair and swung into the hall where the cellar door waited for her.

Tristan's shiny padlock still gleamed against the faded green paint. Arlo smiled at it. Then she hoisted the dumbwaiter and locked it on the top floor.

Climbing down in this long, narrow skirt would be a little more challenging than it had been in her uniform or nightgown, but that was fine. She had all day. Mrs. Hollister had told the innkeeper that Tristan wouldn't be back until tomorrow evening. So she took her time, knowing that if she fell, there would be no one here to help her.

The darkness didn't seem so dark when she landed, and sure enough, she could see three narrow bands of light defining the edges of the snake-covered door. She let out her breath in a huge, relieved sigh. The door was still here, still open.

Still waiting for her.

She waited in turn. Last time, the carved snake had greeted her and the door had swung open, but this morning, nothing moved. All the intricate snake carvings stayed caught mid-writhe, soundless and unchanging.

Arlo's brow twitched just a little bit downward, her eyes narrowing as she registered the change. Perhaps Lucien and his guests were asleep, recovering from another night's revel. But someone had left the candles lit, and with the light leaking into the cellar, it was easy enough to find the handle.

She gripped it and pulled.

The first thing Arlo noticed was the change in the candelabras.

Several of the candles had burned to the nub, leaving nothing but sconces overflowing with solidified wax. Those still lit left the air smoky and acrid as they guttered one by one. Shadows leaped and danced across Arlo's vision in the shifting light. She thought something skittered by her feet, but when she looked down, nothing was there.

Nothing but that stain. Arlo peered down, holding her skirt back and out of the way. Was it...larger? She'd only glanced at it last time, but something about the edges seemed different than they'd been before. She knelt, prodding at the stone with one finger.

It came away wet.

Arlo blinked at her fingertip, covered not with water but with something thicker.

Something red.

Oh God, what had happened?

Lucien hadn't come to greet her. She'd thought he might be sleeping, but what if it was something more sinister? What if he'd gotten tired of waiting? Had he tried to come to her and gotten hurt somehow? Was he somewhere nearby, bleeding out? Did he need help? Arlo listened for the call that always seemed to come from the door, but heard only the hiss of burning wicks in the silence. She plunged through the room, leaving its stuttering gloom behind her as the snake-door slammed shut.

"Lucien?" she called, beelining straight for the stairs she knew would take her up. "Lucien?"

She burst into the hallway at the top of the stairs and nearly tripped over a woman in an iridescent black dress that appeared as though it was made of overlapping fish scales. Her cold eyes were black marbles in bruised hollows, her lips so pale they looked nearly blue. She tilted her head back with a heavy roll and stared at Arlo, saying nothing but for the thin hiss that escaped between tongue and teeth.

Arlo backed away, stepping carefully around the woman until she reached the main hall.

It was more of the same. Guests dressed for a grand ball dotted the hallway in ones and twos, their faces smudged, their bodies limp, but they were awake, watchful. Music wobbled from the ballroom, lumbering and off-kilter, a drunken dirge played half-asleep. She followed it, peeking in, but didn't see Lucien anywhere.

The music limped after her as she hurried to the great hall. Lucien wasn't here either; no one was.

It occurred to her that her past two visits had been at night, when the parties were in full swing. Was this the usual aftermath?

Or had something happened?

A heavy haze of oily smoke writhed against the ceiling outside the drawing room toward the end of the hall, and everything smelled like damp, moldy earth. Arlo tried to look inside but couldn't see anything past the solid wall of pollution. She checked the conservatory, calling "Lucien?"

A door opened behind her and she whirled. A man stepped out of the library. He looked haggard, exhausted, his long white hair the mark of very great age.

But no—Arlo shook her head.

No, it was Lucien.

"What's going on here?" Her voice quavered. "What happened?"

Lucien looked up, and the exhaustion on his face melted away in an instant, though the gleam in his eyes looked a bit harder now than it had before. Arlo started to flinch back, but Lucien had her in his arms before she could back away, his mouth and nose nuzzling the flesh of her neck under her ear.

"You came back," he said, his voice low and warm with laughter and desire and something a little like triumph.

Her stomach fluttered, but it wasn't entirely with pleasure.

"Lucien. I—need to talk to you."

"Come." He grabbed her arm and pulled her up the nearest stair, climbing beyond the library to the upstairs hallway.

Arlo's heart stuttered into a faster rhythm; there was nothing but bedrooms up here.

Where was he taking her?

He steered her into the suite that, in the other Calderwood, sat across from Tristan's. Wait, no. The houses were mirrors of each other. This *was* Tristan's room. At least, it was in Calderwood-above.

"Lucien," she started to say, but his mouth was on hers, his hands roaming over her waist and back and brushing her breasts as he walked her backwards through the sitting room to the bedroom beyond. He tasted like sweet smoke and candied cherries as he pushed Arlo down to sit on the edge of the bed without breaking the kiss.

"You can't know how much I hoped for this." Lucien took her wrist in his hands and unbuttoned her long sleeve to kiss her palm and the delicate veins beyond it. He trailed his hands up her arm to unbutton her blouse and plant kisses on her exposed collarbone while his hands held her wrists like manacles, pinning her to the bed.

"How I hunger for you." Arlo shivered from head to toe as she felt his tongue slide a long trail from the base of her neck to the hollow behind her ear.

Then he pulled away, leaving Arlo to sit in a shuddering, dumbfounded heap.

"No," he said, rubbing the corner of his mouth with one thumb. "We must wait—"

"Lucien—" Arlo started to say, breathless, still reeling from the boldness of his touch. She needed to focus. She needed to ask him about Tristan, about Calderwood, about why he'd let his family believe he'd disappeared.

"—for the feast." Lucien's mouth quirked on one side into a devilish smile.

"Feast?" she echoed.

Lucien nodded slowly, never taking his night-dark gaze off hers.

"Call it...the wedding feast."

"Wedding feast." Part of Arlo raged at her dumbly repeating his words back to him like some kind of trained bird, but most of her brain seemed to have stopped working in the onslaught of his advances. Oddly, the one thought she could hang on to was something Tristan had said about his brother's eyes.

His eyes were like yours, such a light blue they were nearly clear.

What had happened to Lucien, to turn his eyes such a swallowing black?

"Of course," he said, his smile widening. He crossed the room and stepped into the hall, then turned back. "This is your forever now." He shut the door, leaving Arlo alone.

Her vision swam with dancing spots while her chest and fingertips tingled.

Forever.

Not long ago, the idea of forever with Lucien had filled Arlo's body with excited flutters. Now it crawled up her throat like a corpse dragging itself from the grave, slow and sour and sickeningly wrong.

20

SHE COULDN'T STAY HERE.

Tristan might never want to see her again, but Lucien wasn't the answer. Arlo needed to follow him, to demand to talk to him. To tell him that while his offer was immensely flattering, she wasn't planning to stay. She just needed to understand, and then she needed to go.

She stood up so fast it made her head swim, then staggered out of the bedroom and across the sitting room, landing on the doorknob with all her weight behind her, ready to wrench it open. The knob didn't turn. It slid only slightly around before clicking to a stop, and Arlo's heart sank into her stomach.

He'd locked the door.

Her mouth flooded with the metallic tang of bitter irony. She'd spent months locked out of this room, and now she was locked in. Tears spilled down her cheeks, sudden and hot.

"No," she said to the empty room. "No, no, no."

She had to get out of here. The door was locked, but the room had two windows, one of which overhung the lip of the conservatory roof. If she could shimmy out onto that ledge, she could make her way around to the far side and drop, and run. No one would see her through all the heavy greenery, and though the only way she knew of to return to Calderwood was through the cellar, maybe she could find help, or another way back outside these walls.

She opened the drawn curtains and jerked back at the sight that awaited her.

It was night, the shadow-draped new moon leaving the grounds as obscured as the sea's murky depths. But it hadn't been noon yet when Arlo descended, and she'd only been here for half an hour at most. Was that part of the magic of this place? Well, the darkness would help to cover her escape.

But when she tugged at the crank to open the casement, she met her second nasty surprise: the window was fixed shut.

Fury and panic mixed in her, building hot and fast from her feet to her knees to her stomach to her chest, forcing a huge inhale as she surveyed her surroundings. There had to be *something*. She tried the other windows. Locked again.

"Bloody fucking damn."

She crossed to the mantel where she'd seen Tristan have his own crisis, leaning on it just as he had, slamming the side of her fist against it as she let out a long string of curses under her breath.

No windows, no door. No windows, no door.

Arlo squeezed her eyes shut, breaths coming fast and shallow as the litany repeated over and over in her head. What else was there?

Eventually, her gaze landed on the generous, unlit fireplace. She flung herself at the opening and craned her neck to look up the chimney. Could she fit? She'd probably have to take her skirt off and she'd emerge a terrible mess even before making the dangerous jump from the roof to the ground...but it would be worth it, if it worked.

She sat on the floor and leaned backwards into the space, trying and failing to get a better view. Everything was pitch, and the moonless night didn't help.

There was nothing else, though. Not if she wanted to get away.

She'd just moved her hands to unbutton her skirt when a knock came at the door. Arlo barely had time to look up before it opened, revealing a tall, statuesque woman with a regal, knowing smile on her face.

"Time to come down, my lady," she said, dulcet and breathy.

From behind her, Arlo heard the constant whispers drift up from the lower floor.

So nice, they seemed to say, or maybe *surprise.*

"Down to where?" Then she remembered what Lucien had said. "The feast?"

The smile turned into a smirk as her eyes flashed in the dark.

"Just as you say. Come." She beckoned, one brow arched with an expectant look.

Arlo's vision danced with spots while her chest and fingertips tingled. She didn't want a surprise from Lucien, no matter how nice it was. She just wanted to go home. But it was looking more and more like the only way to do that would be to find a way back to the door in the cellar.

She followed.

Returning to the main floor of Lucien's Calderwood was like stepping back in time. Lively music and all kinds of laughter, tinkling and hissing and dangerously suggestive, spilled from the ballroom into a hallway now free of its earlier occupants. The whole place sparkled, as if they'd brought in an army of cleaners to do a day's job in a little under an afternoon, and the smell of moldy earth had vanished in favor of rich spices and sharp, heady perfumes.

Lucien stood at the end of the hall, between the ballroom and dining room doors. Once again resplendent in his pristine tuxedo, he'd added a cape that fell nearly to brush the ground, its white silk lining almost as luminous as his loose-flowing hair. He held out one hand toward Arlo, an invitation to run to him.

Her heart thrilled while her stomach clenched, a strange double sensation. It was as if she were two people, one who feared him and wanted to flee, and another who'd been waiting all her life for this, who knew that fulfillment was just at the end of the hall if only she'd run to him.

The flavor of candied cherries erupted in her memory, a potent sweetness that turned to rot as her stomach seized again. Cold sweat prickled at her hairline, each pore exploding like a tiny star as a wave of hot nausea rolled up through her shoulders and throat. She tried to shake her head without obviously doing so.

Why had she thought of the cherry *now*, when there was no food in sight, and why had such a pleasurable memory turned to so violent a revulsion?

Then a shiver blossomed from her spine down her arms as a line came into her head from the first book she'd ever borrowed from Tristan.

> *We must not look at goblin men,*
> *We must not buy their fruits:*
> *Who knows upon what soil they fed*
> *Their hungry thirsty roots?*

Her face tingled as the blood drained, leaving her pale and almost shaking with revelation.

Dear God, how could she have been so stupid?

She'd been sick with longing since her first night here, wanting nothing more than to taste this again, just like Laura in the Rossetti poem. And while she'd admired brave, clever Lizzie for her strength and ingenuity—she'd told Tristan as much!—she'd acted in all ways like Laura without even thinking. She'd bought her heart's desire with a golden curl and found, too late, that it came with an even greater price.

The goblins had disappeared after selling Laura their forbidden fruit. Lucien was still here. It should have reassured her—he couldn't be like those cruel, monstrous creatures, not if he hadn't left her to waste away after a single illicit taste. Yet his smile seemed too wide now, his eyes too demanding, his reaching hands too much like grasping claws.

For the first time since stumbling on this enchanting nighttime world, Arlo wanted to run not toward him, but away.

If she could, she would do it now. But she stood bracketed, with Lucien before her and her enigmatic escort still behind. She couldn't help feeling that their placement was intentional. Blocking the stairs meant she couldn't get back to the cellar, to the only door that could let her out of Lucien's world. She fought to keep her expression neutral as despair and panic warred within her.

She was trapped.

At least, for now.

But these parties had always been such flamboyant, colorful affairs. Surely, if she stayed careful and alert, Arlo could find a way to melt into the fringes and make her way downstairs unobserved while everyone else's focus was, as always, on Lucien.

Escaping his notice would be the hardest part, since on all other visits he'd seemed to have eyes only for her. But Arlo would find a way. She had to. She'd bide her time, play his game a little longer. And then, when she found her chance, she'd slip away. It wasn't a foolproof plan, but it was the best she could do.

She took a deep breath, straightened her shoulders, and walked to Lucien, taking his offered hand.

"Good evening," he said, his voice ambrosial, his smile a promise of pleasure to come.

When Arlo touched him, skin to skin, his need pulsed through her like a ravening wave, blurring the lines of where he ended and she began. He caught her when she reeled, holding her close to him.

"Come."

Once she was steady, Lucien tucked her hand through the crook of his elbow and led her into the ballroom. It was decorated as Arlo had never seen before, draped with huge swaths of fabric, creating a wonderland of drifting shadows and gauzy caresses that all seemed to glimmer in the light of what had to be more than a thousand candles.

At the far end of the room, opposite the fireplace, stood a dais topped with a huge chair of smoky black glass, almost more of a throne, though its lines were hard and flat, not plush and soft like Arlo had always assumed a throne would be.

The music ceased as they crossed the threshold. In the quiet left behind, Arlo could hear the swish and rustle of fabric as every single guest turned in perfect, eerie unison to watch them enter.

So nice, someone whispered, soft as a distant wave hissing up an abandoned beach. *Surprise,* came the reply from across the room, and Arlo thought she heard *his bride,* though she couldn't be sure.

She knew one thing, though—the sooner she found a way to leave this place, the better.

Lucien gestured to the musicians. They struck up a lively song, and he whirled Arlo into a dance that took them around and around the room. In any other circumstance, she might have made eyes at someone, anyone, a silent plea for them to cut in. But this crowd made her palms slick with sweat, her legs weak with their watching.

So nice, she caught as they passed, and Arlo wondered what was so nice about this. Lucien looked resplendent, of course, and the house was back to its former glory, but something felt...off-kilter about the whole thing. They hadn't watched her like this before. Was it because she hadn't come back three times?

Was it because she hadn't been *his bride* yet?

"Lucien." She needed to tell him that she wasn't here to be his bride, but it was as if he didn't hear her.

"Isn't it exquisite?" he asked, nuzzling her neck with lips as cold as if he'd just come in from a winter's day, despite the warmth of the room. Arlo jumped at the shock of it, but Lucien pulled her close again.

"Please," Arlo said.

Lucien put his fingertips over her mouth.

"Not now, love. Just enjoy it."

So nice reverberated, a low susurration that added texture to the music.

He wasn't going to let her go. Unless...

There was one other way out of here that she could think of. But she'd have to get to it first.

"Lucien, I need…that is…" She shied a little away from him, doing her best to look embarrassed. "I need to…see to my necessaries."

"Ah," Lucien said, letting her go and breaking their contact for the first time since she'd taken his hand. "Hurry back."

She forced a smile. "Of course."

Outside the ballroom, she saw one of Lucien's guests standing where he'd been before, in front of the wall that opened to the servants' quarters and one of the house's staircases. She flashed a tight smile and went to the other end of the house. Someone stood at the foot of the grand staircase, and there was another guest stationed at the far end of the house by the stairs that led to Tristan's room. The staircases at either end of the house would take Arlo to the cellar, but she knew Lucien's minions would halt any attempt at travel in that direction.

"Excuse me." She pointed up the stairs outside the closed library. The guest—guard, really, Arlo knew—stepped aside, letting her pass. She walked to not-Tristan's room, opened the door, then shut it again without going in.

With another peek behind her, she tiptoed down the hall as one thought spun over and over in her head: please let this house have a working dumbwaiter.

She crept to the servants' end of the upstairs hall, sliding away the wall panel and opening the dumbwaiter's door to find the system of ropes and pulleys intact. She took a deep breath, exhaled shaky hope, and grinned in triumph as the car came into view. Then she reversed its direction until she couldn't move it anymore, counting pulls until she was relatively sure it was all the way down in the cellar.

She curled her fingers into fists and then straightened them, shaking out her nerves. This had to work, or she'd be trapped here. She climbed in through the hole and found the support bars to take her weight. A slow descent would be safer, but Arlo wouldn't have much time before they realized she was gone. This was her last chance.

She climbed down as fast as she could, holding her breath the whole way, listening for any sign of an alarm or search. Her luck held, though it did nothing to stop the racing beat of her heart.

Whoever had fixed up the house had also seen to the candelabras. Their new candles filled the room with a warm glow that set Arlo's teeth on edge. This was where she'd met Lucien the first time. It had seemed so warm and welcoming then.

It still did. But now she knew better.

She eyed the rungs that blocked the gap between the dumbwaiter car and the cellar ceiling. The largest opening still looked like it would be a tight fit, but she didn't have the tools to remove the wooden slat and couldn't risk the noise of trying to kick it free. She took a deep breath and then let it all out, flattening herself as much as she could while she shimmied and twisted feet-first through the opening. As soon as her feet hit the ground, she pelted for the door.

Lucien was already there, his hard face cut with an arch, cruel smile.

"Lost, my pet?"

"No! I—" Arlo jumped to the defensive, then checked herself. She was so close. If she could just get him to listen, to understand. "Lucien, why are you down here?"

He cocked his head at her, smug as a cat with a cornered mouse.

"Why?" He drawled, slow as thick syrup, as if he didn't understand the question while also giving the impression that he knew exactly what she meant. "This is my house."

"*Calderwood* is your house," Arlo countered. "Tristan said you were the elder, that you ran away. Does he know you're here? That you've been here all this time?"

"Calderwood." He said it like a curse, like a slur; derisive, dismissive, and full of hate.

Arlo's body flushed with heat, her fingernails biting crescents into the palms of her hands as she stared at him.

"How can you say it like that?" she demanded, her voice shaking as it grew in volume. "Tristan misses you. He's been staying alone in that house for years, on the off chance that you'd come back." She threw her arms wide. "He's your brother!"

Lucien blinked at her. His plush mouth curled up in a smile that parted into a grin before he started making a curious wheezing sound that took Arlo a long moment to place as a laugh. The sound grew until it boomed through the space, shaking the candle flames in his immediate vicinity before stopping abruptly.

"Come." Lucien seized Arlo's arm so tight her hand tingled and all but dragged her away from the lit space, up the cellar stairs and back toward the party. "We'll be late."

Arlo struggled, yanking so hard she thought her shoulder might dislocate, to no avail.

"I didn't come here to marry you," she said as they cleared the stairs outside the dining room.

He thrust her back against the wall and loomed over her.

"You came back a third time." He undid the buttons down the front of her shirtwaist and peeled it away, stripping her down to her shabby corset cover and leaving her arms and neck bare as his guests crowded around to watch. "That makes you mine."

So nice, came the whispers.

Arlo balked. What was nice about this? But the partygoers looked on as though this were a normal occurrence, a sweet lovers' moment. *Surprise.*

No, that wasn't quite it. Arlo listened harder, trying to make the whispers come into focus. *The price?*

Lucien grabbed her arm again and brought her back into the ballroom, where the rest of his scintillant horde waited for them. He pulled her to the base of the throne, then threw her to the foot of the steps while he ascended and fixed her with an imperious gaze. The music sawed to a stop, plunging the room into expectant silence.

Arlo stood on trembling legs in the midst of perfect stillness, the gentle wafting of the layered, gauzy drapes the only sign that she hadn't somehow stepped into a painting.

Then, one guest broke from the edge of the crowd and approached her with a swaying, jerking movement that put every one of Arlo's hairs on edge.

The man stood there, unmoving, then darted both hands out and grabbed her wrist, lifting it to his nose and inhaling as though she wore some intoxicating bouquet.

She attempted to flinch back and failed. Her bladder pressed, wanting to empty. She jerked her face up at Lucien and saw someone she'd never glimpsed before. His once-chiseled cheeks were hollow, his eyes as hard and dark as obsidian, his hair loose in messy silver strands that fell past his shoulders and brushed against his sensuous, cruel mouth.

"Lucien?" Arlo asked, strangled and shrill.

"I think you've come to a mistaken conclusion," Lucien said, gazing down at her with an entire ice age behind his stare. "Tristan's brother is long gone. And when I told you this was a wedding feast, I...may have taken liberties."

Sweat beaded on Arlo's forehead.

Her whole body shook as, one by one, others broke from the crowd to hold and sniff and, God help her, *lick* her skin.

"What kind of liberties?" she asked, a tremulous whisper.

"I'm not going to marry you, my dear," Lucien said, looking at his hand as he drew a careless, casual finger along the length of one armrest.

Then he snapped his attention to her, swallowing her in the void of his endless gaze.

"I'm going to eat you."

Arlo's blood ran cold. She swallowed hard, though her heart and stomach both threatened to rise up and spill from her mouth.

The silence broke, spinning into a concert of thin strings and reedy winds and the low murmur of a building whisper rippling through the crowd. As they got louder, Arlo finally heard what they'd been saying all alone.

Not *so nice*. Not *surprise*.

Sacrifice.

He was going to kill her. Eat her. He'd been planning to do it from the start. And Arlo had no illusions that he'd meant it figuratively, not with the way his minions were lapping at her tender, exposed flesh.

Whoever this creature was, he was *not* Tristan's missing brother. Yet he knew his name, and he looked just like an older version of the portrait she'd seen on Tristan's bedroom wall.

Which meant that, gone though he may be, the real Lucien had been here. And, in all likelihood, this monster had eaten him.

Arlo's stomach soured, clenching with hopeless despair and the inevitability of her own impending doom. Her recent past flashed in sequence—her father's death, the single available job opening outside the city. Arriving at Calderwood, and getting to know its odd rhythms, its singular owner.

Tristan. Good Lord, did he know about this, too? Was *this* why he'd done his best to bar her access to the cellar?

Did he already know, or at least suspect, that his brother was not only lost, but gone?

All the secrecy, all the awkwardness...what if it was because he'd been trying to protect her from *this*? This man—this *creature* and his door had shattered Tristan's family and stolen the better part of his youth. And while Arlo wished he would have just *told* her, she knew why he hadn't. What would a stranger say to a story like this?

It was too outlandish to be true. Except, here she was.

All at once, heat surged in her cheeks and belly while defiance popped like a burning log in her ears.

"Why?" She practically bit the word, flinging it like a glove to open a duel.

Lucien leaned, resting his chin on one hand as he looked at her.

"Why what?"

"Why put a snake to guard the door?" she demanded. "Why set a price?"

Lucien glowered.

"Once upon a time, I was able to move freely between my world and yours, to hunt as I needed; to eat my fill. But then your *precious* Tristan's family came." He sneered, making a dismissive, angry motion with one hand.

"They dug their foundation and laid their stones right over my door." He gripped the ends of his armrests until his knuckles went white, though his face remained composed. "It didn't keep me from going up, of course. But when they realized what I was, where I came from...they stopped me."

He spat the words like a cobra spits venom, then stood and took the steps slowly down to stand before her. The others scuttled away, leaving the two of them alone at the center of the room.

"They found a way to lock me out."

He squeezed Arlo's chin so hard she felt her teeth cut the inside of her cheeks and tasted blood. All at once, she understood what the stain on the threshold was.

"Yes," he said, seeing realization dawn in her eyes. "Unfortunately for me, they knew the old stories. Their blood sacrifice kept me out, but it didn't stop anyone on their side from coming through."

Lucien sighed, fond and wistful, his mouth curved in a self-satisfied, scythe-blade smile.

"The original Calders lost several maids before they figured that out and stopped hiring live-in help. Pity for you that this one was stupid enough to let you live here."

Arlo's marrow turned to ice as she remembered something Mrs. Hollister had told her on her very first day at Calderwood.

Since Tristan and his parents before him had kept the house mostly closed, they didn't need much in the way of help beyond basic cleaning and seeing to meals and laundry.

But did they *really* not need the help? Or was it just that they'd pared back the lives they should have been able to live, because the alternative was having to find new and plausible ways to explain ongoing disappearances among their staff?

Lucien released his vise-grip, snapping his hand down to Arlo's waist and pulling her close. Her bones squirmed with horror, as if they could claw their way out of her skin. This was exactly the way he'd held her before, only now she knew that his fervor wasn't—had never been—love.

It hadn't even been ardency.

It was appetite, the furious, desperate hunger of a predator who'd been denied a meal for far too long.

"How...often?" The words trembled out of Arlo, halting in her throat, tripping over her tongue. But if Lucien—no, if this *creature* had been down here for this long, starved except for the occasional soul who wandered downstairs...

He tilted his head, an amused smile hovering on his lips.

"Hm?"

Arlo drew in a shaky breath and let it out again.

"How often do you need to eat?"

Her host lifted a hand to brush against her cheek.

"Oh, my dear. I don't *need* to eat." His fingers found a stray curl, guided it back to tuck behind her ear. As he moved, the softness of his mouth went stiff, the ends curling too far, revealing sharp teeth. He leaned in, brushing his lips against her ear, his voice a caressing whisper. "But I hunger."

Arlo tried to flinch away, but his hand gripped her chin, holding her immobile. He spoke in the same bored, bemused tone she always imagined rich people used at afternoon garden parties.

"The maids were amusing, in their way, but they weren't... fulfilling." He sighed again, his breath a threatening plume of heat in her ear. "They last longer when they have...spirit." He dragged his mouth across her cheek, "intelligence," and planted a kiss on her mouth before adding "cleverness."

Arlo squirmed against him, but he kept his hand splayed over her back, an iron grip holding her tight. He went on talking, ignoring her distress and, more likely than not, enjoying it.

"I put the puzzle in place to make sure we receive only the highest quality...guests."

He lingered on the hiss, saying *guests* the way others might talk about a fine meal.

He flicked his tongue into her ear and pulled away, grinning.

"Lucien Calder had all those things, and he lasted much longer than the ones who came before. And I liked his face," he said, his severe lines shifting momentarily back to the Lucien she'd met when she first came down here. "But it's been fifteen years, and I starve. *We,*" he said, gesturing around to his cohort, "starve. And we will savor you immensely."

He opened his grin wider than Arlo had ever seen to let two fangs unfold from the roof of his mouth like tiny, glistening daggers. Her knees turned to jelly as he lowered his mouth toward her neck, opening it impossibly wide.

She fought not to shudder as his hands snaked down her body to hold her by the waist and his lips brushed the flesh just over her vein.

21

"Wait!" Arlo turned her chin toward the creature, forcing his face away from her neck.

He pulled back, hissing, but gave her an expectant look.

Hell, she hadn't actually expected him to stop, but hope rose in her as bubbly as shaken champagne, recklessness careening madly through the depths of her soul.

She remembered her first meeting with Tristan.

Arlo Reade, she'd said, introducing herself.

And do you? Read?

Yes. She did. She had. She didn't know exactly what manner of creature this was, but she *did* know her fairy stories. And if he liked cleverness, if he liked spirit...she could do that.

She forced herself to take a deep, steadying breath and held his gaze in silence until she was sure she could speak without her voice trembling.

"It cost me three things to come here." She matched his imperious tone as best she could. It felt a bit foolish, but then she remembered Tristan's acting, the wild delight with which he'd thrown himself into mumming Hyde, and took strength from it. "Shouldn't you give me three things as well?"

Lucien pulled back, fixing his bottomless gaze on her.

She returned it as best she could, watching the slow creep of delight as his open mouth pulled back into too wide a grin and his eyes danced with some unholy light.

"Oh," he mouthed with a hot exhale on her cheek. "Oh yes, I *like* you." He stepped back and flung his arms wide as if making some grand presentation. "Very well," he said, raising his voice so the room could hear. "I will grant you three gifts." He held up one finger. "I will not grant you your life," he cautioned her, "nor more time to live. But anything else is yours for the asking, if there is anything you wish before you meet your end."

Arlo took a slow, deep inhale through her nose and nodded to buy time. Fairy tales. How did they bargain in fairy tales? How could she out-trick a trickster, outplay this cunning beast who'd fooled her so completely?

She thought of how Victor Frankenstein had hated his creation because he couldn't see him as anything but a monster, despite evidence to the contrary. Not unlike Lucien, who told her he valued her cleverness yet didn't seem to believe she had any.

She didn't feel clever, just now. She felt like she wanted to sink into a screaming, weeping puddle and beg for her life.

But that wouldn't work, not here. Not now. Not against him.

What were his exact words? *I will not grant your life.* That assumed he was in a position to grant it, or not.

Right now, he was.

But maybe Arlo could change that.

"First," she said, "I want a dress." She looked down at her corset cover and her sap-green skirt, shabby now with coal dust from Tristan's cellar floor and oil streaks from the climb down Lucien's dumbwaiter shaft. "I've never had anything fine like your guests wear. And If I'm to stay, even for just a little while…"

She let the sentence trail off, but Lucien nodded and gestured to the crowd.

A woman in an elaborate gown came forward. She was oddly familiar, but it took Arlo a moment to place her as the one she'd tripped over in the hall when she came back, the one whose gown looked like several layers of black fish scales coruscating in the light. Her smudged face was resplendent now, dark-rimmed eyes gleaming as she approached. She rippled as Arlo watched, shedding the top layer of her dress as a snake sheds its skin, leaving another dress exactly like it underneath.

The woman draped the discarded garment across both arms and drew closer to Lucien, reverence plain on her face, as though he were some kind of king. And he *was*, Arlo realized, or close enough that it made no difference.

These hills had been his once, before the Calders came. They may have cut off access to his hunting grounds, but this subterranean realm, this dark mirror of the house he so hated, was still unquestionably his.

He took Arlo's elbow and guided her to a shadowed space behind the black glass throne. Grabbing either side of his cape, he lifted it like great black wings to block Arlo from sight, though she could see a blur of guests through the throne's dark translucence, and she knew they could see her as well.

He stared down at her.

"Strip," he said. Arlo backed away from him, shivering as her naked shoulders hit the glass. She turned away from him and undressed, hating every moment that she could feel his gaze like pinpricks on her neck, until she was down to her corset. She stopped, uncertain.

"That, too," Lucien prompted her. When Arlo didn't move, he slid his arms around her front to unfasten her corset peg by slow peg, then let it fall to the floor before sliding the straps of her shift down her arms and catching his thumbs in the band of her drawers. When they, too, pooled at her feet, he handed her the gown.

Arlo shrugged into it as quickly as she could, grateful to cover her nakedness even as her skin rioted at every touch of what appeared to be not clothing but a layer of that woman's flesh. Once on, it fit perfectly, as though it had been tailored specifically for her, and was long enough to conceal her dull boots, the only thing Lucien hadn't made her remove.

The gown's deep hue made Arlo's fair skin and gold ringlets glow, a beacon in the dark.

She caught her reflection in the throne and frowned, projecting for all she was worth the image of a woman concerned only with vanity.

"I'd like cosmetics like theirs," she said, waving one hand toward the crowd. "It's a shame to bedeck myself in such a splendid gown while wearing the face of a poor relation."

Lucien laughed, shaking his head.

"You think so small. But I will give you what you ask for, as promised." He placed a hand over her face like a makeshift cage and closed his eyes. Arlo watched his face contort a little, his brows coming down as he seemed to concentrate for an instant before letting her go. "There."

Arlo turned toward the throne and found a stranger standing there. Her pale-blue eyes gleamed under dark, heavy lashes, and her lips pouted with the stain of stolen berries. He'd somehow made her hair fall out of its loosely-braided and pinned coiffure to spill in unfettered ringlets down her back.

She stepped out from behind the throne to an appreciative murmur from the crowd.

"And your third gift?" Lucien asked, pitching his voice for all to hear. "Would you like one last dance? A meal, perhaps? Rare fruits? Or your name written in the stars that only we can see?" He smiled and granted graceful nods to the tittering, appreciative crowd as he offered each suggestion. "What will you have?"

Arlo took one last deep breath, clenching her hands in front of her to keep them from shaking as she steeled herself to meet Lucien's gaze one last time.

This was it. Now or never.

Her words were like lightning, fast and sizzling.

"I will have your crown," she said. "This little kingdom is mine now."

Lucien gaped at her, his whole face gone slack, then feral with terrible understanding.

"But—"

"You said anything," Arlo reminded him. She crossed her arms, trying to appear as haughty as the queen he'd once insisted she was.

He cringed back, hissing. His mouth split in a ghastly rictus almost all the way back to his ears.

But he had no choice.

Arlo hadn't asked for her life, and he'd promised to grant anything else she desired.

He struck his own face with both hands as if attempting to hold himself together and took a single, staggering step toward her.

Arlo's smile fell from her face. She watched his approach with doe-wide eyes, her whole body rocking with terror she fought not to show.

This was it, her final option. If this didn't work, she was done for. Apologies flitted through her head in anguished rapid-fire: to her mother, for failing to recognize the truth in the fairy tales when they'd seized her by the throat. To Lucien, the real one, for the fate he'd fallen into.

To Tristan, for...everything.

The monster took another step, his face twisted with a furious scowl. Then he stopped, legs visibly wobbling before he fell to his knees before the dark fall of Arlo's borrowed finery. Miserable, furious indignation flashed in his eyes, but he didn't stand up again.

Arlo clamped her mouth in a grim line to hide the force of her relief, so overwhelming it was a wonder she didn't collapse, too. She could do that later, if she survived. But just because she'd won against him didn't mean she was safe from the rest of them. She had to get away before they realized she was still only human, vulnerable and alone.

This wasn't over yet.

She took a deep breath, blinking for the scantest of moments before snapping her eyes open with all the imperial force she could muster.

"You're all hungry?" she asked, her voice ringing across the space so loud that not even the excessive draperies could muffle it. She surveyed Lucien's courtiers—*her* courtiers—with an icy glare before stabbing one finger down at the quivering thing on the floor.

"Eat him."

They hissed and spat, their shoulders jerking as if on the verge of some awful transformation. Then one dashed forward—the same one that had first come to her—and stopped just in front of her, trembling with want.

"I mean it," she said, glancing at the fallen lord of this fallen place. "This kingdom is mine now. You'll do as I say." A snarl curled her lips, born of disgust and the desperate hope that this would work. "Eat him."

The little monster swooped. The others followed, converging on their former king like a host of rats on a fallen cat.

Arlo backed away, then ran, pausing only to retrieve her oil-stained skirt and tip over one of the heavy candelabras in the direction of a massive drape. She pelted down the stairs, back to the cellar, back toward the door.

Her footsteps echoed in the brief silence before screams erupted above her. They rang through the house and through her head as she ran, and she knew the sound would chase her even into her dreams.

Her skirt was heavy in her arms but she held on, determined to reach the door. She seized the handle and hoped for the best, nearly crying out with relief as it opened. Then she turned, just short of the threshold, and eyed the candelabras.

Their flames seemed much higher and hotter than before. Arlo seized one tall, many-branched candle holder and dragged it across the floor. It screamed against the stone as she brought it over the threshold, over the blood, into the world where neither Lucien nor his dark host could follow.

As she started to push the door shut, the little snake who'd set her challenge spoke to her, surprise clear in its tone.

"You?"

She glared at it and gave one grim nod.

"Me."

The snake regarded her warily, darting its forked tongue out and then pulling back, shocked.

"Mistress," it said, hissing the word, evidently tasting the change on her skin. "How may I serve you?"

Arlo looked at the snake for a long moment, then glanced past it and back through the door. Smoke coiled up the corridor towards her, and she could smell wood burning in what she could only hope was the entire house falling to flame.

She reached out with a steady finger and stroked the snake's diamond-shaped head. It leaned into her touch, not noticing until too late that she'd grabbed it where it couldn't bite her. She held it up in front of her face and said only one word while it gaped in shock.

"Burn."

She hurled it through the portal before slamming the door behind it. Then she stuffed her grease-streaked skirt in among the writhing carvings and tipped the candelabra until the candle flames reached up from below it, holding it there while her shoulders trembled until the fabric caught fire. The heavy metal fell to the floor with a crash when she let go. She stood there, panting, flames dancing in her eyes as the conflagration grew.

After a while, she didn't know how long, stinging eyes roused her from her daze.

Larger parts of the door glowed like the logs at the heart of a fire while the smaller curls and flourishes had already crumbled to a dark, oily ash. Every breath seemed to dry Arlo's mouth and throat, and she realized too late that she was breathing more smoke than air.

She forced herself up, stumbling half on hands and knees toward the stone stair that led to the cellar door, only to realize once she'd reached the top that she'd come down via the dumbwaiter shaft. The door was locked from the other side, and the thick smoke had risen so that it was even worse up here than down below.

Arlo turned, casting a helpless, hopeless glance at the dumbwaiter shaft as she realized she didn't have the strength to climb it.

A whimper squeaked in her throat as she squatted and leaned against the green-painted door, trying to get below the worst of the roiling haze. The burning portal to Lucien's world glowed from all the way across the room, falling in pieces to the floor to dissolve into a dark stain. Everything blurred behind tears she couldn't stop.

She'd defied a dark, ancient creature of these hills, played for her life against impossible odds and *won,* only to end up trapped here and likely to die anyway.

Tristan wouldn't be back until tomorrow night and, since he never entered this unlit cellar unless he had to, who knew how long it would take him to find her. At best, it would be in a day or two, when they needed more coal for the stoves.

At worst, not until she started to smell.

She sank into a crouch and sat curled against the cellar door, so close to freedom, yet so far away.

"No," she told the darkness, choking on every syllable. "No, no, no."

The words took shape in her fists. She pounded on the cellar door, slowly at first and then faster, fueled with rage and fear and utter despair. Ragged sobs erupted as her fists fell, her wordless screams etching the night until her anguish condensed and solidified into a desperate resolve.

She didn't want to die here. If climbing that damned shaft was her only way out, so be it.

She covered her mouth with one arm and staggered down the stairs, trudging step by dragging step across the cellar, navigating by the light of the burning door until she reached the dumb-waiter shaft. She gripped one of the vertical rails and held onto it with her head bowed, her chest heaving for breaths she couldn't find.

Arlo sank to her knees in front of the shaft, bracing on her arms, her locked elbows the only thing that kept her from falling as hacking coughs wracked her body, wringing her lungs. A bang sounded from above, but she barely noticed it as her eyes fluttered, lids too heavy to do anything but close as her golden hair fell in a curtain around her face.

Footsteps scuffed down the stairs, followed by a wordless, horrified shout.

Arlo looked up into the spill of light from a hand lantern to see dark blue eyes in a face frantic with worry. Smoke billowed away behind him, seeking higher spaces through the cellar door, which now hung wide open against the wall.

She gasped, delirious with relief, then coughed again.

Tristan knelt and dragged her into his arms, holding a clean handkerchief over her mouth and nose.

"Arlo! What the hell are you doing here?" His voice shook with equal parts fury and fear, but his arms were like iron bands around her.

Arlo turned her face into his shoulder and sobbed, helpless as a child. Tristan held her tight, pulling her back up to standing. Then he pushed her gently away to take in her dark dress, her dramatic makeup, the disorderly fall of her unbound hair, and softened his tone.

"What happened?"

Arlo didn't answer, only stared at the scorch marks on the foundation stones where the door had once been.

Tristan's mouth fell open as he looked at the wall, then at Arlo and back again several times.

She tried to speak, then coughed and had to swallow several times before she could try again.

"I told you." She gasped and curled forward as a coughing fit wracked her. "I met Lucien."

He flashed her a wide-eyed look of absolute horror.

"You—" His voice was stern and afraid in equal measure, but Arlo cut him off.

"I met him," she said, "and I killed him. And you were right. He wasn't your brother at all. He was... something else." Her last words dissolved in a fit of coughing that galvanized the stunned Tristan into action.

"What am I thinking?" He slung one of Arlo's arms around his shoulders and slid his other hand under her knees, holding her close to his chest as he stood. "Let's get you out of here."

Arlo nodded, already slipping into unconsciousness as he carried her step by careful step out of the cellar and into the light.

22

ARLO WOKE HALF-SLUMPED IN the library's deep, wide window seat with a blanket tucked carefully around her. Glancing through the window, she shivered at the long stretch of Calderwood's shadow over the grounds.

She'd had enough of shadows for right now, thank you.

Tristan came elbowing in a little while later with a tea tray and an apologetic smile.

"You're awake!" He hooked a foot behind one of the ottoman stool's legs and dragged it over from the desk to place the tray nearer to her. Steam wafted up, fortifying her with the familiar, comforting scents of black tea and bergamot. She relaxed her shoulders with a sigh, hunching a little over the hollowness in her chest.

"Miss Reade," Tristan said, pouring a cup and handing it to her. It clattered ever so slightly on the saucer as it moved, belying the tremor in his hands as he sat.

Arlo took it, not much steadier, and Tristan rubbed his palms several times down his trouser legs before clasping them tightly together in his lap.

"I find myself...I don't..."

His flustered stammering was charming, in its way, but Arlo's exhaustion dragged at her body, and the guilt of having fallen for Lucien's lies until it was almost too late was an iron fist squeezing her soul.

She was done with games.

"You're back early." Her tone wasn't accusatory, nor even curious. It was simply a fact. "Mrs. Hollister told the innkeeper you wouldn't return until this evening."

Tristan scraped a hand through his loose, dark curls with an awkward laugh more breath than sound.

"That was the plan. But…I can't explain what happened. I had a nightmare about…" He looked at her, shame and nervousness writ plain in his gaze, then pushed on. "Hang it. About the Door."

When he said 'door', Arlo could hear the capital letter.

"And I had this sudden, overwhelming need to get home as soon as possible. Jonathan drove the horses like blazes to get back here when we did."

He poured his own tea and sipped it while Arlo stared into her cup's glimmering reflection. Her eyes still bore smudges of the dark, kohl-like markings Lucien had given her, and the snakeskin dress bared her shoulders and chest almost to the cleft of her breasts.

She hadn't been thinking about that, underground. Now she held her saucer with one hand while surreptitiously trying to hitch the lap blanket just a little bit higher.

"Here." Tristan put his own cup down, then stood and hovered so quickly he nearly fell on her. He had an awkward moment trying to place his hands before he managed to arrange the blanket so it covered her up past the shoulders. "There." He tucked it in behind her. "Better?"

Arlo nodded.

Tristan sat back down, started to get up again, one finger raised, and sat down once more. Finally, as a last resort, he lifted his cup and looked away.

Arlo set hers down, too tired to hold it up, and dozed. She drifted in and out of dreamless sleep, her body too drained to care that she was curled up in a window seat instead of a proper bed.

She wasn't aware of it when Tristan left, but he wasn't there when she woke to find that the sun had come all the way around the front of the house. Light poured in on her, a benediction of warmth and safety after the nightmare she'd escaped. A step in the doorway made her turn to find Tristan returning.

His jacket was gone, his sleeves rolled up, his collar unbuttoned and his entire upper body blackened with streaks of soot.

"You burned the door," he said, by way of greeting, his voice ringing with awe. "I went down to look...but it's *gone.*" He rubbed the side of his face, leaving grime on his cheek. "How did you burn the door?" He shook his head, mouth hanging open in speechless, grateful disbelief. "Miss Reade—"

She smiled then. It was a small thing, but it reminded her of something he'd said earlier.

"What happened to Arlo?"

Tristan flinched. "What?"

"Downstairs," she said. "You called me Arlo."

"I—" He moved closer and knelt by the window seat.

She freed a hand from under the blanket.

He took it, clasping tight, intertwining his fingers with hers, and turned over the ball of their hands, looking at it as though it were some rare discovery, some new wonder of the world. Then he looked up at her.

"Arlo."

She met his gaze, watching as the sun picked out different layers and shades of blue.

"That's why you looked sick, isn't it?" he asked, his voice quiet, gentle, not at all the accusation she thought she'd receive. He reached up to brush a thumb against her cheek, though his other hand still held hers tight. "You'd already been down there once, before last night."

Arlo closed her eyes and nodded.

"Twice. Last night was the third time."

Tristan's hand froze, then pulled back from Arlo's cheek leaving cool absence in its wake.

Arlo opened her eyes to see him staring at her.

"That's not..." His eyebrows furrowed. "That's not possible. You should be—"

"Tristan." Arlo relished the opportunity to address him by the name she'd secretly used for so long. "I'm sorry for keeping secrets from you. But you've been keeping secrets too, I think."

She raised an eyebrow. Tristan nodded, guilty gaze turned down and away.

"I'll tell you everything." She slid her fingers down his jaw to lift his chin toward her. "If you'll do the same."

He swallowed. "All right."

Arlo took a deep breath, then told him about how the house had whispered to her, how the door had called her from the very first time she went downstairs.

"When I found you by the wine cellar?" he asked, his glance sharp, mouth hardening just a touch. It twisted when Arlo nodded, bitter regret plain on his face. "I knew it."

"The first time," Arlo continued, "Lucien—well, the thing wearing his face," she amended when Tristan winced. "He brought me to the most beautiful party I'd ever seen. His house was as full as this place is empty. He offered me food, and I..."

Tristan swallowed, wide-eyed. "No."

Arlo nodded. "I guess I was more Laura than Lizzie after all." She breathed a weak laugh.

"But how did you get through? The riddle—"

Arlo blinked, shooting him an incredulous look. "You *knew* the riddle?"

"Of course. Why do you think I keep no precious metals in the house? My—but without those, how did you satisfy the terms?"

Arlo freed one hand from his grip to run it through her loose curls and flicked the ends toward him.

"Something gold," she said. "For the intangible, I sang a song my mother used to sing when I was afraid."

He huffed an amazed breath out through his nose, shaking his head as he drank her in with wondering eyes.

"And the silver?"

"Do you remember that night in the garden, when you told me my eyes looked silver in the moonlight?" Tristan nodded. "I...waited for the full moon, then went out and stared at it, closed one eye, and didn't open it until I got downstairs."

His eyes shot wide with surprise. "And that *worked?*"

Arlo shrugged. "It's magic. I don't think it ever had to be literal."

"Magic." Wonder hushed his voice. He met her gaze and, this time, didn't look away. "Arlo." He rubbed his thumb over hers, gentle but firm. Searching. "Last time, you ran from me. But I...would like to ask you one more time. And if you say no, I promise I won't ask again." He cleared his throat, but he didn't look away. "May I kiss you?"

Arlo's smile grew as she nodded.

Tristan leaned forward, brushing his lips against hers as a relieved sigh escaped his chest like a buoy finally freed from being held underwater.

Arlo threw her arms around his neck, not caring a bit that he was all-over grime as, to be fair, so was she. He tasted of tea and orange and *life,* and she shivered as weeks of built-up longing for him crashed over her all at once.

When he brushed tentative fingers along her exposed neck, she leaned into his touch like a sunning cat. Her gasp against his mouth made his kiss deeper, his own longing clear in his answering moan. She slid a hand down his throat and into his open collar, exploring, until she touched the scar below his collarbone.

Tristan caught her hand in his and met her gaze for a long moment before he turned her wrist up and pressed his lips to her pulse. Then he took her face in both hands, as gentle as if he was lifting a fallen baby bird back to its nest, and met her eyes again.

"Arlo."

Yes, she wanted to cry. *Yes.* She would listen to her name in the music of his voice for eternity, if he'd let her.

He took a deep, shuddering breath, giving the sense that he was barely holding himself back.

"You've just been through something terrible." He brushed back golden curls that seemed to spark in the sunlight. "I'd hate to...that is, I don't want to take advantage..."

Arlo bit her tongue. Months ago she would have thought this was extravagant: all the gentleness, the softness, the making sure that she wanted this as much as he did, especially when passion lay so thick between them it was nearly tangible.

But she could thank Lucien for one thing, at least. Now she knew that the most delicious thing a man could do, especially a man in a position of power, was to make sure she wanted to give whatever he wanted to have from her.

Even so, when it came to Tristan, she was tired of waiting. Arlo took his face in her hands and spoke to him without blinking.

"Tristan Calder, I have been in love with you since the day I walked into this house. If you can tell me you feel the same, if you can tell me this isn't going to shame us both, then I give myself gladly."

Tears brimmed in his eyes before he answered her with another kiss. Where his first had been joyful, reverent, this one blistered with the heat of his desire, a raw hunger so similar to Lucien's that it sent fear rippling through Arlo until she looked into his eyes. Not black but blue, fever-bright with the need he'd finally allowed himself to succumb to, as wild as Lucien's had been controlled.

His hands roamed over her as though he needed to reassure himself that she was real. Her breaths quickened until she was panting at the increasing pressure of his touch. His flexing fingers dug between her ribs in response, clutching hard enough that she wondered if she'd wear the shadow of his hands for a day or two after this and found she didn't hate the idea.

Then there was a quiet pop and the sensation of something tearing away from her skin, and Arlo gasped with surprise and then pleasure as she realized that her dress had given way under the pressure. Aside from the blanket, there was now nothing between them but the tattering remains of a flimsy snakeskin gown.

Tristan froze in that moment, his mouth open against the slope where her neck met her shoulder. A low almost-growl rumbled out of him as he came to the same conclusion, and Arlo gasped as his teeth pressed ridges into her tender skin. He paused, then took a slow, shuddering breath before drawing back. Meeting her gaze, he lifted a thumb to brush over the swell of her bottom lip with conscious gentleness, soft as the edge of a butterfly's wing.

"Are you sure?"

Afternoon sun poured like honey through the windows, haloing the mess of his dark curls in a bright corona as he waited for her response. Arlo's heart nearly burst with the rightness of him, of this, of them. How could she ever have wanted anyone else? She reached up to guide his dark hair away from his face. Her lips pulsed a little, tender from the scratch of the stubble that had just started to shadow his jaw.

He said he'd dreamed of the door, that he woke from a nightmare and knew he had to rush back here. She had a vision of him riding on the carriage bench with Jonathan, shouting at the horses to go faster, faster. Of him scrambling to unlatch the padlock and fling open the cellar door. Of him finding her in the billow of escaping smoke and carrying her upstairs. Of him, lighting the stove to heat water for tea and forgetting all the while what a mess he was because he was too preoccupied with taking care of her.

"Yes." She held his hand against her cheek, her silvery gaze steady on his. The blanket fell away as she sat up, leaning closer and reaching for one of his shirt buttons. "I'm sure."

He swallowed, then helped her unbutton his shirt the rest of the way, baring his shoulders and chest. The scar she'd noticed before on his left collarbone was now a bright, angry line, a new cut beginning to heal on top of the old tissue.

Their blood sacrifice kept me out.

She ran a gentle fingertip over the stroke, remembering the fresh blood on the threshold of the ruined door. Tristan captured her hand and brought it to his lips before he sank to kneel before her, slowly guiding her legs apart to taste the slickness between them.

Arlo writhed, throwing her head back, and only then recalled that the curtains behind her were open. Anyone walking in front of the house would have gotten quite the show. She gasped a breathless laugh, making Tristan look up, and pointed at the window.

He laughed too, then drew her down to the floor with him so that only the tops of their heads might be visible to any passers-by. Chance visitors were rare and Mrs. Hollister wouldn't be back until tomorrow, but Arlo didn't mind the excuse to be closer to him.

She knelt beside him, heart jerking sideways with every hitched breath that rasped in her smoke-tender throat. Her skin hummed and burned wherever he'd touched her, and she hated that he wasn't touching her now.

She reached for him instead, feeling the lean muscles in his arms jump when she grazed them, as if he was even now trying to restrain himself. His effort delighted her, but not as much as his hands did. She gripped his arm and swung one leg over his lap to kneel astride. He looked surprised. He looked hungry.

He looked wonderful.

Arlo moaned as Tristan dug his thumbs deep into the hollows under her hips. She took his face in both hands again and kissed him. The stubble of his hurried morning scratched her fingers and lips, but she didn't care. He'd been so gentle with her, and right now, after what she'd gone through—after escaping a monster by becoming just a little monstrous herself—Arlo was in the mood to dare.

She skimmed her palms over the sharp line of his jaw to tangle in the dark curls she'd so admired and pulled, lifting her hips as he tilted his head back with a fervent groan.

Then he was beneath her, inside her, and Arlo's heart went effervescent with a fierce joy that she *hadn't* given this to Lucien, that she could be with Tristan without any taint of his dark counterpart staining her soul.

The last of the monster's shadows fell away in a raptured delirium as she kissed Tristan again, her head all bubbles, her whole body buzzing with the need for him, only him, always him.

Forever.

"You know what I still can't figure?" Tristan asked, stretching under the blanket that only barely covered them as they lay together along the length of the library carpet. He ran a languid hand up and down Arlo's arm to stir the hairs there into standing.

Arlo looked up at him, propped on one elbow beside her. "Hm?"

"How you got downstairs in the first place. I locked the cellar door as soon as I suspected you might have found that wretched portal."

Arlo bit her smiling bottom lip as a quirk of mischief overtook her.

"Come on," she said, leaning over and picking up his shirt from where they'd discarded it. "I'll show you." She buttoned the shirt and stood so it hung scandalously short, just brushing above mid-thigh, then slipped into her unlaced boots. With any other person, at any other place or time, she would be mortified. But right now, with Tristan beside her and the dark door irretrievably far behind her, she felt absolutely safe.

He stood, stumbling into his trousers and shoes before following her down the hall and to the kitchen. They each lit a hand lamp before venturing down to the cellar.

Most of the smoke had cleared, thanks to the strong breeze blowing from the propped courtyard door through the open kitchen windows. Arlo led him all the way down into darkness, stopping where the dumbwaiter car would slide into the room and making a one-armed flourish.

Tristan looked blankly at her. "I don't understand."

Arlo grinned, eyes twinkling. "I climbed down the dumbwaiter shaft."

His eyes bulged. "You *what?*"

She shrugged. "I hauled the car all the way upstairs from the kitchen, then climbed down the shaft."

Tristan stared at her for a moment, aghast.

"What if it had fallen on you? Arlo, you have no idea—"

She laid a hand over his mouth and smiled as his admonition trailed off into silence.

"I made sure it was locked in place."

"But...why didn't you send it all the way down? There's a gap between the ceiling and the top of the car; surely that would have been safer?"

With a laugh, Arlo explained the same logic she'd once worked through herself, about the dangers of trying to wriggle in and out through the close-set rungs.

Tristan shook his head, then took her in his arms and crushed her to his chest, burying his face in her hair.

"I knew you were too smart to be a maid."

It had been an insult the last time he'd said it. But this time, Arlo felt no sting, no gut-punch of uncertainty. She pushed him playfully away and winked.

"Don't be ridiculous, *sir*. Maids are often the cleverest of creatures." She gave an airy, theatrical sigh and laid her cheek on one hand with an impish smile. "It's only that no one ever seems to notice."

To her surprise, Tristan's expression went serious.

"I noticed." He captured her wrist with one hand and brought it to his mouth to kiss her knuckles. "Right from the start."

She raised her eyebrows. "You did?"

"As soon as you walked into the library." He grinned, open and rascally and totally captivating. "You should have seen how your eyes lit up at all the books."

She smiled and looked away, a little embarrassed and very much pleased that he'd been watching her so closely for such a long time. Her gaze landed on the scorched wall where the snake-door had once stood.

"Lucien didn't."

Tristan winced, and Arlo bit her tongue, remembering that the real Lucien had been Tristan's brother, before the monster had stolen his name and his face.

"I'm sorry. I meant...whatever his true name was. We should both be grateful that he underestimated me."

Tristan shook his head, wonderment still plain on his face.

"You have no idea how glad I am that he did. You shouldn't have been able to come back, not after the third time. No one else ever did."

Arlo stepped back, crossing her arms.

"Which brings us rather neatly to your turn. Tell me what you know about that door. The riddle. The blood. Everything."

"The blood..." Tristan lifted a hand to the cut on his chest, running his fingertips over the healing scab.

"The creature told me that the Calders who built this house did so on top of the entrance to his ancestral hunting grounds, and took on the task of sealing him in with their blood. He has hated your family for a long time." She leveled a look at him. "But he wore your brother's face."

Tristan sighed. He paced slowly over to where the door had been, holding his lantern out with one hand and Arlo's wrist in a loose grip with the other. When they reached the far wall, he dropped Arlo's arm and spread his palm and fingers flat against the newly-bare stone.

"We used to play down here, Lucien and I. We found the door when we were children. When we asked, our parents told us what they knew of its provenance, and that it was our responsibility to seal it shut with our blood. But we wouldn't have to worry about it until we were adults. So I didn't worry. But then Lucien started looking sick. Drawn, as though...as though he'd eaten fairy fruit, and pined for it."

He put the lantern down on the floor and pushed both hands through his hair, making it stand in wild disarray around his head.

"He told me there was a king down there who wanted to make him a prince, to give him a world, and all he had to do was return three times to prove his loyalty. Branston—our butler at the time—reported some silver missing, and my mother lost a gold ring. And then one morning, we found that Lucien had vanished in the night. We put out the word that he'd gone missing, but..."

Arlo put her lantern next to his on the floor and put one hand on his bare shoulder over the scar while her other hand stroked his cheek, his jaw.

"You knew exactly where he went."

Tristan nodded into her hand.

"How could I not? He wanted me to go with him, but...I couldn't leave, not with the family responsibility to keep that door closed. I could have stayed in town, come out only once a month to replenish the blood, but I thought if I stayed here, if Lucien ever did find a way back, I'd be here. But he never did. I don't...think he lived very long, after that final crossing."

"Tristan." Arlo kissed his cheek, his jaw, his mouth, then hugged him tight. "I'm so sorry."

"But you did," he said. "How did you break free? And how did you destroy the door? I tried so many times, with fire, with axes. Nothing so much as put a scratch on it."

Arlo tilted her head.

"Well..." The word curled up at the end with the promise of more to come. "I sort of...tricked him."

"Tricked," Tristan said, flatly. *"Him."*

Arlo nodded.

"How?"

She told him about the bargain then, three things for three things.

"So it was actually *my* kingdom in the end, you see. Not his." She shrugged. "Which meant the door was mine, too. I could do anything I wanted with it."

She laid her hand in the space where his had been, the outline still faintly visible in the layers of soot.

"And I wanted it to burn. Ah!"

She squealed that last as Tristan yanked her hard around and pressed his mouth to hers, crushing her to him, his heartbeat galloping against her palms.

"You are without a doubt the most extraordinary woman I've ever known," he said, breaking only as far away as he needed to in order to speak. His hands were hot and strong on her back as he spoke, his gaze in that moment more intense than Lucien could ever have hoped to achieve.

"I can't begin to tell you how sorry I am, that bringing you here put you in peril of your life." He stroked her cheek with a thumb, his lips beginning to spread into a smile. "But I also can't tell you how glad I am that you came. I know that Calderwood has been strange, in several ways. But for the first time in my life, I think we can change that. If you'll help me."

Arlo went still in his arms, searching his gaze as she took a deep, trembling breath.

"Arlo Reade," he said, with a smile so radiant it almost shone in the darkness. "Will you do me the honor of becoming my wife, and the lady of this house?"

She had a vision then, a flash of what a future here might look like. This beautiful old house, no longer creaking and ominous but thrown open to light and air, to people, to joy. Calderwood had been Tristan's prison for so long. Together, they could make it a home.

She threw her arms around him, squeezing him as tight as she could, wanting in that moment to absorb him, be one with him, to be as close to his body as she already felt to his soul.

She took in a shuddering tearful breath, every inch of her skin tingling with a surreal levity, as though she might at any second float away on a cloud of happiness.

"Yes," she said, half a sob, half a laugh. "Of course I will."

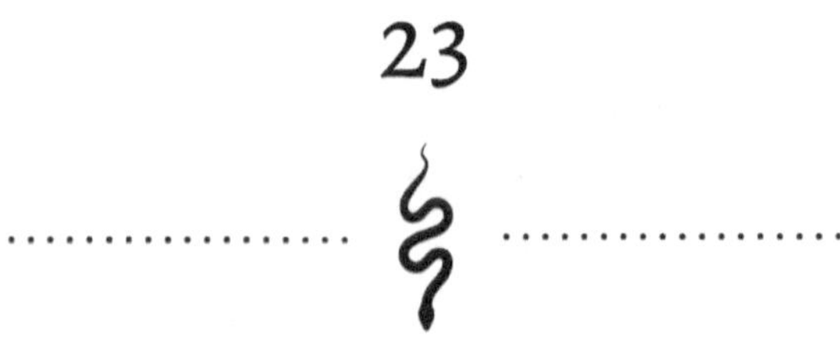

Epilogue

ARLO TUGGED HER SHAWL closer around her shoulders as she made her way down the terraced steps that hugged the sunken garden. She nodded to the new team of caretakers planting autumn bulbs that would erupt into springtime color. They touched their hats as she passed.

The sounds of a bustling household floated through the open windows behind her, a welcome change from the silence that used to hang so heavy over this place. She looked back as the terrace door opened and caught the eye of Mrs. Carmichael, the new housekeeper, who bobbed her head. Arlo had to look away to hide her smile—she'd been the one bobbing, not long ago.

Mrs. Hollister had chosen to retire from Calderwood. She'd said she wanted to rest her back and spend more time with her grandchildren, but Arlo couldn't help wondering whether those were the only reasons. After all, Hollister had been the woman in charge of Calderwood for a long time. It would be strange and likely unpleasant for her to serve someone she'd once supervised.

When Arlo had mentioned it to Tristan, he'd snorted and asked whether it might *also* have something to do with not wanting to work for two godless reprobates who neither attended church nor had waited until they were married to gain carnal knowledge of each other.

On reflection, Arlo had to admit it was a distinct possibility. But, whatever the reason, she wished the woman well.

Turning left from the garden wall, Arlo went past the servants' wing of the house and into the little wood she'd sneaked through in her final desperate rush toward Lucien's siren call. A memorial stood among the trees now, topped with a draped urn, its letters and dates carved so deep they filled with shadow in all but the most direct light.

LUCIEN AMBROSE CALDER

17 DECEMBER 1863 — 26 MAY 1880

"Tristan," she called, her voice soft with tenderness.

Her husband turned from where he knelt before the stone, brushing a hand over the scarlet chrysanthemums that bloomed in stone pots on either side of the memorial. Leaves crunched under his feet as he stood and walked to her, putting his arms around her.

"My love," he said, resting his cheek against hers.

Arlo laid a gentle hand along his other cheek, humming a wordless, happy sound.

"It's getting so cold." She snuggled in closer to his warmth. "Will you come inside for something warm?"

He looked down at her, his eyes sparkling with amused mischief.

"Why, Mrs. Calder," he said, his tone playful and just a little suggestive. "What sort of *something warm* did you have in mind?"

Arlo tossed her head and laughed, then winked at him.

"I thought we could start with tea..."

He picked her up and whirled her around to the sound of their laughter. Then they turned as one, stumbling like giddy children, never taking their gaze from one another as they found their way back to the house.

In their absence, the wind sighed through the trees of Calderwood, and the ash-white snake that had been watching them from under a nearby rock slithered silently off into the hills.

Acknowledgements

Writers write alone until they don't, and I have so many people to thank for helping me make *Calderwood* a reality:

My CMWB crew, who read every iteration of this book from its inception as a short story. They're the ones who demanded I turn it into a full-length novel so, you know, this is kind of their fault. Special thanks to Ali and Katie Beth, the best cheerleaders and problem solvers a girl could ask for, and to Jessamyn, whose terrifying knowledge of everything always comes in handy.

André Meister, my cover artist. I knew from the second I saw his work that his incredible blend of expressive and unsettling would be perfect for bringing this cover to life. Not to mention, he's a cool dude. (Still kind of amazed he let me hire him, TBH, but super glad about it.)

@liz.potent, whose character art of Arlo, Tristan and Lucien melted my brain with joy. As a writer with aphantasia, it brings me a special thrill when artists make pictures of my characters, because it's the only time I get to see them and not just understand the concept of them. It never stops being amazing.

Andrew Belonsky, whose writing, advice, and conversation are always something to look forward to.

Jason J. Marchi, whose grand ideas and willingness to play make-believe with a little kid had a big part in shaping my lifelong love for stories.

And, of course, a huge thank-you to my family for putting up with my (probably annoying) need to always be writing.

About the author

Leila A. M. Martin has written many novels and published several. She's had poetry and short fiction published in *Verbicide* and *Three Stories* magazines and edited VENUS REMEMBERED by Ray Bradbury and Jason J. Marchi.

She publishes new short fiction weekly at leilaammartin.com.